PARIS INFORMATION

A Novel of Spies

by

Robert E. Huber

1

This book is for Frances.

Where is the wisdom we have lost in knowledge?

Where is the knowledge we have lost in information?

T.S. Eliot

Chapter 1

A freak storm out of the east had turned the November gray of Paris white.

Wilson might have ridden out the blizzard in his room in the Latin Quarter rereading Gibbons' *Decline and Fall of the Roman Empire*, except for the letter he had received two days earlier from the U.S. Department of State.

United States citizens residing in Occupied Paris are directed to attend an urgent briefing in the Grand Palais at 5 p.m. Nov. 4, 1941. To accommodate attendees, the government of the German Reich has granted the United States government temporary use of the building's main exhibition hall. Access to the hall will be restricted to the entrance on the Cours de la Reine opposite the Seine. Proof of U.S. citizenship, in the form of a valid passport, is required for admission.

With his passport secure inside the buttoned pocket of his raincoat and an open umbrella over his shoulders, Wilson navigated the slippery pavement of the Pont Alexander III, homing in on the Nazi flag flying atop the steel-and-glass dome of the Grand Palais. Coming off the bridge onto the Right Bank, he joined a long queue of Americans braving the snow-swept afternoon along the Seine. The line snaked into the Palais through two massive bronze doors, where a taut-faced Foreign Service officer checking passports sat behind a reception desk. A blonde and affable Wehrmacht lieutenant stood a few paces behind him. The German nodded politely at each American passing before him, an advertisement for the civility of the New Order.

An hour after joining the queue, Wilson proffered his passport to the Foreign Service officer, who glanced at Wilson's photograph, then at Wilson.

"Same square jaw. Same fair hair. Six feet tall. Age 27. Tell me, Wilson, what brought you to France?"

"History. I'm researching my doctoral dissertation."

The man fingered through a sheaf of papers on the desk in front of him.

4

"Wilson ... Wilson ... Wilson ... there you are. Strange first name."

"I go by my middle name. George."

"I suppose so. Galahad's not a name you see every day."

The foreign service officer held out Wilson's passport, then snapped it back, asking, "That team Ed Williams plays for in Boston, it's the Reds, isn't it?"

"You mean Ted Williams. He plays for the Red Sox."

The officer returned Wilson's passport.

"You're a young man, Wilson. Stand in the rear. There aren't enough chairs. Next."

Wilson turned away, drawn by the din of hundreds of Americans milling in the building's cavernous central hall. The vast art nouveau interior, enclosed by soaring ceilings, marble floors and plaster friezes, had been built for the 1900 Exposition, a showcase for the optimism of fin de siècle Europe. Now, it reeked of motor oil, a consequence of the Nazis having converted it into a military depot to service their tanks, troop carriers and staff cars.

Wilson was passing a huge wall frieze entitled *Progress Leading the People*, when a lithe young woman with milky skin and urgent green eyes diverted his attention.

"I must attend this meeting," she pleaded in a Parisian accent to the taut-faced Foreign Service officer. "To get information for a friend. She is in Le Havre. She cannot be here."

"Your friend's name?"

"Ilena Bloch."

The Foreign Service officer consulted the papers on the desk. "No Ilena Bloch on my list of Americans in Paris."

"She is not an American but desperate to come to America."

The Foreign Service officer stole a glance over his shoulder. The Wehrmacht lieutenant was speaking to a Wehrmacht sergeant.

The Foreign Service officer lowered his voice.

"That is another process, madame.   Miss Bloch may apply for refugee status by making an appointment when she returns from Le Havre. I would not advise you to pursue the matter at this time and this place."

He looked past her to the next person in line, but the woman did not move.

"Is there anything else, madame?"

She ran her left hand through her snow-wet black hair.

"I *must* attend this meeting."

"It is open only to United States citizens. Are you an United States citizen?"

"My name is Smith."

"*Are* you a U.S. citizen?"

"My name is Smith."

The Foreign Service officer rolled his eyes but consulted his papers again.

"Your Christian name?"

"Jane."

"Yes, there is a Jane Smith listed."

The woman pivoted quickly toward the great hall.

"But," he said, his voice halting her, "Jane Smith's already inside. I checked her in myself. Have you a passport, Miss Smith?"

She brought her hand tentatively to the pocket of her black coat, then said softly, "I forgot it."

"If you are not on my list and have no passport, you may not enter. That is the way things are."

Again, he tilted his head furtively toward the Wehrmacht lieutenant.

"There is nothing more to be done. Not now. Not here."

The woman stepped back from the desk. Her eyelids fluttered. Her shoulders slumped. Her hands dropped to her sides. Wilson saw her swoon and rushed to her, cinching his arm around her waist. His grip steadied her ... and unnerved him.

From beneath her snow-damp coat, a wave of gardenia-scented perfume rose on heat from her body. The fragrance consumed him.

"I'll get it for you!" he whispered urgently.

She pulled away, her posture straightening, her eyes focusing.

"Get what!?"

"The information you need! Nothing could be easier! Just wait here."

She stepped back further, her face strained in disbelief.

"You Americans!" she said, her tone almost an indictment. "Your national motto should be *Nothing could be easier!* Nothing could be more difficult! This American won't let me in, and that German will never let me wait."

She shook her head in despair and stepped toward the bronze doors.

"No!" Wilson said louder than he knew, turning heads among those in line.

She stopped. He was at her side again, lost in the desperation of her face. Words tumbled from him.

"That little park along the Cours de la Reine, no more than 200 meters from here … the Garden of the Swiss Valley. Go down the stone steps. There's a stone arch by a stream and a little bridge. The bridge will protect you from the storm. Wait there. *Please.*"

She had never heard a man say please that way, a harmony of hope and fear. Her incredulity gave way to hope of her own. He might be helpful, and she needed help. Putnev had given her an assignment. She had to complete it. God, how she had to complete it. The American might be a means to that end.

"You would do this for me?" she asked.

A*nd so much more,* Wilson thought.

"Take this," he said. "I'll meet you in the park in 30 minutes. I promise."

He handed her his umbrella.

In the exchange, their fingers touched.   Wilson froze.

A nervous little man pushed past him.

"Excuse me," the little man said. "They're going to start. I need to know what's going on."

Not half as much as I, Wilson thought, breathing in the scent of gardenia and watching her pass back through the bronze doors and into the storm.

Chapter 2

The State Department's letter announcing an "urgent briefing" had routed the American trademarks of smiling faces and easy jokes. Now, hundreds of Americans - standing, sitting, pacing amid fuel tanks and mechanic bays in the grandeur of the main hall of the Grand Palais - succumbed to a grave tension.

Except Wilson.

Dinner, he thought, his mind racing ahead. Yes, dinner. With her. He had the cash, having withdrawn all his money that morning in anticipation of his trip home. His father, on advice from an old friend from college, had provided Wilson with more than enough funds.

"Make sure," Dr. Sumner Jackson had written to Dr. Clyde Wilson a year earlier, "your boy has at least double what he needs. Since the Occupation, there are rumors America will limit the amount of dollars coming into France. It wouldn't do for George to be stranded. Besides, I'm sure he's sensible. Won't squander it."

Wilson hadn't. His bank account that morning stood at more than $2,500 or just over 200,000 French francs. He had lived frugally, but now a more-than-frugal dinner – perhaps at Balzar - would not unduly ruffle the Puritan standards of Dr. Wilson.

What Dr. Wilson's son had in the back of his mind might. She had captivated him and left him with a longing to venture where Wilson had gone only once before with an unsure Classics major from Wellesley. His fantasy reached such a pitch that Wilson shook his head in amazement at the lurch of his imagination. He returned to the moment, summoned by a gaunt American diplomat approaching the lectern, flanked by ten other Foreign Service officers. The crowd fell silent.

"My name is Stewart Holmes, U.S. consul in Paris. Our embassy in Vichy has asked me to share with you significant developments on the international scene that have occurred in the past 96 hours. We consider this information vital to your decision making."

The weight of the consul's darkening voice momentarily displaced Wilson's plans for dinner.

"Four days ago, October 31, off the coast of Iceland, German U-boat 552 torpedoed the American destroyer *Reuben James.*"

Sighs and gasps.   Consul Holmes raised his hands for silence.

"The Reuben James sank within five minutes; its forward magazine having taken a direct hit from the German torpedo. Of the 160 crew members, 115 sailors drowned, including all officers. At the time, the *Reuben James* was escorting a commercial convoy from Halifax to Great Britain. This escort duty was within the bounds of international law. It should be noted; the German government has expressed regret for the attack on the *Reuben James.* Your government considers this response inadequate."

The hall was dead silent.

"We have called this briefing to alert you that due to the extraordinary volatility of the international situation, we urge all Americans in France to return to the United States as soon as possible. We have assurances from the German Foreign Ministry that travel between Paris and Lisbon, via Spain, will be unobstructed for U.S. citizens. From Lisbon, ships to United States ports continue to cross the Atlantic. German authorities further assure us that these ships, if properly identified and not advancing the cause of the Reich's enemies, will be allowed to cross the ocean without interference. We, at the consulate, are prepared to assist you in arranging transport.   While we believe sufficient accommodations are available for return passage to the United States, your prompt attention to this matter will help facilitate your timely and safe departure. Our staff will remain here to answer any questions you may have. Please save any further questions for them."

The crowd was stunned to silence except for one.

"Mr. Holmes," said a gray-haired woman, pushing back her folding chair and rising. "One question, please."

"Very well, madam," the consul said, deferring to her age, "but only *your* question."

"I have lived in Paris since a girl. I love Paris and am loathe to leave her. Hence my question: is your request that expatriates abandon Paris an order or a recommendation?"

Consul Holmes's back straightened.

"My remarks are not an order but represent your State Department's most adamant wish. While we are not at war with the German Reich, the situation is fraught with tension and uncertainty. Should hostilities come to exist between the United States and another power, American citizens remaining in Paris could be subject to internment ... or worse."

Hysteria erupted.

Folding chairs were shoved aside and the nicety of ladies before gentlemen forgotten, as the crowd of overwrought Americans besieged the Foreign Service officers and Consul Holmes.

Wilson did not join them. Two weeks earlier, he had shipped a copy of his dissertation to his mentor and scheduled its day-long defense for Monday, December 8, at Harvard. Then he had booked transit back to the States on the American Export Line's *Excalibur* sailing November 12 from Lisbon, arriving New York, November 17. He had even telegraphed the Boston & Maine Railroad to make connections and reserve tickets for him from New York to Waterville, Maine. There, his father would meet him and drive on to the family home in Unity, where his mother had promised a welcome-home dinner and reunion with his fiancée, Mae. His homecoming from his year-long sojourn across the ocean seemed natural to Wilson. It would commence the tidy life Mae had planned for them. Together, they would face the future hugging the shore, cosseted by the secure and the familiar.

But as he maneuvered through the agitated crowd and headed out of the Grand Palais to the Cours de la Reine, an alternative life, scented with gardenia, had begun to roil his soul and beckon him into deeper water.

Chapter 3

Outside, snow covered the parterres and streets surrounding the Grand Palais and was silently gathering on the German staff cars and troop carriers parked along the Cours de la Reine. Wilson slip-slid across the roadway and between the vehicles. He reached the Garden of the Swiss Valley and quick-stepped down its uneven stone steps to the stone arch where he had promised to meet her.

In an awkward pirouette, Wilson spun 360 degrees, his eyes searching the confined sights lines of the cramped little garden.

She wasn't there.

He ran to the other side of the bridge. Then returned to the stone arch. Nothing. He sighed and slumped into its wall, the cold of the stones piercing him to the bone, snow swirling about him. It conjured in his historian's mind, Henry IV bare-footed in the snow of Canossa in humiliation before the pope. Now, in Paris, a thousand years later, Wilson was enacting another humiliation: his penance for a wild romantic fantasy.

He pushed off from the wall and retraced his steps up the stone stairs. Regret consuming him. He hadn't even learned her name. Another blast of cold air unsteadied him ... and then overwhelmed him.

It bore the scent of gardenia.

He spun around and saw her approaching the staircase, her overcoat windblown to her back and whipping out at the hem, her feet ankle-deep in slush. He bolted down the steps.

"Good God, I thought I lost you!"

She was too cold to catch the depth of his emotion.

Tears coursed down her cheeks, the product of the storm howling across Paris. For the second time in an hour, Wilson slid his arm around her waist. He guided her past the little stream and its snow-covered rocks and up to the street.

As they emerged onto the Cours de la Reine, Wilson looked up at the moment a Paris taxi slid to a stop in front of them, and without wondering why in the middle of a blizzard in a city where taxis had been all but eliminated by the Germans, he should find a taxi, he threw open its back door and guided her into it.

11

"Balzar, rue des Écoles!" he ordered and pulled shut the door behind them.

She leaned into him, her body shivering. Wilson pried the umbrella from her hands and began to massage them between his own. Her labored breathing eased, and warm air from the car's heater began to relax the tension across her shoulders.

The cab crossed the Pont Alexander III, passing the National Assembly building, its façade draped with a huge banner proclaiming *Germany Is Winning On All Fronts*.

Ten minutes later, they arrived at Balzar and stepped beneath the red awning and five white globes where patrons dined outside in warm weather. They ascended the three steps to the restaurant and opened the door. Warm air swept over them, carrying the aroma of garlic and roasting meat and tobacco smoke, a sumptuous descant to Balzar's polyphony of muted voices and tinkling glassware.

The maître d'hotel took her wet coat and showed them to a banquette in the back of the dining room. Without waiting for one of the white-aproned waiters, Wilson ordered a bottle of Gigondas from him.

"Weighty wine from the south to warm you," he told her. "It wouldn't do for you to become the first woman in the 20th century to freeze to death in the Latin Quarter."

She didn't smile. Perhaps, it was his botched idiom for *freezing to death*. He tried again. There was no idiom for *what is your name.*

"Clotilde. Clotilde deBrouillard. I'm not American."

With a wave of his hand, Wilson brushed aside her confession and came to the only issue that mattered to him.

"But is it *Miss* deBrouillard?"

"Mrs."

Wilson frowned, a reflex beyond his volition.

"I'm a widow. The invasion."

The usual response to that information was a sympathetic tilt of the head, not the look of relief softening Wilson's face.

"Yes, the invasion," he said, regrouping. "A terrible thing. I'm sorry."

She looked straight ahead.

12

"One month, Paul was lecturing in philosophy at the university. The next, dead, shot by the Germans days before the armistice. That was 17 months ago."

She cupped her hands over her mouth and blew warm air on them and looked at Wilson.

"And you are?"

"George Wilson. American."

She forced a smile.

"You Americans have this feeling for us French. Paris is – was – full of Americans. Writers, painters, musicians. George Gershwin took us by storm. *An American in Paris* used real Paris taxi horns. Did you know that? Real horns. I miss those horns so much. Someday cars will return to our streets, and it will be noisy again. Tell me, George Wilson, why are you in Paris when everyone else is leaving?"

"I came to research my doctoral dissertation in history. Early Middle Ages. The transition of the Church from a religious institution to a political force in Europe."

"Old history."

"But in some ways contemporary. It parallels my country over the past half century. Our emergence from isolation onto the world stage."

"You sound like that other Wilson. Woodrow. He made quite an impression on us after the war. I was a girl, but I recall our embrace of him. Vive Wilson! I wish you Americans felt the same way about us now."

The waiter uncorked the wine and poured a sip into Wilson's glass. Wilson pushed the glass toward her.

"Taste it. You need it more than I."

Her surprise at a man deferring to a woman the masculine prerogative of first- tasting brought another smile to her face. She swirled the wine in the glass, inhaled its bouquet without sipping.

She nodded at the waiter. He filled each glass a third full.

"One has little chance to drink good wine. Each week, it becomes harder to get what we need. The ration cards offer only the minimum."

She sipped the wine.

13

"Tell me, George Wilson, will you Americans come and save us French again?"

A good time to get to business he thought.

"Have you heard about the *Reuben James*?"

A glass of Gigondas later, she had, and what the American consul had said it meant for an American in Paris.

"Then you will be leaving Paris," she said.

He couldn't bring himself to say he was scheduled to depart the next morning.

"I have a ticket to return to America."

"When?"

"Soon."

"You must know when."

Then a moment's respite. The waiter returned to the table and pointed to the chalkboard on the wall next to the kitchen door.

"The menu," he said.

She looked where he pointed. Her voice turned light.

"Sweetbreads! I did not believe I would see such a thing again."

Wilson dismissed the waiter with a promise of ordering later.

"I think America will enter the war soon," he said, deferring discussion of his departure. "I know it's taken time, but we've grown accustomed to the Atlantic protecting us."

His words stung her.

"Protecting you!? There's no protection from them! Do you know what they are like, these Germans? Twenty years ago, they slaughtered an entire generation, including themselves. Now, they've become Nazis. Unspeakable. My neighbors, the Werbs. Gone. Overnight. Where? For what? And you Americans talk about an ocean that protects you!"

She heard the ingratitude in her voice. It shamed her. This sincere young man had just given her information that Putnev had assigned her - commanded her - to obtain. George Wilson deserved something more than her anger.

"When are you leaving for America?"

Wilson exhaled in defeat.

"Tomorrow," he admitted, as if his departure were a sin, and the sin would drive her away.

14

But she slid closer to him, and he felt her breath on his face and inhaled again the scent of gardenia.

"Thank you for helping me, today. I was at the Grand Palais for a friend."

It was her cover story, what Putnev had told her to say to gain entry.

"She teaches with me here in Paris. She is a Jew. Desperate to get out of France."

Wilson shook his head no.

"The Nazis will never allow it. But what of you?"

Now, she shook her head no. No more need for a cover story. She could be honest.

"I am a citizen of a conquered country. France has become hell. None of us is getting out."

Her despair pierced him.

Then a brainstorm, sired by an overwhelming need to protect her and stay with her.

"Clotilde, I *can* get you out. Don't think me crazy or forward or ... but it *can* be done. A marriage of convenience. There's this English poet, Auden. He married Thomas Mann's daughter to get her to Britain. It happens. We could. Here in Paris. At the American Cathedral. We could marry. Think of a marriage certificate as an exit visa. You'd be a U.S. citizen by marriage, and you could leave France under protection of the American flag. It would entail nothing more on your part. I mean you wouldn't have to ..."

She pulled back from him.

"You Americans! One doesn't just marry!"

"It would save your life!"

She couldn't help but smile, nor could she stop herself from reaching out and stroking his cheek.

"Clotilde, we can do this. If we are married, the Germans will grant you a visa. It's simply a matter of ..."

"Nothing in Occupied Paris is *simply a matter of.* Even if we did this crazy thing, this marriage, it would take weeks to get a license."

"I'll stay in Paris until the marriage license is issued."

"And if your country should enter the war before we get the license? What then? You'd be imprisoned. Deported to Germany. Killed. I'm already a widow."

"It's a risk. But also a choice."

She shook her head wearily, her tone bitter.

"Choice. They spoke highly of it at the Sorbonne. The philosophers adore choice. It makes us human, they say. Even absurd choices. That's what my husband said. That's what Paul said the night before the Germans entered Paris, and he and a friend went to the outskirts of the city to tear down road markers, cut telegraph wires, anything to slow the German advance. But why, I pleaded with him? The French Army had all but surrendered; the government had abandoned Paris for Tours. I told him it was suicide. Yes, he said, but suicide is a choice, even an affirmation. If there is no sanctuary, he said, no place where hope lives, death is nobler than life."

She slumped into Wilson, her head to his shoulder, her breasts into his arm. It ignited him.

"The check," he blurted.

And not waiting for what he sought, threw 2000 francs onto the table and took her hand and led her out of the restaurant and into the storm.

Chapter 4

Not knowing where she was going but knowing what she would do when she arrived, Clotilde slid her arm around Wilson's waist, his arm already about her shoulders. They walked quickly down rue des Écoles then up rue Laplace to his building at number 16, both oblivious to the taxi that had brought them from the Grand Palais and now crept silently behind them through the falling snow.

They passed the darkened ground-floor lodging of the concierge and ascended the three flights to Wilson's room. He unlocked the door. They stepped inside, his free hand to the light switch. In the damp November room, where the smell of burnt coal lingered and the overhead bulb emitted barely enough light to dispel the gloom, the dam that had stopped her emotional life since her husband's death gave way.

She drew him toward her. In an ecstasy of necessity, coats fell and in a moment his hands were fumbling with the back of her bra, his trousers half unbuttoned.

Then their quickening breaths were caught short by the door thrown open.

"German security!" yelled a man in the doorway, backlit by weak light from a hallway sconce.

Wilson stumbled backwards. Clotilde darted in front of him, her blouse open, her skirt riding on her hips.

"You have no … "

The man slammed his forearm into her chest, sprawling her into the corner and with a brutal right fist caught Wilson full in the jaw. The last thing Wilson saw before collapsing to the floor was a scar, shaped like a checkmark, beneath the man's right eye.

Chapter 5

Wilson came to three hours later. His head swirled, his mouth full of blood. He was alone and wobbled to his feet, staggered down the hallway to the bathroom, washed out his mouth and descended unsteadily the ill-lit stairs to the street. The snow had stopped. The street was deserted. He began to run, as much as his spinning head allowed, up rue Laplace and past the baroque complexity of St. Etienne du Mont and the spectral enormity of the Panthéon, until he reached the prefecture's office on the far corner of Place du Panthéon. He stumbled up the limestone stairs into the dimly-lit reception area. A gendarme sat behind a desk, smoking a cigarette and typing.

"I need to know if a woman, Clotilde deBrouillard, was brought in tonight by German security!"

The police officer coughed and rolled his neck.

"First, you are in violation of the curfew. I won't report you … if you go home, now. Second, if you are correct, and German security has brought her in, it is best not to know."

"But I need to … "

"You *need* to know nothing."

"Would such a person be brought here?"

The police officer stubbed his cigarette into a filled ashtray, then looked around, his voice low.

"I will tell you this and nothing more. No one has been brought here since I came on duty four hours ago. However, if German security agents were involved, Clotilde deBrouillard could have been taken anywhere, and even if you knew where to look, it would be dangerous. I can be of no further help to you. Accept that she is gone for tonight. If she is a Jew, accept that she is gone forever. It is the way things are in Paris."

"But …"

"Leave. Now. The curfew."

The next morning, Wilson settled with his concierge, took his two valises by horse-drawn carriage to the Gare Montparnasse and boarded the 11 a.m. train with connections to Lisbon and never saw the man with the scar beneath his right eye who had followed him from rue Laplace and had waited behind a kiosk on the platform until the train with connections to Lisbon had rolled out of sight.

Chapter 6

They met in the nave of Notre Dame, its crush of German tourists and French worshippers cover for their secrets. Sergei Putnev was already there, seated in the back. With no gesture of welcome from him, Clotilde lowered herself into the thatched seat next to him. He slid his own chair closer, and she smelled his unwashed body and felt the pressure of his thick shoulder against hers. Without looking at his jowly and oily face, she told him what she had learned from Wilson the day before and what had happened to her.

"I only went back to his room, Sergei, to get the information *you wanted*," her voice almost a plea. "But nothing happened. *Nothing.* Nothing to make German Security suspicious. You must believe me."

Putnev did. Her story had been confirmed to him hours earlier by the muscular if bungling Maxim Trafanov, who had provided more information about Clotilde's evening than Clotilde. Putnev and Trafanov had sat on a faded red sofa in the tiny lobby of the Hotel Splendide in Pigalle. To an onlooker, their encounter as random as two strangers sitting in a doctor's waiting room. Both men had opened newspapers and held them up, obscuring their faces. Putnev had spoken first.

"You followed her, as I ordered?"

"Yes, comrade, in my taxi."

"And?"

"You were right, comrade. I have learned things. You will be pleased."

"After what happened three weeks ago, I hope I will be pleased. You remember three weeks ago?"

Trafanov remembered. Cringed. Continued.

"After the Grand Palais, she was with a man. American. Fair-haired. A student. They went to his room. To fuck. I entered and removed her to our safe house by the St. Martin Canal. She's there now."

"Will she stay, as Mrs. Verskya stayed?"

"She will stay. She thinks I am Gestapo. Scared what I will do to her if she is not there when I return."

"And the man?"

"She told me about him, how she met him by chance *outside* the Grand Palais, but she denied trying to get into the Grand Palais."

"Did you follow this man?"

"Yes, comrade, this morning. I returned to his apartment building and trailed him to the railway station in Montparnasse. He carried two valises. I asked the agent at the station about the ticket he purchased. It was to Lisbon. He told the agent he was making connections for a boat to America on the 12th. I watched him pass through German security and board the train. He has gone. I am sure."

Putnev nodded, not in approval of Trafanov's work but as a precursor to the next steps to be taken.

"In that case, you will do this. Return to the safe house and release her. But warn her that German State Security knows who she is and is watching her. Then, when I tell you, send her the letter. When she gets it, it will set things in motion. And when things are in motion, she'll do whatever I demand. *Anything*."

With the prospect of *anything* in his mind, Putnev had folded his newspaper and left for his debriefing with Clotilde in the rear of the nave of Notre Dame.

"You know, Clotilde," he whispered, looking over his shoulder making certain no one had sat behind them, "I wonder if you've invented this story about the Gestapo arresting you to force me to relieve you of your duties. I know that's what you want."

Her voice was a plea.

"Sergei, I am only a school teacher and a widow. I was wrong for this kind of work. I am not a spy."

"Nonetheless, you know too much to walk away. I made it clear to you. Your commitment to The Party could not be a sometime thing. It requires obedience. Obedience is the inviolable rule of The Party."

She stole a nervous glance at the faithful lighting candles in a side chapel.

Putnev waved a dismissive hand at them.

21

"Fools. All of them. Making sacrifices. Genuflecting to the Great Unseen, certain that some cosmic father figure has their best interests at heart. Even if God exists, He's not reliable. You never know if He will answer your prayers. But people? People can be very reliable … if properly motivated. Such as your late husband."

Paul deBrouillard had been reliable, recruited by Putnev at the Sorbonne, where Soviet Intelligence had planted Putnev as a right-wing émigré writing the next great Russian novel. The cover story had given Putnev access to White Russian salons.

Putnev spied on White Russians so well, his Soviet handlers expanded his responsibilities to include recruitment of French students to do the bidding of the Moscow-directed global revolution. His liaison to the student cells was a young lecturer in philosophy, Paul deBrouillard.

Putnev had recruited Paul for two reasons. Paul was ideologically committed to a worldwide communist order lead by the Soviet Presidium … and Paul was married to Clotilde.

From first meeting, Clotilde deBrouillard obsessed Putnev. A combination of her innocence and shy beauty consumed him. He could not have sex with any of the prostitutes he frequented in Pigalle without fantasizing the woman was Clotilde. Only his considerable discipline and lack of opportunity prevented him from pursuing her. Yet, his desire for her never waned. So, he waited. Time, he thought, might be on his side. He was right. When Paul was killed by the advancing Germans, a path to Clotilde opened.

Within days of Paul's death, Putnev had set upon the path. He lavished attention on the bereaved Clotilde: dinners, advice, help getting her a job teaching in a Paris primary school, even money to pay her expenses. It seemed to work. She confided to him, she always responded to kindness, one of the reasons she had fallen in love with Paul.

As it turned out, Putnev had been too kind. When she finally emerged from 13 months of mourning, her affection for him had not evolved into anything approaching romantic interest, only a grateful appreciation, what a niece might feel for a doting uncle.

But Putnev did not object. She might not sleep with him, at least not yet, but she was beholden to him. So, when he asked her to join him in the work of The Party, she felt obliged to say yes. Her first assignment had been to infiltrate the Catholic Resistance in Paris.

"You won't even have to act," Putnev had told her. "You were once a Catholic. Now, I want you to return to the fold, to St. Séverin in the Latin Quarter. Catholic students and professors worship there. They are likely candidates for the Resistance. Join them. I want to know - Moscow wants to know - who they are and what they're up to."

At first, her work as a double agent was painless, but within a month, her acquaintances at St. Séverin had evolved into friendships, especially with Josephine LeMans, a university lecturer in theology who planned to take vows in the coming year. LeMans had warmed to the young widow, and it did not take long for her to recruit Clotilde into the Catholic Resistance and share political secrets with her. Clotilde passed these secrets along to Putnev. With each confidence she divulged, her guilt grew.

But it was not only betrayal of her new friend that wracked Clotilde. It was her betrayal of the faith itself. She was returning to it, not to the fairytale stuff of childhood but to a darker belief, ambiguous yet grounded in the hope that the last word in the fallen world might yet be The Word.

From the steps of the chancel at the far end of the Cathedral, a priest announced afternoon prayers. Clotilde clutched the top of the chair in front of her and pulled herself up. Putnev grasped her right arm and pulled her back down.

"I'm not finished, Clotilde. You will go when I say. Remember the inviolable rule. Obedience."

He released her arm and gently stroked the side of her face.

"Perhaps you need a man, Clotilde. That would explain your behavior last night with that young, fair-haired American student you picked up at the Grand Palais. After all, you were once married. You grew used to men. You're only 26. Dark eyes, milky flesh, sinuous limbs ... still very desirable."

A sudden wave of dread swept over her, voiceless and undefined, deeper than the unexpected lechery of Putnev's words or his touch. *But what?*

"In any case, Clotilde, I can't release you from your work for The Party. This is not child's play. You're no longer the daughter of

23

a doting tailor who sewed you little frocks. You're a soldier of the Soviet Communist Party, fighting the occupying Germans and the Russian émigrés who are their stooges. More important, you know who I am, and what I do. I must keep you close, as I kept Paul close."

"Please release me, Sergei. I would tell no one of our work together or anything about you."

"What if your loneliness should lead you to the bed of a German? Pillow talk has betrayed more spies than torture. I can't take the chance."

Putnev saw her arms tighten to her sides, heightening his frustration with her, and, at the same time, his desire for her.

"What am I to do with you, Clotilde? I thought I'd given you an easy assignment: join the Catholic Resistance and get me information.   But you couldn't manage that.   Then I gave you a less demanding, assignment: Attend yesterday's closed-door meeting by the American consul at the Grand Palais. It was simple information gathering. Nothing more."

She had tried to get out of it.

"The consulate will require identification," she had pleaded with Putnev.

Putnev had had an answer. He always had an answer.

"Tell the Americans you attend on behalf of that friend of yours, the Jewess you teach with. The one whose cat you feed when she visits her sick uncle. You even have a key to her flat. What's her name? Ah, yes, Bloch. Tell the Americans, Miss Bloch seeks asylum in the United States and doesn't know where else to turn. Americans love to think their country is the holy destination for oppressed people ... except their own Negroes."

He had chortled at his observation.

"They will hear my accent, Sergei. Know I am French."

"They'll think nothing of your French accent. Just act American. Demand your rights. Loudly. And wear that perfume I gave you, the one that smells of gardenia. That way, they'll *know* you're American. French women can't afford perfume, anymore."

"But my name. It's French."

Her litany of excuses had angered him.

"Then change your name for Christ's sake! Become American! Be Jane Smith! There must be at least one Jane Smith

24

among the hundreds of American expatriates who will be at the Grand Palais."

"The Grand Palais?"

"The meeting is at the Grand Palais. The American consulate is too small. Enter through the Cours de la Reine entrance along the river."

She had, and she had met George Wilson, and believed the Gestapo had detained her, and now she was trying to explain it all to Putnev in the rear of the nave of Notre Dame.

"Please, Sergei, I know you're disappointed in me."

Ah, he thought, a confession and consequently a need for appropriate penance. Now, everything was in place. For more than a year, he had sown her with sweetness. Now, it was time to reap the harvest. He had hoped she would give herself to him – if for no other reason than gratitude – but she hadn't. Which, in its own way, was better. Had she submitted in affection, he couldn't do everything to her he wanted. Family friends didn't do the things he wanted to do to her. Unseemly things. But soon, after she received Trafanov's letter, she would be desperate. Then, she would beg him for help – the begging was essential - and he would exact his price, as unseemly as he wished. But for now, play her along.

"Very well, Clotilde. Although you seem unable to keep faith with me, I will keep faith with you. I relieve you of all assignments for The Party, including your infiltration of the Catholic Resistance."

He heard what he expected. What he had played for.

"Thank you, Sergei. Thank you."

She rose. This time, he did not stop her.

"We should continue to meet, Clotilde. Three weeks from now, here, at the same time."

She nodded agreement and exited the cathedral, navigating through the late autumn gloom toward her flat across the river in the Marais quarter. She was midway across Pont a'Arc, when she halted so abruptly that a couple walking arm-in-arm behind her split apart to avoid bumping into her.

The silent dread that had broken over her moments earlier in the cathedral had returned.

But now that dread had a voice. Putnev's voice.

That would explain your behavior last night, he had said to her, *with that young, fair-haired American student you picked up at the Grand Palais.*

But she had not described George Wilson to Putnev -- not what he did, not his nationality, not the color of his hair.   Yet, Putnev knew.

A blast of cold wind off the river caught her full, sending a shiver down her spine. She resumed her pace, only now faster, almost desperate to get to her room and lock the door behind her.

Chapter 7

From across the plaza in front of the cathedral, Trafanov had watched Clotilde until she disappeared around the corner of Notre Dame. Minutes later, he saw Putnev emerge onto the plaza. Putnev knew where to look and spying Trafanov's cab, made for it, barging past a half-dozen pedestrians who had stopped to stare at one of the few taxis still plying the streets of Paris. He climbed into the back seat and slammed shut the door. Trafanov eased up the clutch. The taxi pulled from the curb.

They drove in silence, Trafanov the soldier awaiting orders from Putnev the officer. It had been that way since the Eastern Front in 1916, where Private Maxim Trafanov had been assigned by the Czar's Army as subaltern to Sergei Putnev, a young lieutenant. Within three days, Trafanov had taken the tip of an Austrian lance meant for Putnev. The action left Trafanov with an angry scar shaped like a checkmark beneath his right eye. Trafanov's sacrifice, however, did not yield friendship. The men's different social status - Trafanov the abandoned child of a Kiev prostitute, and Putnev the indulgent son of a dissolute estate manager near St. Petersburg - prevented it. But it did not prevent a certain familiarity.

"First things first," Putnev said, as the taxi crossed over the Seine, heading north toward Pigalle. "The Borodin woman. Is she at the Splendide?"

"Room 8."

"Where did you find her?"

"Working the Gare du Nord. Fucking in empty train compartments to pay the rent. She was once rich. Her husband some big-shot doctor in Moscow. They fled the Revolution, but the New Guard caught them before they got out of Russia. Condemned him an anti-revolutionary and shot him. Let her go. But took her money and raped her blind for a week. Somehow, she got to Germany, then Paris. Desperate."

Yes, Putnev thought, desperate. She would beg him, a fellow émigré, to help her. Begging was an aphrodisiac for Putnev. He had learned about it from his father who introduced his son to the

27

pleasures of powerless peasant girls on the estate he had managed. Before sending his 13-year-old boy to the back of the piggery for his first sexual experience, the elder Putnev had said, "Make her beg you. It's better."

The confused boy had asked, "She'll beg?"

The father smirked.

"If you threaten her the right way."

The boy had threatened her with a beating. She begged him not to. His father had been right. The begging had excited him, as much as the touch of her dirty hands.

Putnev worked a Gitane into his tortoise-shell cigarette holder.

"I suppose the Borodin bitch is old and full of wrinkles

"Not so bad."

"Did you tell her what I want?"

"Yes."

"Can she deliver?"

"Already arranged. I brought Borodin and the girl an hour ago to the hotel. The girl is in pigtails and school uniform. What you like."

Putnev's voice turned arch.

"It's not only a matter of what I like. It is a matter of *you* getting it right. And too often you don't. Remember what happened three weeks ago with the desk clerk at the Hotel Etoile? What *were* you thinking, Maxim? The little slut the clerk procured not only looked 12, she *was* 12! And ran to the gendarmes, afterwards. Thank God, I have Captain Azuir of the Paris police on our payroll. Even then, we just made it. By the time I reached him, the gendarmes had turned the matter over to their Nazi masters. Azuir told me German State Security had already sent one of their own, some German cop named Halle, to investigate. The prick is obsessed with persecuting men who fuck girls. What are we supposed to fuck? Dogs?"

Putnev shook his head in disgust.

"Just once, I want one of these moralizing Aryans like Halle to ask the girls how they feel. He'd get an earful. The little tramps enjoy it. Remember the one we found a few months ago walking alone by Sacré-Coeur just before curfew? Said she liked what I did to her. Said it reminded her of what her father did to her. She loved it."

Putnev lit his cigarette.

"In any case, Halle is a dangerous man. And powerful. Azuir couldn't rein him in. Halle was already on his way to see the desk clerk at the Étoile. The clerk would have ratted us out. Fortunately, you got to the desk clerk before Halle. At least you handled *that* correctly."

Trafanov heard the rising anger in Putnev's voice and sought to placate him.

"It will be correct this time, Comrade Putnev. I promise. Any girl the Borodin woman procures *will be* 18. I personally guarantee that Madame Borodin will ..."

Putnev lunged forward, grabbing the back of the front seat with such force it jarred Trafanov's grip on the steering wheel.

"I don't want your personal guarantees! You guaranteed me the desk clerk at the Etoile would find suitable girls. He didn't. Get it right! The girl must be 18!"

Trafanov righted his swerving car.

Putnev eased his grip on the seat and leaned back, his voice again under control.

"Does Madame Borodin know what became of the desk clerk at the Etoile?"

"I told her it wasn't suicide ... no matter what the cops said."

Putnev crushed his cigarette into the chrome ashtray in the car door and let his fury subside before continuing.

"I have a job for you, Maxim."

Trafanov had first heard those words on an April afternoon in 1916 in Pinsk.   Intelligence Officer Sergei Putnev had just learned through the brutal interrogation of an Austrian colonel that the German government was financing Lenin's return to St. Petersburg to foment civil strife and accelerate Russia's withdrawal from the war. It was extraordinary information. Revolution was coming. It was not a matter of whether the revolution would be good or bad, only that a man be on the winning side. With the information Putnev had just learned, he knew what side that would be. That evening, Putnev commandeered a car, 30 gallons of fuel and set off from Pinsk. Forty-eight hours later, he made contact with the St. Petersburg's Soviet and told them what he knew. Sergei Putnev's driver that night had been Maxim Trafanov. Within 48 hours, Putnev had deserted the Czar's Imperial Army and become an operative in the Soviet's nascent Ministry of Internal Affairs, with Trafanov attached to him to carry out his directives.

Putnev's career flourished. He had a gift for identifying White Russians and killing them. So well, that 20 years later, Soviet Intelligence thought he might be as able an assassin outside of Russia as in and posted him to Paris under cover as an émigré novelist. Putnev requested Trafanov as his aide. The Party agreed, and in three months, Maxim Trafanov was driving a Paris cab, reporting to Putnev in secret and killing whatever émigrés Putnev and The Party ordered liquidated. The Putnev/Trafanov partnership was so effective, Russian secret service maintained it even after the Nazi Occupation. Once a month, Putnev withdrew 2000 Reichsmarks from a Swiss bank account in Paris to bribe the appropriate Nazi, allowing Trafanov to keep his taxi.

Trafanov stopped his cab in front of the Hotel Splendide, a ramshackle building, its rooms rented by the hour. Putnev stepped onto the sidewalk, then looked back at Trafanov.

"Your new assignment is this: in two weeks, send Mrs. deBrouillard the same letter I composed to Mrs. Verskya. But with one change. Do not threaten Mrs. deBrouillard's children, as you threatened Mrs. Verskya's. Mrs. deBrouillard has no children of her own, so threaten only her students at the Louis Pasteur Primary School in the Marais. Write the letter in Gothic script. Room 8, you say?"

"Yes, comrade. Madame Borodin will be there with the girl. Do you want to know the girl's name?"

"No," Putnev said sharply and ascended the stairs into the hotel.

Chapter 8

Thirteen days after her last meeting with Putnev in the nave of Notre Dame, Clotilde dismissed her class at the Louis Pasteur Primary School in the Marais and prepared to leave for the day. In the faculty lounge, she hung her smock in her locker and retrieved her coat. As she pulled her woolen gloves from the coat pocket, a folded piece of paper fell to the floor. She picked it up. Read its Gothic script.

Clotilde deBrouillard,

You are being watched. Your interest in Americans disturbs us. Remember. If we want to kill you, it will be done. Or if we want to make angels of your little girls on their way home, you cannot stop us. Do not forget the power we have over you. Your stay with us by the Canal St. Martin SHOULD have been an ample reminder.

Clotilde ran to the lavatory and vomited.

An agonizing day later in the back of Notre Dame, seated in the gathering gloom of the solstice, she was begging with Putnev.

"Sergei, you must protect my children!"

Putnev suppressed a smile of anticipation. The harvest was about to be his. He asked her to tell him everything. She did and showed him the note.

"The script," he said, after reading the letter. "Very artistic. Sad that someone with such a beautiful hand could be so monstrous."

"I beg you, Sergei. Help me."

Her begging excited him.

"You want my protection. You shall have it. We don't want Nazi thugs doing unspeakable things to your little girls. You need only be obedient to prevent that. Do you know the Hotel Splendide in Pigalle, Clotilde?"

She shook her head no.

"Then you will. Next week. This time. Room 8. It's where I write. Room 8 will be our new rendezvous place. In this matter, it is

31

best we stay in close contact. When you arrive at the hotel, ask for the baron."

A week later, an ingenuous Clotilde entered the Hotel Splendide. She had taken only a few tentative steps into the little lobby before the desk clerk confronted her.

"I don't know you. If you're meeting someone, you must pay for the room now."

She blinked in confusion.

"I'm meeting the baron."

The clerk eyed her.

"You don't look like his type. In any case, wait there."

He nodded toward the faded red sofa across the room.

Putnev arrived five minutes later.

"Room 8 is upstairs," he said matter-of-factly to her. "Come with me."

The grimy white walls of room 8 enclosed a wood-frame bed, an armoire and a smudgy window overlooking Rue Duperré. Clotilde stood by the armoire. Putnev stood by the bed and beckoned her with a sly smile that vanquished her innocence.

"Don't look so shocked, Clotilde. Remember the cardinal rule. Obedience."

She backed toward the door, her left hand outstretched behind her searching for the porcelain door knob. Putnev shrugged.

"Of course, Clotilde, you *can* run away. I wouldn't dream of forcing you to do anything distasteful. But consider that note you showed me, the one in Gothic script. If you walk away now, where will you turn when the Gestapo comes for you and your students? To the gendarmes? They're in bed with the Nazis. I, alone, stand between you and the mayhem Paris has become. To protect you and your students, I have taken risks and am willing to take more. But I want something in return."

"Sergei, I beg you ..."

His chest tightened. His voice lowered to a breathy intensity.

"It's good that you beg, Clotilde. But tell me *exactly* what you're begging for."

She did not answer. He grasped her jaw. Squeezed it.

His next words exploded on her face.

"Get down on your fucking knees, Clotilde!"

She hesitated.   He did not and pressed his fat hands into her shoulders, driving her knees to the floor.   He dug into his pants pocket and pulled out a slip of paper and held it to her eyes.

"Memorize the telephone number written on this paper!"

Then he wadded the piece of paper into a ball and jammed it into her mouth.

"Eat it, Clotilde."

She was crying.

"Eat it, Clotilde!"

He watched her eat it.

"Now, swallow it."

He watched her swallow it and sighed.

"Very obedient, Clotilde.   If you need me, call the number you have memorized and say to whoever answers, 'I want to speak with the baron.'   The person knows how to contact me."

He patted her head.

"Now that you understand our arrangement, Clotilde, be here next week.   And wear something more exciting than that dowdy frock."

He stepped past her, flung open the door and descended the stairs.

Chapter 9

Wilson's journey home was agony. In his train compartment on the Sud Express, he had sat paralyzed, his inability to help Clotilde rendering him unwilling to help himself. His Atlantic crossing on the *Excalibur* was worse. Each night, he had drunk himself to sleep, only to be beset by the same nightmare: the *Excalibur* torpedoed and slipping beneath the waves of the Atlantic, that ocean Clotilde hated.

But the *Excalibur*, each side painted with a huge American flag to alert U-boat commanders of the vessel's neutrality, had crossed the Atlantic in five unmolested days, reaching New York City and its Jersey City pier at dawn on November 17.

Although Wilson had reserved a first-class ticket from Grand Central Station to South Station, Boston, he destroyed it and purchased - as if in atonement for his desertion of Clotilde - a third-class ticket. But the discomfort of being cramped into a stiff-backed seat next to a chain-smoking consumptive was meager penance for his inability to have saved her. By 1 p.m., he sat aboard a Boston & Maine Railroad train heading north out of Boston to Waterville, Maine.

Two hours later, in moral misery, he stepped onto the wooden platform of the Waterville train station, where his father had promised to meet him. Dr. Wilson had kept his promise.

"Son!"

The six-foot surgeon in the dark three-piece suit and impeccable Chesterfield exuded a patrician's confidence. He removed his gray fedora and waved it at his only child. In a moment, the doctor was extending his hand.

"Your mother would have come, but she's preparing the fatted calf. A grand dinner it will be. The Cadwalladers are joining us. I knew you'd like that."

Dr. Wilson took one of his son's suitcases, and the two men walked through the late autumn air toward the black Packard parked by the end of the platform. And through the closed window of the backseat, Wilson saw her, saw Mae.

She had not changed: thin, bright brown hair in a bob, a Peter Pan collar buttoned up, her smile conveying warmth without heat and a certitude that God had created an orderly world with her in mind.

As Wilson slipped into the front seat, Mae leaned forward and beamed, "Your father invited me, Georgie!"

She handed Wilson a five-cent bag of Hershey Kisses.

"I remembered you liked them. They say everything is rationed over there."

"You kept up with the news?"

"With you there, I wanted to know all I could. It sounds so awful. We're so thankful you're back with us. For good."

The 23-mile trip from Waterville to Unity took 40 minutes. The clapboard farm houses set back from the road amid fallow fields and pine forests recalled his childhood. For years, he had told his big-city friends at Yale and Harvard that Maine was not a quaint repository of New England life, but a hard-scrabble landscape in North America, a state masked by pockets of charm along its southeastern coast, deflecting the poverty of its interior.   Still, the farmsteads and weathered barns along state highway 202 warmed him, free as they were of Nazi flags.

Conversation with his father and Mae skimmed across quotidian life in Central Maine: births and deaths, pregnancies and disease, achievements and disappointments and a forecast of light snow by nightfall.

"Six o'clock, then," Mae said, as she exited the car in front of the fieldstone parsonage of St. Mark's Methodist Church.   "My parents will be so happy to see you."

Father and son drove another five minutes to the grand Italianate mansion with its wrap-around porch and sprawling grounds that Dorothy and Clyde Wilson called home, built a half-century earlier by a Maine railroad magnate. Six bedrooms and eight fireplaces, a double salon and a large dining room with French doors afforded abundant space for a family of three.   But the Wilsons were generous with the space.   Dr. Wilson made rooms available to surgical residents at Thayer Hospital in Waterville, where he presided as head of surgery. And student-teachers at

Waldo County High School, where Dorothy Wilson served as principal, could always find temporary accommodations.

The smell of roasted lamb greeted Wilson as he stepped into the center hall.

The whoosh of the opening door drew Dorothy Wilson from the kitchen, a lacy apron over her black woolen dress. She ran down the turkey-carpeted center hall, hugged her son, then backed off, stared at him.

"I've prayed so hard for this day."

Two hours later, having arranged and rearranged and rearranged again his cufflinks and toiletries atop the mahogany bureau in his boyhood room, Wilson heard the chime of the front-door bell.

The Reverend Arthur Cadwallader, his wife Virginia, and their only living child, Mae, had arrived for dinner. Wilson readjusted the three sets of cufflinks, this time to point toward the tip of a faded Boston Red Sox pennant he had hung on the wall as a boy.

"Son," Dr. Wilson called upstairs, "our guests, your guests, have arrived!"

It astonished Wilson how quickly a desire for alcohol had overtaken him after only five days aboard the *Excalibur*, and now as he descended the center hall staircase, he wanted a drink. But even if his father had stocked whisky, it would never be on display when the temperance-proclaiming Reverend Cadwallader visited. His aversion to spirits had been passed along to his daughter.

"I'm sure it tastes as bad as it smells," she had proclaimed brightly at the Colby College Senior Cotillion, where Wilson had escorted her three years earlier. Most of the night, he had sipped a gin martini, but she remained quiet about his exhibition. Later, when he asked if she had objected, she had said resignedly, "I don't like it, but at something like the Cotillion, all the boys do."

The Reverend Cadwallader's handshake was as robust as his deep look into Wilson's eyes, while Virginia Cadwallader deferred her usual plump decorum with a solid kiss on Wilson's cheek.

"My boy. My dear boy."

Having observed the laying on of hands and lips from her parents, Mae was free to stand to the side and smile and add to the merriment by saying, "We're so happy you're home!"

Coats shed, hot punch served, Paris became the object of their questions.

"What was it like?"

"What about curfews and rationing?"

"Are the churches still open?"

"We hear the Germans have behaved well in Paris. The papers said Paris was an open city. There was no destruction."

In ten minutes, the party had moved from the double salon into the dining room and to the high-polished Georgian table lit by a three-tiered brass chandelier. In a furtive glance through the French doors, Wilson watched the season's first snow drift through the weak light from the street lamp beyond their front lawn and felt again his last moments with Clotilde.

His mother's guiding hand brought him back.

"You sit here, George, at the seat of honor, next to your father."

In a moment, their heads were bowed.

The Reverend Cadwallader's grace exceeded a simple thanks by two minutes, ending with his hope that world leaders would be wise enough to spare America the folly of the Europeans and keep the peace. After all, God had placed America between two great oceans for a reason. The pastor's stentorian "Amen" was punctuated by a pop from the burning logs in the white marble fire place that made Wilson jump. It brought laughter and commencement of dinner. After the roast lamb and Brussel sprouts and mashed potatoes, the Reverend Cadwallader picked up his coffee spoon and tapped the side of his water glass.

"George, as you know, I'm not only a proud alumnus of Colby, but I've been on the board of trustees for more than eight years. It's a fine, fine college, even though my dear friend Clyde believes his Bowdoin is the best school in the state of Maine."

"In all New England," Dr. Wilson corrected to laughter.

"In that time," the Reverend Cadwallader continued, "I've made important connections with many people at the college. One with the chairman of the history department, my good friend the Reverend Doctor Stephen Moseley."

The Reverend Cadwallader paused, took a sip of water as much for dramatic effect as to lubricate his throat.

"And Dr. Moseley has informed me that when he learns you've successfully defended your doctoral dissertation at Harvard, it will be Colby's pleasure to offer you ..."

He paused again and rose from his chair.

"... an assistant professorship in the history department this spring semester."

"Oh, Daddy, you never said anything!"

The Reverend Cadwallader was not done.

"What's more, George, for this spring semester, arrangements have been made for you to stay in Dr. Gorham's home."

"Daddy, that's so beautiful!"

"He's on sabbatical, collecting fossils in the Dakotas. His house is right off campus, and as Mae knows, quite beautiful. Not up to the grandeur of the Wilson manse but a very comfortable and affordable accommodation until you get a place of your own."

"Arthur, how can we ever repay you?" Dorothy Wilson stammered

Her display of indebtedness was not necessary. Two years earlier, Dorothy had interceded with the Waldo County Board of Education to secure Mae the position of second-grade teacher at the Unity Day School.

The Reverend Cadwallader waved a convivial hand.

"All I want, Dorothy, is a slice of your mincemeat pie."

Much laughter and Wilson took it as his cue. He pushed back his chair and began to collect the now empty plates.

Mae rose to help him. Neither Virginia Cadwallader or Dorothy Wilson objected. It was where Mae belonged.

Chapter 10

The last of the plates removed, Wilson and Mae stood alone in the kitchen. With his mother's mincemeat pie already on the sideboard in the dining room, Wilson knew he and Mae would not be interrupted ... as if the moment had been planned.

"Don't you just love kitchens," Mae said twirling toward the porcelain sink and picking up a plate to dry, the hem of her Scotch-plaid skirt rising an inch above her knees. "Especially this one. It's so homey. Can't you just see it with children and friends and ..."

"Mae ..."

She held the plate to her chest and stepped toward him, close enough to be intimate but not touching.

"I know, Georgie, it's all so much. The position at Colby, you being back home, your defense at Harvard, us, the wedding ..."

"Wedding? You made plans?"

She giggled.

"Not exactly plans. But after Daddy's announcement, it all suddenly made sense. Part of a plan. First your return, then the position at the college, then, well, a June wedding. We had discussed it before you left. Remember?"

Wilson remembered. It had been the night before he left for France. His father had loaned him the Packard. Back from dinner in Waterville by ten, he and Mae had sat in the idling car in front of the parsonage. No, she had said pulling back, as he slipped his hand beneath her coat, there would be time for that kind of thing after they were married. He hadn't contradicted her assumption of wedlock.

Now, at least, he would challenge it.

"Mae, there's the war."

Her voice turned defensive.

"*We're* not at war. That's *their* war. The Germans and French and English. That's all they ever do. War."

"You know about the *Reuben James*?"

"Yes, but the Germans said they were sorry. Besides, you came across with no trouble."

"Mae, listen to me. War is coming. It's a war we must fight. You don't know what these Nazis are."

She slipped the dried plate into the wooden dishrack.

"What I do know is we love each other, and we can't let every unfortunate thing that happens in the world dictate what we do. The big things are beyond us, Georgie. We can't control them. It's the little things that matter in life. That's what's real. You and me and our families and the hopes that hold us together."

Wilson relented, retreated.

"We'll talk when I'm back from Harvard. I'll be going down to Cambridge for a few weeks to prepare for the defense. I really can't focus on anything until the defense is over."

"Oh, I understand Georgie. When you're back in a month, we'll have Christmas and New Year's, and then set you up in Dr. Gorham's house. We'll have plenty of time to make plans."

She cocked her head toward the swinging door that led to the hall that opened onto the dining room.

"We should go back. They'll think we got lost. I just love your mother's mincemeat pie."

Chapter 11

The conference room in the second-floor History Department off Harvard Yard seemed an unlikely venue for life-changing events more often reserved for altar or battlefield. But the men and women who came there to defend their doctoral dissertations emerged either to triumphant university careers or, failing, disappeared into academic obscurity.

What had unfolded on December 8th was no less life changing.

Laurence Hazell, chairman of the Harvard History Department, glared in incomprehension at Wilson. The professor's shock of white hair, hawk nose and six-foot-four-inch frame were intimidating enough but seemed almost trifling compared to his lacerating baritone.

"George, do you fully understand the magnitude of the honor we have bestowed on you, today? You have not only successfully defended your doctoral dissertation, we are going to publish your work. The Harvard University Press. We consider your dissertation seminal in illuminating the Church's triumphs and failures as it transitioned from the ease of philosophy to the agony of governance. And yet, you seem ready to throw your success away."

Professor Hazell's classes, from Introduction to Western Civilization to his seminars on Medieval France, had transcended the appraisal of "interesting" for Harvard history students to "indispensable." Across the Western academy, dozens of his students not only taught what he thought, but delivered their lectures with the same conviction, more akin to revelation than exegesis.

"George, you have impressed us, and we are not an easy audience to impress. Professor Lane is, to my thinking, the premier medievalist in American academe; he was your mentor. He directed your research. Make no mistake. It is your skill and scholarship that produced *The Great Transition: The Church from Prayer to Power*, but it is Jonathan Lane who shares some of the bright-light attention this work will receive. He deserves your consideration."

The stately plump Professor Lane flashed a temporizing hand.

"Laurence, these are extraordinary times. Scholarship is subsumed by larger concerns."

Lane knew those larger concerns well. He had accompanied Woodrow Wilson to Paris in the diplomatic orgy following the 1918 armistice. The President had made no decision about regional partitions or national destiny or treaties without first consulting him.

"What George did this morning is understandable."

It had been a brilliant autumn morning in Cambridge. Although the trees had lost their foliage weeks earlier, the bright air and mid-50s temperature had bestowed a last gasp of autumnal warmth before the onset of New England winter. Even the Army private stationed at the door of the recruiting station on Boylston Street had allowed himself a smile as Wilson entered.

Wilson's induction had been easy. No more than ten minutes to enlist, with an unexpected addendum from the recruiting officer, a trim second lieutenant with enthusiasm made for his work.

"With your background, Mr. Wilson, I hope you'll consider Officer Candidate School. The U.S. Army needs men with your intelligence: fluency in German and French, not to mention Latin and Greek, a Yale education and about to receive a Harvard PhD. After basic, it would only involve an additional 18 weeks of training."

Wilson's answer erupted.

"When can I report?"

"After the first of the year would be ..."

"No. Sooner. Now."

The second lieutenant arched his eyebrows at the enthusiasm.

"If you can reach Ft. Benning, Georgia, within six days, you can begin basic on Monday and enroll in OCS upon completion. You'll have to pass a physical, but that should be no problem. Does that meet your needs?"

Wilson said it did.

"Professor Hazell," Lane continued, "it doesn't take the Harvard History Department to tell us where the country is headed.

What happened yesterday at Pearl Harbor has made war inevitable. I know the left-wingers of our university do not countenance patriotism and the isolationists counsel disinterest, but we should understand the impulses of a young man."

Hazell exhaled heavily, shook his head in defeat, turned to Wilson.

"Still, George, I can't deny the brilliance of your work. I shall continue to hope for your safe keeping in what lies ahead and your eventual return to our world of scholarship. You have a gift. I regret it will be spent – I hope not wasted – by the U.S. Army."

The chairman extended his hand, but his eyes did not meet Wilson's. Hazell was out the door in a moment, leaving Wilson with Professor Lane. The two men shook hands.

"George, keep in touch. I'm disappointed, but I understand. If I were your age, I might have made the same decision. Best of luck."

Then Wilson was alone. The weight of telling Professor Hazell he had enlisted had lifted, now replaced by the heavier burden of having to tell his father and Mae.

His father would be incredulous, then angry, then resigned. But Mae ... Mae was another story. The only defense he had was to call his decision a moral imperative. And that was true. As far as it went. He would not tell Mae of the oppression he had felt as she twirled about his mother's kitchen with a dried plate in her hands, nor of the relentless ache in his soul for a woman he had met a month earlier in a snow storm in Paris.

Chapter 12

Returning to Maine, Wilson barely made his connections.

But at 7:31 p.m., his train from Boston pulled into Waterville Station. Once again, Dr. Wilson was there to meet his son. This time alone.

In a moment, he and his boy were walking toward the Packard.

"Well, what happened?"

"Your son has a PhD. in history from Harvard University. What's more, they were so impressed with my dissertation, they want to publish it. The Harvard University Press."

Dr. Wilson laughed, a loud explosion not unknown to him but employed only on the rarest of occasions.

"My boy, I'm beginning to think you should reconsider that offer from Colby. You're too good for them."

"I already have reconsidered it, Father."

"Don't wonder. Colby's a good school, but once your book is published, I'd wager that Bowdoin comes courting."

Then added with a sly smile, "Although, your mother will never want you and Mae to leave central Maine for Down East."

Dr. Wilson slid behind the wheel of the Packard. His son sat next to him. They were pulling out of the parking lot when Wilson spoke next.

"I'm not going to Bowdoin or Colby, Father. I'm not going to teach. I've enlisted and leaving for Ft. Benning, Georgia, in the morning. Basic training and Officer Candidate School."

They were out of Waterville on Route 202 when Dr. Wilson next spoke. His words weighted.

"Your mother and I have been close friends with the Cadwalladers for more than 20 years. Do you know what they're expecting? What your mother and I are expecting? Jesus, George, have you thought about Mae?"

He had never heard his father say Jesus in any context but prayer.

"I can't marry her. Not now."

"Not ever, it sounds to me."

Wilson ignored the accuracy of his father's observation.

"The world is coming undone, Father. Being ripped apart. I have a higher obligation."

Dr. Wilson snorted.

"There was a woman in France, wasn't there?"

Wilson didn't answer.

"I'll take that as a yes."

Wilson braced himself for what was to come. And yet, it did not come at once, but a mile further in the cold Maine night and then in a voice of resignation.

"The older I get, the less certain I am of anything, George. A month ago, I performed an emergency craniotomy on a Penobscot Indian, who had tried to blow his brains out with a shotgun. I opened his skull, removed three pieces of buckshot from his brain and sutured him back together. The man lived. That is, until last night, when he opened the jets on the gas stove in his shack on China Lake and committed suicide, killing himself and two young daughters. All my life, I have tried to protect you from such freak insanity, the abject violence that runs just beneath the surface of our lives. The position at Colby, marriage to Mae, the union of our two families, all seemed to offer a great bulwark against the universal mayhem. Now, you're throwing that safety away and stepping into a catastrophic war."

Wilson could no longer argue, only clarify.

"Father, no matter what you tried, you couldn't keep me safe. Yale and Harvard and Unity all protected me, but it can't last. Sooner or later the horror breaks through. I saw it first hand in Paris. Yes, I met a girl. And in the blink of an eye, she was carried off. Probably to her death. After that, I couldn't return to the pleasantries of a well-ordered life. Colby and Mae and the safety of Maine are no longer luxuries. They are unrealities. One of my professors today spoke of the Church making its transition from the ease of philosophy to the agony of governance. It's the same for people. The false hope of a well-ordered life has to give way to the reality of making decisions invariably between bad and worse."

Dr. Wilson's voice was subdued.

"I know you well enough, George. Your mind's made up. Your decision is as irrevocable now as when you told me you weren't going to Bowdoin but to Yale.   At the time, your mother said it was just the son expressing his independence   But that day, I heard something else, as well.   Your voice was hard as flint.   That hardness has returned."

A four-point buck bolted across the roadway. Dr. Wilson swung the steering wheel. The Packard swerved. The deer disappeared into the dark.

Another minute of silence.

"I'll tell you something son ... you've overwrapped your decision in too much philosophy.   Philosophy is a menace. It makes painful reality a game of logic, an exercise in sophistry at the expense of honesty. The issue is far simpler than your moral hijinks about choice. Do you love Mae as much as you love the woman back in France, regardless of her fate?"

Expecting no response, Dr. Wilson continued.

"I'm sorry for Mae, especially after the death of her sister, Anna. And I'm sorry for you. I'm sorry for our friendship with the Cadwalladers.   All casualties of your coming of age."

Chapter 13

When the Packard came to a stop in the long driveway leading to the Wilson home, Dr. Wilson exited the car but left the engine idling. He looked back through the driver's window.

"I assume you're going to the Cadwalladers," he said coldly.

Wilson did.   Mae ushered him into the foyer of the parsonage.

"Oh, Georgie, I've been calling your mother every half hour! Daddy said Dr. Moseley hadn't heard from Harvard. I began to worry."

She shut the door behind them, a swirl of cold air tightening her shoulders.

"Father and Mother are at Monday night Bible study. They should be home, shortly."

Wilson led her by the hand into the front parlor.   They seated themselves on the green velvet settee draped by a hand-crocheted afghan of faded greens and reds and yellows, the product of her grief at the death of her sister.

In a minute's explanation, the painless part of the evening was over - the successful defense. The offer of publication brought the buoyant Mae to the edge of the settee. Then a pause that she knew foreshadowed shadow, a darkness she had first felt twelve years earlier, when her father had gently sat her down on the same settee and told her Anna had drowned in a boating accident on Unity Pond.

"Mae, our wedding in June. I can't …"

"Oh, no, no, no, Georgie, I've been thinking, too. Why wait? We can get married right after Christmas. That way we can set up house in Dr. Gorham's for the spring semester, and you wouldn't have to wait for, well, I know you don't want to wait any longer."

She was breathing rapidly. Her eyes blinking.

"Not January, Mae, not June. I don't know if ever. I've enlisted. I leave for the army tomorrow morning. I don't know what else to say. I …"

Without looking for it, she slid the afghan from the back of the settee and pulled it tight around her shoulders, then rose, walking out of the parlor and up the stairs.

"Mae!"

The last sound Wilson heard in the rectory was the click of her bedroom door closing.

Chapter 14

It was the only letter for him in the morning mail call. Wilson read it on the spot, standing in front of his cot in the wood-frame barracks at Ft. Benning, surrounded by three dozen other soon-to-be second lieutenants who were opening letters from their families.

June 17, 1942

My dear son (Or should I write Lt. Wilson?),

We are so proud! Colonel Cashman called this morning to tell us you will be graduated first in your Officer Candidate class and will be acknowledged as class leader at the graduation exercises. He seems to be a very thoughtful man, and said he had invited you to luncheon with him and Mrs. Cashman on graduation day. He asked us to join you. Of course, we would love it, but I have graduation exercises of my own to preside over at Waldo County High School, and your father is addressing the Central Maine Medical Society. He notes, with considerable delight, that attending graduations where you are the central point of veneration is nothing new for us. At the Unity Day School and at Waldo County High, you graduated first. And then Phi Beta Kappa at Yale, summa cum laude from the history department. All this has preceded your latest accomplishment in our nation's armed services.

Your father is most interested in speaking with you about your future plans. As you know, he contributed to the campaigns of Senator Hale and Senator Brewster and introduced both men to prominent citizens here in central Maine. He would like to contact them on your behalf, perhaps for a position in Washington. Of course, you will have to discuss all this with him.

In any case, I fear for so many of our young men. Most of the boys in this year's graduating class at Waldo have expressed their intent of enlisting, as soon as they graduate.

We love you and are so proud, George, and eagerly anticipate your return next week for your ten-day leave.
All our love,
Mother and Father

His parents' absence did not disturb him; his mother had already informed him of that during their once-a-week telephone call. But his father's wish to contact Maine's senators did. It would not be the first time Clyde Wilson transmuted paternal concern into paternal interference.

Nine years earlier, he had, without telling his son, called the director of admissions at Bowdoin to "put in a good word" for George. Thanks to a telephone call from the director to congratulate George on early admission, son discovered what father had done. Wilson thanked the director of admissions but informed him he was going to Yale. The subsequent confrontation with his father resulted in a one-week standoff of silence, ending only after Yale informed George he had been accepted. Dr. Wilson dutifully congratulated his son, and the matter was dropped, but the clash of wills was not resolved and now seemed certain to arise again.

Then there was Mae, or rather the absence of any mention of her in his mother's letter. He hoped he wouldn't see Mae during his ten-day leave. To that end, he had scheduled a visit with his cousin, Melchior, in Portland on the one Sunday his leave allowed him to be in Unity. Otherwise, his parents would insist he join them for morning service at St. Mark's. Still, in a town of 600 people, meeting Mae would be inevitable and avoiding her too contrived. But what was he to say to her? Act as if that evening in December had not happened?

Wilson did not see the interruption coming.

"Unlike other graduations you've starred in," the rotund Colonel Cashman grumbled, coming up behind him and adjusting Wilson's cot to put it in perfect alignment with the other 36 cots in barracks, "you won't be speaking. Army doesn't approve of that. We simply call you to the stage, tell the audience what you achieved, give you a citation and shake your hand."

Wilson snapped to attention, saluted.

"As you were, Wilson."

Colonel Cashman ignored the salutes from the other recruits and nodded toward the barrack door.

"Come with me."

Wilson followed three paces behind, wondering how a man of 280 pounds had survived the Army physical.

Colonel Cashman passed through the front door and stopped under the tarpapered overhang above the pay phone. Perspiration glistened on his forehead. He waved a perfunctory hand at the young man on the telephone. The young man hung up and hurried away.

"Just as well you're not speaking, Wilson   A mid-afternoon graduation ceremony on a parade field in June in South Georgia is no one's idea of a good time.   But I didn't come here to discuss the weather. Our luncheon today must be cancelled.   Too bad.   Mrs. Cashman has perfected egg salad. Just the thing in this heat."

He pointed down a sunbaked lawn the length of a football field toward an oval, where a limp American flag hung at full mast.

"See that Jeep down there, parked at the oval?   It and its driver will take you to the Ft. Benning Officers' Club.   Since you're not an officer for another four hours, you won't be admitted ... unless you tell the guard you have been invited by a fellow calling himself St. Patrick. That's all Wilson. Good luck."

Chapter 15

Viewed from roadway, the Ft. Benning Officers' Club offered little more polish than the enlisted men's mess, but inside a richer environment greeted Wilson. He walked down a long corridor, its paneled walls adorned by brass sconces and paintings of American Presidents and the triumph of American arms at Yorktown, San Juan Hill and Belleau Wood. The parquet floors creaked beneath his step and led to an oak-paneled tap room. Behind its bar stood a tall man, his craggy face softened by a gray goatee. He wore a crumpled white suit and sipped what appeared to be a martini.

He waved Wilson over to him but did not extend his hand.

"Bartender doesn't show up until 11:30. I wasn't prepared to wait another hour for the day's first drink, so I made it myself. Care to join me?"

"No, thank you, sir."

"Call me St. Patrick," he said, raising his glass and smiling a smile of good cheer ... and duplicity.

"Yes, Mr. St. Patrick."

"Just St. Patrick. As you might suspect, it's not my real name, but it pays homage to my Irish ancestry."

St. Patrick's suit had the nipped waist and tailored cut of Saville Row, except with St. Patrick there was no trace of an English or Irish accent, only the lilt of a Southern aristocrat.

"Colonel Cashman will be pleased by my commandeering you. It means more food for him. I can vouch for the excellence of Mrs. Cashman's egg salad ... if your taste runs in that direction. I'm sure you prefer pate de foie gras from your days in Paris, or Yankee pot roast from your boyhood in Unity, Maine."

St. Patrick tapped a tan envelope lying on the bar in front of him.

"First in class deserves some recognition," he said, "such as receiving your orders before everyone else."

With a flick of his right index finger, St. Patrick sent the envelope sliding along the polished bar. It came to a stop in front of Wilson.

"Open it later, but I'll tell you what it says. Following a 10-day leave, you will be sent west through San Francisco, assigned to the 7th Infantry Division, Third Battalion, 10th Regiment, Bravo Company. What your orders don't say, but what I know, is you'll then be shipped to Portland, Oregon, where you'll join Bravo Company as assistant commander and from there be assigned to the Aleutians. Yes, certainly the Aleutians. Wonderful spot, the Aleutians. Do you know the Aleutians?"

It wasn't really a question. Wilson had heard the answer in St. Patrick's voice. The Aleutians were the last place on earth you wanted to be stationed.

With a pleased-with-himself smile, St. Patrick took a long sip of his drink.

"Infantry," he mused. "Well, that's what they've trained you for these past weeks, not to mention your basic training before that. Looks like you'll be killing Japanese. Unless your father gets his way. He's already contacted two U.S. senators. Told them you'd be a great asset in Washington. That means he wants you safe, if you consider Washington safe."

Wilson's back stiffened.

"I have no intention of going to Washington, sir. I will go to the Pacific. To the Aleutians and fight Japanese. Infantry is what I want. I'd prefer Europe, but ..."

"Why Europe?"

"I've lived there. Know some of the languages."

Which was true. That Clotilde was there – or might still be there – was truer.

With remarkable agility for a man of his height, St. Patrick ducked beneath the bartender's bridge and emerged on the other side, where he lifted a bottle of Beefeater gin from the back counter and poured himself another drink.

"Sure I can't tempt you?"

Wilson shook his head no.

"Perhaps, I can tempt you in another way. By getting you out of the Aleutians, out of the Pacific Theater of Operation and away from Washington."

Wilson did not weigh his words. He was too surprised.

"To Europe?"

"Europe seems to be on your mind. But I didn't say that. However, you're justified in asking what it is I am saying."

St. Patrick held up the bottle of Beefeater, examined it.

"Used to drink bourbon. Well, I really had to considering where I was born. But over the years and across the ocean, I've found gin a more engaging libation. A friend of mine, Bill Donovan, loves the stuff."

Wilson knew better than to say anything more. By now it was clear; the conversation would unfold only as St. Patrick wanted.

"It's not quite a state secret, George, although no newspaper has written of it, but President Roosevelt just signed an executive order creating something called the Office of Strategic Services, OSS. It's a clandestine service, fighting the enemy not with infantry and airplanes and ships, but with guile, subterfuge and surprise. And it's looking for recruits. Not volunteers mind you. Of course, you must want to join us, but we do the asking. Which brings me around to why you're here listening to me and watching me drink. We'd like you to join us."

"But my existing orders."

"Countermanded ... providing you come with us. Regular Army has no choice. If OSS wants you, and you want us, they're out."

"Where would I go?"

"Oh, I couldn't possibly say."

"What about training?"

"Couldn't possibly talk about that until you join us."

"Precisely, what would I be called upon to do?"

"I told you. Guile, subterfuge and surprise."

"With whom would I serve?"

"An assortment of God's creatures. No two quite alike."

Wilson rolled his eyes.

"I know, George, I'm not very forthcoming. It's the nature of what I do."

St. Patrick sampled his fresh drink.

"I can't be more specific than that, at least for the moment. But feel free to ask more questions. You're bound to come up with one I can answer."

"If I were to join you, when would my tour begin?"

"Good show, George, a question I will answer. Immediately."

"As in ..."

St. Patrick looked at his wrist watch.

"... as in three hours and fifty-two minutes from now, or ten minutes after you receive your commission. We'd do it sooner, but we thought you might want to graduate with your class."

"How long do I have to consider your offer?"

"Three hours and fifty-two minutes. If you say no, we have our eye on another man in your class."

"Why not both of us?"

"I'm afraid that's another question I can't answer."

"If I turn you down?"

"You'll never hear from me again, and you can go to the Aleutians, lead your men into battle and return to Unity with a chest full of medals, the rank of captain and the adulation of friends and relatives. I hope to hear from you before the ceremony begins."

"St. Patrick, this is extremely ambiguous, even confusing."

"In a way, it's a good test for you."

St. Patrick sipped his drink then lifted his head, seeming to address an invisible figure suspended above Wilson.

"Many years ago, I was a freshman at Harvard University. Part of the first week's ritual for incoming freshmen was a physical examination. In truth, it was really an opportunity for a bunch of green medical students to get clinical experience. Anyway, our entire freshman class was paraded into the field house where young medical students, only a few years older than ourselves, poked, probed and questioned us. I'm afraid they didn't learn very much. We were a healthy lot. No venereal diseases, no TB, no anything. Yet, the would-be doctors went about their tasks overseen by their professors. It was all pro forma, except for one extraordinary interlude: the proctology examination. We were ordered to strip from the waist down, bend over, grasp our ankles and await a digital probe. In search of hemorrhoids, no doubt. Well, as I stood there, half naked, bent over, grasping my ankles and looking backwards and upside down between my legs, I noted a pair of black patent-leather high-heel pumps leading up to a pair of shapely ankles disappearing beneath a white lab coat. No doubt, they belonged to the only woman medical student in the class. It's something you don't forget. Ever since I entered intelligence work, I have been

55

reminded of that day and that examination, because, in its own way, it sums up what we do and what the OSS will do: view the world upside down and backwards from an implausible posture in hope of making sense of the unexpected. George, if you join us, ambiguity and confusion will be your constant companions. They will be your best weapons and worst enemies. If you like things cut and dried, stay in the infantry. We thought your background, especially your doctoral dissertation, suggested otherwise."

Struggling to get past a vision of St. Patrick awaiting a rectal examination, Wilson managed, "You've read my dissertation?"

"A colleague has. He was most impressed."

Wilson made the connection.

"Professor Lane?"

"I really couldn't say. Although, Lane is a first-rate fellow. President Wilson's right-hand man in Paris. Extraordinary diplomat."

St. Patrick finished his drink.

"Hope to hear from you," he said.

His hope was well placed.

"You will. Now. I'm in."

St. Patrick leaned across the bar and extended his right hand.

"Welcome to the OSS, George. Now, one last thing. How about that drink?"

"No, thank you, sir."

St. Patrick smiled broadly.

"Good. You passed your first test. Had you accepted a drink, I would have discussed the weather and then cheerfully seen you to the door, leaving you to wonder what this meeting had been about. We don't like men or women who drink this early in the day. In the OSS, you'll need all your wits about you."

Wilson glanced at St. Patrick's empty glass.

"Oh, this," St. Patrick said cheerily. "A stage prop. I emptied out the gin before you came in. It's water. An example of the deception you will be engaged in, except the goal won't be to enlist a bright young man into a new government service. It will be to kill and confuse as many Germans and Japanese as possible. Guile, subterfuge, surprise. No heroic infantry charges; just ruthless mayhem. That's why we're sending you back to school. We'll teach you how to do things that aren't spoken of in polite company."

'Where's the school?"

"You'll know in a day or so, after you get to wherever it is we're sending you. Be prepared to leave immediately following the commissioning exercise. For the next few days, don't think. Just follow orders, and no calls to your family. They're not expecting you for three days. When the time comes, we'll tell you what to say. A car will be waiting for you after the ceremony."

"But ..."

"No buts. Only ambiguity and confusion."

Wilson nodded.

"Viewing the world upside down and backwards from an implausible posture?"

"Bravo, George, so nice to be quoted correctly. You understand. Nice to have you aboard."

Chapter 16

Forty-five minutes after receiving his commission as a second lieutenant in the United States Army, George Wilson was delivered by Jeep to the Ft. Benning airfield. In the sweltering heat of the Quonset hut next to the tarmac, a 50-year-old staff sergeant, all sinew and grizzled hair, saluted him and asked, "You from St. Patrick?"

"Yes, I'm ..."

"OK, lose the uniform and get into these. No one is supposed to know you're Army, not even Army guys."

"But ..."

"Too bad about the uniform. It's good for picking up broads."

The sergeant handed Wilson the same navy-blue suit, white shirt and rep tie Wilson had worn when he had arrived at Ft. Benning, six months earlier.

"Get into these and go outside. A plane's waiting for you. And take this."

He handed Wilson a black attaché case.

"Don't ask me what's inside, 'cause I don't know. It's locked, and I ain't got the key."

Ten minutes later, Wilson found himself seated next to the bomb-bay door in a Douglas B-18 Bolos medium range bomber that was banking north, and heading, well ... Wilson didn't know. The pilot and co-pilot weren't saying, nor was the navigator sitting behind them but near enough to Wilson to have carried on a conversation had he wanted. He hadn't. It was well into the night before the plane descended through a heavy cloud cover and came to an easy stop on a misty runway. The pilot turned to him.

"As far as I go. There's probably something to eat in the control room."

Wilson disembarked and walked through cool air toward another Quonset hut. Inside, he announced to a sergeant who he was and asked where they had landed.

"There's some food over there," was all the sergeant said.

Over there was a metal table with a coffee pot and a wax paper-wrapped sandwich. Wilson poured himself a cup of cold coffee and took a bite of a stale ham sandwich, before eyeing a newspaper lying on a metal chair. It was a day-old copy of the *Bangor Daily News*. It was an easy deduction to make. His plane had landed at Presque Isle Army Air Field in northeast Maine.

"Your plane's leaving as soon as it's refueled," the sergeant said. "If you need the head, it's over there, but hurry up."

Wilson reboarded and saluted the new pilot, who was already in the cockpit.

"Listen, pal, no need to salute," the new pilot drawled, as he pulled a St. Louis Cardinals baseball cap tight to his head. "I'm not military, and I don't know shit. I'm an independent contractor for Air Transport Command, 23rd Army. I fly the Atlantic with whatever cargo the Army wants. Usually, it's the aircraft itself. I fly 'em over, hand them to the Limeys and get ferried back. I'm doing the same this time, but I was told to drag your ass with me. It's a long flight, and you won't sleep. No one sleeps crossing the Atlantic, unless they're shitfaced. Plus, we make stops. Newfoundland, Greenland, Iceland, Northern Ireland before we land in Surrey. That's southern England. There we part company. Me back here, and God knows what the fuck they're going to do with you. Enjoy the flight."

Wilson didn't. He sat, squirmed, stretched out and squirmed some more on a wooden bench retrofitted into the small cargo area. He had been handed a parka, but after seven months in Georgia's heat, no flight suit could keep him warm.

Twenty hours later, unshaven, fatigued, hungry and cold, Wilson emerged into the late afternoon light of South England.

On the dirt airstrip, the pilot wished Wilson good luck and pointed to a gloomy British Army private standing by a British Army staff car.

"He's for you."

Wilson climbed into the back and, in the comparative luxury of the soft upholstered seat, fell asleep. He awakened an hour later as the slamming of the car door gave way to the private announcing, "We're here."

Wilson rubbed his eyes, pulled himself out of the car and was immediately offered a hand of welcome from a balding middle-aged man in an open-collared white shirt and white flannel slacks. He spoke in an English accent that did not engage his upper lip.

59

"Welcome to Britain, Lieutenant Wilson. My name's Venerable, if you choose to believe that."

"From The Venerable Bede, the Church historian?"

"Your PhD. does you credit. Yes, The Venerable Bede. I'm late of the British Expeditionary Force, ferried out of Dunkirk a year ago aboard a yacht."

Venerable looked over his shoulder.

"And behind me is Perran House. Quite a barrack. Built by two earnest gentlemen in 1894. A glorious bit of Victorian architecture, cavernous enough to accommodate classrooms, dining area, bedrooms. It comes with 20 acres out back for the fun and games we have in mind for you lads. Follow me."

Inside, Perran House was a catalog of English architecture: lead mullioned windows, parquet floors, oak paneled rooms, and a four-sided gallery overlooking a formal reception area topped by a stained-glass oculus 50 feet above the floor. Off the reception hall, a half- dozen sturdy oak doors opened to dining room and salon, library and music room, cloak room and study. A brass plaque on the wall noted that in 1913, the house had received George V.

"We appropriated Perran House from a rather put-out City banker - War Powers Act, you know - and turned it into the OSS English campus. It's the first espionage school in history. We're setting up another one outside Washington. But for now, this is it. You're in the first class. To have earned that distinction, someone on your side of the Atlantic thinks you're pretty impressive. By the way, I'll take that."

He pointed to the black attaché case Wilson carried. Venerable produced a key and opened it. He withdrew a manila folder.

"We need your health records. Physical, dental X-rays, blood types. You never know. We may have to identify your remains ... assuming we get any."

Venerable smiled to deflect the implication of what Wilson had gotten himself into.

"There's tea and sandwiches in your room. Get a good night's sleep. We begin 7 a.m. tomorrow. Almost two months of training. During that time, you're restricted to Perran House. You start in the classroom, end in the field. They'll be some physical conditioning, as well. By the way, at Perran House forget George Wilson. Your new name is Number 765. Your fellow students are numbers, too. Indeed, at Perran House, keep your interactions with others to a minimum. It doesn't do to know too much about anyone. Our philosophy is what you don't know you can't tell, even under torture. Of course, I'm speaking only about the most unlikely circumstances. So nothing more than good morning and good night to the others. If you need to talk, talk to me. Pleasant dreams 765."

Chapter 17

Wilson had not ventured beyond Perran House's formidable iron gates for six weeks.

"Consider Perran House home," Venerable had said to his seven recruits in opening remarks the morning after Wilson arrival. "It's less painful than thinking of it as prison."

To Wilson, neither home nor prison was accurate. Workhouse was.

Even had he been granted an evening's leave, he would not have found the energy to investigate the modest charms of the village of Woking. Classroom lectures that began at sunrise and lasted into the night, along with hand-to-hand combat instruction and hours of calisthenics, jogging and weightlifting, had exhausted his body and focused his mind on one thing: becoming a competent agent behind enemy lines.

Venerable's definition of competent had gotten Wilson's attention.

"If you're competent, gentlemen, you will survive. If incompetent, the Nazis will kill you, most likely after removing various appendages without benefit of anesthesia."

The 17-hour-a-day, seven-day-a-week regimen demanded far more of him than basic training in Georgia. Ft. Benning had allowed at least eight hours sleep. Perran House no more than six. At Ft. Benning, he had been fed well or at least amply. Perran House limited him to 2,500 calories a day. At Ft. Benning, the only reading requirement was the U.S. Army Manual and the company notice board. Perran House prescribed three hours daily to books detailing how to bomb, extort, lie, stab, escape, blackmail, kill. Each black art to be learned and demonstrated - in simulated tests - to Venerable's satisfaction.

The demands of Perran House pressed not only on his body but also on his soul. At Ft. Benning, he had been trained to meet an adversary in open combat. It was brutal but direct, its very directness conferring a warrior valor.

Not so at Perran House.

Even Venerable's introductory lecture on the seemingly benign subject of an agent's equipment pricked Wilson's conscience.

"When you're behind enemy lines, chances are you won't have a gun," Venerable had said. "Guns are problematic. If you use one, its discharge can be heard, although we do supply silencers. The real problem is guns are difficult to conceal. If the Nazis stop you and find one, they'll pull out your finger nails to learn why you're carrying it. So, instead of a gun, we'll issue you one of these. I call it Grandad."

Venerable withdrew a pen knife from the pocket of his white flannel trousers and held it up to the class, a prosaic article amidst the splendors of Perran House.

"Something my grandfather would have carried. Hence its name. Even the Nazis can't get suspicious about a pen knife. Of course, if they play with it long enough, it might give them pause."

Venerable pried it open and pressed his thumb and index finger against the knife's housing. A six-inch blade telescoped out.

"Just the thing to plunge into the enemy's ear or to slit his carotid artery. But watch out for the blood. A severed carotid gushes like a garden hose. As soon as you open the artery, get back, or you'll get soaked. Let your victim bleed out. It won't take long, and your victim will be thoroughly neutralized. As soon as the artery opens, blood pressure drops. The result: immediate unconsciousness. Hide the body as best you can. Nothing elaborate. You want to get away. Water is best. Streams, lakes, ponds. If you're landlocked, pile leaves on the corpse. Just hide it fast."

Then there was the lecture about women.

It had been a glorious English morning in late June. Through the conservatory's French doors opening onto the garden, Wilson saw striving hollyhocks, fresh rose blooms and shoots of boxwoods spearing skyward. They had recalled his mother's garden in Unity. There, as a small boy, he would be at her side as she watered seed beds, deadheaded roses and instructed him in the Christian faith and its demands for social action. Years later, when he learned she had, as a student, led a demonstration at Colby in support of women's suffrage, it came as no surprise. Women, she would tell her son, were no less God's creatures than men and always to be respected.

Venerable had a different take on women.

"Use them. Everything is a means to doing your job. Women are no exception. When you're behind enemy lines, don't hesitate to sleep with a woman ... if she can help you. It will encourage her to assist you. A woman's logic in this area is powerful. She rationalizes having sex by assuming she would only do so with a good man. Ergo, if you've slept with her, you must be a good man, and she'll protect you. Just don't forget yourself and fall in love. Sacrifice her if you must. You're wedded to your job not her. On the other side of the gender coin, don't be reluctant to play on a man's insecurity about women. When it comes to his wife or sweetheart's faithfulness, nothing distracts a man more than the fear she is unfaithful. We're beginning to use this very ploy now. As we learn the names of German soldiers in France from our contacts – generally prostitutes servicing the troops – we send those same soldiers anonymous letters posted from within Germany, reporting their beloved is entertaining some bloke back home. It can't help but damage German morale."

Hand-to-hand combat was another subject on Venerable's syllabus and no less disconcerting to Wilson.

Fisticuffs at Perran House was like nothing Wilson had experienced in basic training at Ft. Benning, where hand-to-hand combat consisted of a few semi-comical encounters with a judo expert, who routinely flattened every recruit he urged to jump him, including Wilson. When the instructor helped Wilson to his feet, he had said, "Don't get upset, son. We don't figure you're gonna be in too many fist fights. That's why we issue you M1s."

At Perran House, they figured differently. There were no M1s. Only Grandad and Venerable's admonition, "Be first, be fast, be lethal."

Recruits were given a rubber version of Grandad and ordered to approach a man from behind and slash his throat. The man, dressed as a German sentry, would then slump to earth only to rise a moment later and congratulate his attacker on his stealth. Seven weeks into training, Wilson reckoned he had killed 22 ersatz Nazis on the back acres of Perran House.

Finally, there was the loneliness of OSS training or at least of being alone. He had not fraternized with the other recruits nor they with him. Only sympathetic smiles passed among them that seemed to say, "Sorry, we're under orders. Someday, after the war, we might talk about this but not now."

It was cold camaraderie, but camaraderie nonetheless. Except for one. Number 809, a humorless stump of a man, thick-wristed, no neck, beyond cold in his classroom answers.

"You're inserted behind enemy lines," Venerable had hypothesized late one morning. "It's a night time insertion. By air. Your parachute brings you to a field in the countryside where you have been told a partisan will meet you. The sign and countersign of this meeting begin with you asking the partisan, 'Have you ever been to New York?' and the partisan is to respond, 'Yes, but I don't like New York.' Ten minutes after you glide to earth, a woman approaches you from a hedgerow. You ask her, 'Have you ever been to New York?' She says, 'Yes, but I don't *love* New York.' Number 765 what would you do?"

"Repeat the question," Wilson said, "asking her to rephrase her answer."

"And if she repeats, 'No, I don't *love* New York City,' what would you do?"

"I'd repeat my request for more precision on her part."

"You've already said that Number 765. Anyone else?"

Number 809 rose from the wing chair in the corner of the library, as far removed from his classmates as possible.

"Kill her. She's either stupid and got the countersign wrong, or she is the enemy. In any case, she is of negative value. Eliminate her."

"Anyone else?"

Venerable eyed his students and pointed to the man seated next to Wilson. The man deferred.

"I crack safes. That's why I'd be in France. No other purpose. Not my call."

"True enough," Venerable conceded "most of you will be inserted for a single task: blow a bridge, crack a safe, set up a radio and probably be in tandem with someone else … someone who would have to make a decision about the woman."

Venerable stepped away from the lectern and gazed out the window.

"Nevertheless, it's interesting to see who'd survive if my hypothetical came to pass. If the woman were a Nazi, those of you with Number 809 would survive. If she were a true contact but had honestly garbled the countersign, those assigned to Number 765 would have the best chance of surviving. Other partisans wouldn't look favorably on the man who killed one of their own just because she said *love* instead of *like*."

Venerable returned to the lectern.

"But enough philosophy for one morning. Here's a practical solution to many of your problems. Money. You'll get plenty of it to advance your mission. We'll supply you with Reichsmarks and the national currency of wherever it is you're inserted. They're counterfeit notes but very convincing, especially in the heat of quick exchange. They're also in the largest denominations available. The Reichsmark notes go up to 1000. Flash a few of those around to an underpaid German, and he might look the other way. Our hope is that the bigger the amount you offer, the less likely it will be rejected. In short, money works, especially among the Gestapo. It's said Göring has gotten rich providing exit visas for Jews. If the rotund Herr Göring is on the take, lesser lights may be as well."

Venerable pushed back from the lectern and glanced at his wrist watch.

"All this talk of death and deception has made me hungry. Let's adjourn to luncheon."

They did. Except Wilson, his appetite vanquished by the overwhelming feeling that his decision to join OSS had been a ghastly mistake.

As the rest of the class headed toward mess, Wilson lingered, then slipped into a side garden shaded by a towering beech tree.

Venerable, also, skipped lunch, his appetite suppressed by the feeling that he too had made a ghastly mistake. He came around the matte silver trunk of the tree.

"Feeling distressed, Wilson? Or don't you enjoy seminars on how to tear out a man's testicles or jam a stiletto into his ear?"

Wilson managed a diffident smile.

"We didn't go for that too much at Harvard."

Venerable laughed.

"So, mayhem isn't to your liking? It isn't to most people."

"But not all," Wilson said, unable to repress a moralizing urge.

"You mean Number 809?"

Wilson nodded.

"Interesting character, number 809. Of course, I can't tell you much about him. Or at least I shouldn't. But I sense your concern goes deeper than curiosity? 809's fanaticism has made you question the morality of what we're doing, hasn't it?"

"Well ..."

"I'll tell you something about Number 809. It may help you better understand what we're about at OSS. He was once an officer in your army. That is, until he resigned his commission and volunteered to go behind enemy lines and kill Germans. His commanding officer was pleased to get rid of him. Said he was too hard on his men."

"Surely, 809 could have been reprimanded by his commanding officer."

"Only if the commanding officer were a Catholic bishop. You see, Number 809 was – is – a Jesuit priest. Entered the army as a chaplain. Just naturally drawn to something bigger than himself. First, the Church, then the Army. If he were Russian, he'd have been with Lenin in 1917. If German, he'd have joined the Nazis before the Bier Hall Putsch. He's also a bloody ascetic and, therefore, without vices, except zealotry. Do you know, when we were giving out new names – the numbers you all go by – Number 809 was disappointed. He wanted a real name. He wanted to be called Jerome."

"The ascetic saint."

"Exactly. A saint so disciplined, he ruined his digestive track to demonstrate his disdain for food and drink. The brothers had to dig a cesspit near his pulpit to accommodate his frequent discharges. Jerome was utterly intense, like Number 809. When 809 was a chaplain, every poor bastard who confessed to him was given extraordinary penance. Nothing as humane as a few Hail Marys. For a man who lied to a friend, Number 809 prescribed a week of silence. For another, who confessed to masturbation, 809 ordered the man to wrap his private part in adhesive tape for a week. You get the picture. 809's commander, who was a Protestant padre, tried talking to him but got nowhere. Number 809 is so certain of the world to come, he'll happily sacrifice anything in this world, including comfort, friendship, the esteem of others."

Venerable turned from Wilson and looked up at the beech tree and slapped its massive trunk, as if affirming something in the universe greater than himself.

"The chaplain at Merton College once told me, faith is 23 hours of doubt overcome by one hour of hope. To Jerome, that's nonsense. Doubt and hope don't even exist in his world. He's as certain about his God as you are about your two hands. He knows – *knows* - God has a higher calling for him, and to hell with the rest of the world. As a result of this certainty, 809 resigned his commission and went to basic training for infantry. That's when we learned about him and recruited him. The traits of self-righteousness and fanatical devotion may not be desirable in a chaplain, but they can work well for a lone-wolf operator behind enemy lines. Number 809 would kill anyone we told him to kill. He'd see it as doing his job, being true to his mission."

Venerable paused.

"But, I'm not so sure about you, George. If you were my neighbor, and my house were on fire, you'd do all to save me. But I don't know if you'd slit a man's throat for no other reason than he might – *might* – be a Nazi."

Wilson did not respond.

"George, have no illusions about why you're being trained and what we expect of you. You're no 809. And that's all right. But in the end, I value Number 809's discipline and commitment to mission. I hope you have those qualities. You have everything else - all the tools and skills the OSS wants. I would trust your evaluation of potential agents in a way I wouldn't trust 809's. He's a butcher. You're a surgeon. He's rigid. You're agile. But both skills are necessary, and I need to know that if the occasion calls for it, you can be a butcher."

Venerable looked at his watch.

"Must get ready for afternoon class."

An hour later, Venerable began his lecture.

"For the past 40 days, we've taught you how to kill, how to set up cells, how to blend in and how to strike at the enemy and acquire information that can be used against him. Tomorrow, we're going to see how well you've learned those lessons and how fast you think on your feet. In the morning, you'll be given field assignments, and, for the first time since your arrival, free to wander beyond the bounds of Perran House.   Of course, you'll return to Perran House late in the afternoon, and we'll see how you've carried out those assignments. Think of it as your final examination."

For the first time in a life of academic excellence, Wilson wondered if he might be better off failing. And for the next four hours heard nothing except a warning voice deep inside him – sounding much like his mother's -- that he teetered on the verge of losing his soul.

Chapter 18

Venerable was sitting behind a Boule desk as Wilson, just out of breakfast mess, entered the library of Perran House.

"Welcome to your final examination," Venerable said, without a hint of real welcome. "Your colleagues are already out there. You're the last to go. By the way, if you see any of them, ignore them. We've scattered these trials throughout Surrey, so you shouldn't run into each other, but if you do, mum's the word. We want to see how you work alone."

He rose from the desk, a wad of British bank notes in his right hand.

"Your trial is straightforward. Learn as much as you can about the air defense systems that protect Woking from the Luftwaffe. You have a free hand. Break the law if you must, but try not to kill anyone or damage too much property. I have influence, but not enough if you assassinate the lord mayor or seduce his daughter. We're giving you three assets -- a bicycle, a map and these."

He handed Wilson the pound notes.

"Remember what I said about money. Use it to get what you need. Clock's ticking."

Wilson turned to leave, then looked back at Venerable.

"You haven't made up your mind about me, have you?"

"No," Venerable said, "and I know you haven't made up your mind about us."

Chapter 19

Outside on the gravel courtyard, the gloomy private who had driven Wilson eight weeks earlier swung open the iron gates of Perran House and pointed down the road.

"Woking's that way."

Wilson pedaled the black English racer onto Hook Heath Road, a narrow country lane ambling over an undulating landscape of tall trees and Edwardian homes. As he rounded the first bend and the grounds of Perran House disappeared from view, a giddy sense of freedom came over him, almost what he had felt the afternoon he first met Clotilde. Then, it had been freedom from Mae and the constriction of an appointed life. Now, it was freedom from the ethical conundrums of the past two months. But his giddiness was short lived, killed by his doubts. Maybe, he wasn't OSS material. His reasons for volunteering were anything but patriotic or Manichean or even adventurous. They had been recklessly romantic: a quest for love, a flight from banality. Find Clotilde. Escape Mae. All empty-headed notions. Mae and the life she represented were not trifles, and Clotilde was gone ... forever.

Yet beyond all reason, here he was on a sunny August day in south England on route to a trial that would determine if he were fanatical enough to kill Germans and anyone else who got in his way.

Wilson passed the first shops of Woking on his right. Their X-taped window panes brought him back to his assignment: the town's air defense. He coasted to a stop on the side of a stone bridge above a willow-shaded stream and removed the map from his back pocket.

Air defenses would mean radar, and radar would mean high ground. Hills. Spires. The map showed both. The Surrey escarpment running north of the village, and a high-spired church, St. Mary the Virgin, nestled in the town. Wilson also noted location of the Woking Golf Club. While not high, its fairways would be spacious and shielded from the road and curious on-lookers. Hills, church and golf course would be his first points of investigation. As to civil preparedness and response, what better place than a local pub where money could buy pints that might loosen tongues.

Four hours later, having posed as a religious pilgrim at St. Mary's, a golfer enquiring about membership at Woking Golf Club (where a man in coveralls informed him the course had been converted to farmland to help feed an embargoed island) and an avid bicyclist exploring the escarpment, he knew no more about Woking's readiness to survive a Luftwaffe attack than when he had set out. In fact, had he not known a war was on, the eternal pattern of meadow, low stone walls and Edwardian architecture he had encountered in and around Woking suggested an England at peace with its neighbors and favored by God. He cycled down the lane, stopping at the timber-and-plaster façade of the Angel Inn. He leaned his bicycle against the building and entered. The dim interior smelled of stale beer and greasy food. Wilson pulled out a barstool and ordered an ale.

"Well then," the beefy, red-faced barkeep said, "as I pull you a pint, tell me if you be a Yank or a Canuck. I can't always tell."

One hour, two pints and a greasy lamb pie later, the bartender knew more about Wilson than Wilson knew about Woking's air defense. Another half-pound spent on three lagers for three bar patrons and a pot of tea and Dundee cake for two women lunching at a corner table were equally unproductive. Wilson pushed back his bar stool. As he dropped a pound note on the bar, the door to the Angel swung open, and he heard a booming and familiar voice yell: "Will you look at that out on the High!"

All heads turned toward the window. And as they did, Number 809 nonchalantly walked up to Wilson and plunged a fist hard into his groin. The punch dropped Wilson to his knees.

"Let me help you," Number 809 said loudly, as the patrons, finding nothing unusual on the High, turned toward the disturbance at the bar.

The bartender threw open the bar bridge and rushed forward. The two women asked anxiously if the nice man who had bought them tea and cake was ill, while other patrons circled around the fallen Wilson, who gasped for breath, unable to speak.

"Been like that since I knew him in the States," Number 809 said, shaking his head sadly. "Can't hold a drop. Should stick to tea. He'll be OK. I'll take him back to London."

Number 809 bent down, and in one swoop of his arms lifted Wilson from the tacky wooden floor and hauled him, feet dragging, out of the inn and into the backseat of a black Alvis. The car, driven by the private who had opened the gates of Perran House, pulled away and turned the corner.

But London was not its destination. That was One Webster Way, just around the corner. Moaning and dizzy from the pain in his groin, Wilson offered no resistance as 809 lugged him out of the car, through the front door and upstairs into the dental surgery of Dr. Ronald Brandman. He dropped Wilson into the examination chair and handcuffed his hands and feet to it. Then with an economy of motion and not a flicker of emotion, 809's hands closed round Wilson's neck compressing his carotid arteries. Wilson went limp. As his jaw slackened, 809 wedged a small block of wood into the right side of Wilson's mouth between his upper and lower teeth. Wilson came to, and Dr. Brandman lowered an overhead lamp toward Wilson's mouth and said, "There's one filling in the back. Nicely done, too. Pity."

Then Dr. Brandman dug a dental pick into the filling with such force that Wilson screamed, the pain in his mouth surpassing the pain in his groin.

"Turn on the radio," 809 said matter of factly. "It's going to get noisy in here."

A minute later, with the radio at full volume and Mozart's *Jupiter Symphony* soaring toward its coda, 809 shouted at Wilson, "Who are you working for!?"

Wilson did not answer.

809 turned to Dr. Brandman.

"Remove the filling. Don't be delicate."

He wasn't.

Wilson screamed.

"You have only one filling, but you have a whole mouth full of teeth," 809 said. "And we'll visit each and every one, unless you tell me why you're here, and why you're working for the Nazis."

Wilson shook his head a violent no. The pick again. Screams again.

Then Dr. Brandman put down the dental pick and picked up a pair of tweezers and pinched from Wilson's mouth a little plug of lead. He dropped the filling into a porcelain bowl.

"Should I begin on the rest of the teeth?"

809 shrugged.

"Use the pick again."

The man did. The result was the same. Screams and a refusal to answer.

809 shook his head sadly, and as the last note of the *Jupiter Symphony* died, he said, "We're not going to get anything. It's over for him. Put him under."

Chapter 20

The aroma of sautéed onions and grilled meat brought Wilson around.   From the overstuffed sofa in the reception room of Perran House, he raised himself to his elbows.   Venerable loomed before him. His voice cheerful.

"Feeling better, George? You were unconscious. A sack of potatoes. So, instead of hauling you to your room, we let you sleep it off, here."

Despite the pain in his groin and throb in his jaw, Wilson rose to his feet. He was too drained to audit his language.

"What the fuck is going on!?"

The first time Wilson had used *that* word, it had earned him a once-in-his life slap from his indignant father, who had dragged him off the baseball field at Unity Day School, with the warning, "I don't care if you strike out a hundred times! Never use that word!"

Now, 19 years later, it earned Wilson only a sheepish smile from Venerable.

"Oh, you mean number 809."

Wilson exploded.

"A sadistic son of a bitch. He violated your precious rules! He engaged me and damn near killed me! He's a menace and a ..."

Venerable took Wilson by the arm and escorted him to the dining room.

"Oh no, George, I couldn't reprimand Number 809. He passed his final exam with flying colors. But enough about him. You've had an ordeal. That's why we let you sleep. Actually, we didn't have much choice. Dr. Brandman gave you powerful anesthesia. You must be hungry. That greasy lamb pie you had for lunch couldn't have satisfied. I should have warned you about the food at the Angel. But that's done with. You're going to eat better, starting right now.   You're getting what I believe is the last filet mignon in the British Isles.   We've even violated government rules on the preservation of private property and pinched a bottle of Gigondas from Perran House cellar. Thought you might like a drop of something on the big side. You deserve it. You see, you've passed your examination, as well."

Venerable and Wilson stepped into the dining room. Venerable pointed to the elegantly-laid Georgian table, replete with heavy crystal wine glasses, silver service and china plates.

"Have a seat," he said, pouring a glass of wine for each of them. He brought the glass to his nose.

"This should make some amends."

Wilson's anger returned.

"809 is a maniac! He violated your directive. He engaged me, then practically killed me."

"Oh, that."

"Yes, *that!*"

"He didn't violate my directive."

"But you said ..."

"I said *you* shouldn't engage anyone. Number 809 wasn't given that order. In fact, he was specifically *told* to engage you. More specifically, he was told to abduct you. Be happy he only hit you in the testicles. He might have gone for your throat."

"He had that option?"

"We think it best not to over-restrict our agents."

Venerable sipped the wine.

"It needs to open more, but it's very good. Try it."

Wilson raised his glass. The Gigondas brought him back to his last and only night with Clotilde. Venerable saw the distant look in Wilson's eyes, misinterpreted it.

"You look a little weak, George. Let's get some food in you."

Venerable raised his hand toward the kitchen door. The door opened. The mess sergeant entered and went to the sideboard and began preparing a plate for Wilson.

"Eat on your left side," Venerable suggested. "That was a significant extraction you had."

"And you tell me 809 is no sadist."

"He may well be a sadist, but he's awfully good at following orders. He was a crucial part of your examination. You see, we didn't really care about Woking air defense, although we were pleased with your efforts. Showed initiative. One of your observers reported you did all the right things. You scouted the high ground, St. Mary the Virgin, the Woking Golf Club ... all good ideas. But there was nothing to find. There's nothing in Woking, except Woking."

"Then why ..."

"Why did we send you on a wild goose chase? We were after something else, and we decided to kill two birds with one stone. As you know, I had doubts about you, the kind of doubts I don't have about 809. I could see you had doubts, too. I heard it in your response on how to deal with an agent who fumbles her countersign. Those doubts would do you credit ... as a Boy Scout. But as a spy behind enemy lines, they could prove fatal. We needed to know how deep those doubts ran. So, we put you to the test. Made it extremely painful for you to remain with us. We reasoned you would only endure the pain if you were committed. Number 809 played his part by providing the pain, even asking inane questions about you working for the Nazis. You could have spared yourself the agony of Dr. Brandman's handiwork by confessing – however falsely – that you were a Nazi agent. If you had, Brandman and 809 were under orders to cease the torture and bring you back here, where we would have sorted out the whole thing ... and then let you go. But you didn't confess. You held on. Your doubts didn't get the best of you, and that overcame my doubts about you."

Wilson bit into the steak. It was the first good meal he'd had since leaving Unity. Another sip of Gigondas calmed him further.

"Why didn't you give me truth serum? It works."

"We could have, but that brings me to our two-birds-one-stone approach. You remember that attaché case you toted across the Atlantic? It really did contain your medical records, including dental X-rays from Ft. Benning. You have good oral hygiene. Only one filling. Guess that goes with having a doctor for a father. Anyway, a little-known fact about dentistry is that American dentists fill cavities differently than European dentists. Little known except among German intelligence officers. If the Germans captured you, they'd quickly examine your dental work, revealing your dentist was an American and assume you were an American. Under more clement circumstances, we would have sent you to Dr. Brandman on your own, and he would have removed your American filling – with benefit of anesthesia - and replaced it with a good

European filling. But we figured, why not get the work done *and* see if you talk. Two birds, one stone. How's the wine?"

Wilson glared at Venerable.

"Don't be so delicate, George. In 1917, as part of my induction into British counter-intelligence, they beat me up. Not a university prank with a big paddle across the bum but a bloody bad beating. Fists to the face."

With surprising decorum, Venerable removed a bridge from his mouth revealing a toothless gap in the front of his lower jaw. Then with equal finesse, refitted the bridge.

"Tomorrow, George, you'll feel as right as rain. Tomorrow, I'll still look like a circus clown. I'll leave you to your food. Over the next few days, relax. Get to know some of the maidens here in Woking or even London. Then, we've scheduled three parachute jumps for you. But don't worry about them. We won't be tossing you out at 10,000 feet. No more than 3,000 feet. We even supply a parachute. Once we deem you're no longer a menace to yourself in the air, you'll get your orders. A few days after that ... well, you'll be somewhere on the continent. Have a good night, George."

As Wilson sank into bed, his last thought before falling into a deep sleep induced by the Gigondas was of Paris and a blizzard and the whiteness of Clotilde's neck in the dim light in his flat on Rue Laplace.

Chapter 21

For the teachers of Louis Pasteur Primary School in the Marais quarter of Paris, only one day of work interrupted their summer holiday: the new-term prep. Held in early August, the new-term prep obliged educators to return to school to receive their class assignments for the coming term, confer with administrators over curriculum and review new text books. It was also a day when teachers from one form passed along student records and student appraisals to teachers of the next form. In cases termed exceptional need, students were required to attend the new-term prep to meet their new instructors in person.

It was a heavy and hot afternoon as the dozen women faculty members gathered around the long oak table in the second-floor teachers' lounge. They fanned themselves and talked about life. A science teacher remarked how cooler air over the Atlantic had failed to move inland, leaving the basin of land and river that was Paris to bake in the summer sun. Another teacher opined on the pointlessness of complaining about the weather and shifted the conversation to the consoling fact that new text books had arrived.

"The first in years," she said.

"The Germans are very efficient," a third teacher countered with sarcasm bordering on sedition. "All new books purged of Jewish authors and Jewish contribution."

"Not only have the text books been purged," the science teacher added, "but all Paris, as well. And by our own Paris police! Two weeks ago, just after sunrise, gendarmes swept through my quarter in Montparnasse. I was walking the dog. They entered every apartment marked with a yellow star. Sometimes knocking. Sometimes not. They hauled people away in their pajamas. One old man was naked. There's not a Jew left in Paris."

And then, as an afterthought, added, "I wonder how our Miss Bloch managed to survive."

"Perhaps, she knew someone. Perhaps, she convinced the gendarmes not to take her. After all, gendarmes are men, and men ..."

The conversation stopped as Ilena Bloch appeared in the doorway to the lounge. The yellow star sewn on her paisley frock above her left breast cast the brightest light in the room, like a beam from an interrogator's arc lamp, throwing her frizzy brown hair and green eyes into dull relief.

"Clotilde," Ilena Bloch said, "I'd like you to meet a very special person."

Bloch looked over her shoulder.

"Claire Marie," she said softly, and a seven-year-old girl with cropped black hair came to her side, her eyes cast down.

"Claire Marie Bastian, I want you to meet your new teacher, Mrs. deBrouillard."

The girl did not move.

Gently, Bloch brought her hands to the girl's shoulders and guided her across the room to Clotilde.

"Say hello, Claire Marie."

The girl said nothing.

"Perhaps, if her mother could join us," Clotilde said.

"She works. Claire Marie's uncle will come for her later."

And then in a whisper to Clotilde, "If he is sober."

Clotilde bent down, face to face with Claire Marie.

"I'm sure we will have a wonderful time in the new term, Claire Marie. I know you are a sweet girl who enjoys her studies."

Sweet girl was true enough, according to the report Clotilde had read, but studies were not Claire Marie's strength. She was considered "abnormally slow." Bloch's report added, "Perhaps, someday our schools will provide for the special needs of students like Claire Marie, but for now, we can only be kind."

Clotilde patted down the cowlick at the crown of the girl's head, then kissed her on the cheek. Claire Marie pulled back, and Ilena Bloch said to Clotilde, "I know you will be good to her."

Claire Marie buried her head into Bloch's hip.

"May I tell Mrs. deBrouillard our special secret, Claire Marie?"

The girl looked up, the beginning of a smile on her face.

"Spinoza," Ilena Bloch said.

"You know Mr. Spinoza!?" Clotilde asked in exaggerated wonder. "You must be a very special little girl if Miss Bloch told you the name of her pussycat. When Miss Bloch travels to Le Havre to see her uncle, I take care of Mr. Spinoza and feed him and play with him. We are going to be great friends, Claire Marie."

Claire Marie retreated behind Miss Bloch.

"I know you will be good to her, Clotilde. She is gentle. Don't let the other students bully her. It is terrible when they bully her. It is terrible when anyone is bullied."

Tears welled in her eyes. She looked at Clotilde.

"Three days ago, they came for my uncle in Le Havre. They …"

Ilena Bloch brought her hands to her eyes, then strengthened and took Claire Marie by the hand and left the room.

The conversation at the table resumed, coursing back to the weather, then to the issuing of the new text books, then turning again to the recent roundup of Jews. Clotilde did not join in. She walked to the window overlooking the cobblestone square and looked down at its cast iron fountain trickling water into its circular stone basin.   Yes, she thought, bullies are terrible - those who taunted Claire Marie, those who forced Ilena Bloch to wear the yellow star, those who killed her husband Paul, those who enslaved Paris, and Putnev who enslaved her. Tears filled Clotilde's eyes. She withdrew a lace handkerchief from her pocket and did not see the Paris police van pull to the curb in front of the school or the two gendarmes who got out.

Ilena Bloch walked unsteadily back into the lounge, her face ashen.

"They have come," she said and folded her arms tightly across her chest, one hand covering the yellow star.

The tramp of heavy steps on the wooden staircase echoed through the school. A moment later, the two gendarmes entered the lounge.

"Which of you is Miss Bloch?"

Ilena Bloch stood up, said nothing. She lowered her right hand, revealing the yellow star.

"Please, come with us," the policeman said.

The teachers seated at the table did not rise. Only Clotilde stepped forward.

"What do you want?" she demanded.

It was not a question but an accusation.

"Only to do our job, miss."

"And what job is that?"

The policemen ignored her question.

"Miss Bloch, you will come with us."

The gendarmes came abreast of the woman. A moment later, the only sound in the conference room was the receding tramp of their footfalls.

Clotilde ran after them. By the time she reached the street, Ilena Bloch had been sequestered in the back of the police van. Clotilde tried to open the door. The gendarme did not interfere. The door was locked. As he climbed into the driver's seat, his companion came around to Clotilde. She stood her ground.

"You can't take her away! What has she done!?"

The officer pursed his lips.

"The Germans are understaffed in Paris. They ask us to assist them. In this case, they have asked us to assist with Miss Bloch. I know nothing more, but I give you some advice. The situation is not what any of us would like, but it is better that we French work with the occupiers. If we do not, the consequences for all Paris could be unspeakable. It is the way things are."

Long after the van had pulled away, Clotilde stood on the pavement in the midday heat. When she returned to the teachers' lounge, the new-term prep was all but over. No questions. No discussion. No protracted oration from head mistress Camille Ronsaar.

"In three weeks," Mrs. Ronsaar concluded, sending her faculty on its way, "our students will return to a school and a world increasingly fraught with danger. It is our duty to protect them as best we can. We can only urge compliance with the present order. To urge anything else is irresponsible."

The lounge emptied. Clotilde stood alone.

Her inability to help Ilena Bloch tore at her. All she had managed for her friend was a feeble question to a gendarme. She was as complicit in Ilena Bloch's arrest as he. Self-loathing filled her, not only for what she had failed to do but for what she was about to do. Again.

Putnev was waiting for her in room 8.

Chapter 22

The first time Clotilde entered the Hotel Splendide on Rue Duperré in Pigalle, the desk clerk had confronted her.

Now, eight months later, he ignored her as she passed through the dimly-lit foyer and ascended the worn staircase. She had become a Splendide habitué, a weekly trifle for the Russian gentleman who frequented room 8.

Putnev was fully dressed and standing by the armoire.

"It's good you're on time," he said. "I'm a busy man. What would you like to do?"

He always asked that question because, he told her, he liked to hear her say, "Whatever you want. I beg you. Do it."

After she said those words, he undressed, hanged his suit in the battered armoire. She did not undress. He had talked to her about that, too.

"After I am naked and lying on the bed, I want to watch you remove your clothes. It will excite me."

This afternoon was no different from any other. She undressed. He watched her. It excited him. Then he said, "Come here. You know what I like."

She came and did what he liked, and then something she didn't know he liked. He rolled quickly off the bed, stepped to the armoire, threw back its door and adjusted the full-length mirror hanging inside to reflect her naked and contorted body. Then he was back at her.

"Look up at me when you do that," he demanded. "And beg me for it."

She looked at him and begged, and he looked in the mirror and, observing himself inside her, issued a breathy *ah* of pleasure.

It was over in a few minutes. He rolled onto his back. When his high-pitched wheezing ceased, he asked the same question he asked every week.

"You have heard nothing more from the German who wrote that harrowing note last December, the one threatening your students?"

No, she said. It had been quiet. Her children were safe.

"And I promise you, Clotilde, your children will remain safe. I have arranged it. *There is little in Paris I cannot arrange.* But just to be safe, it is good we remain friends."

She rose from the bed and began to dress.

"Don't be in such a rush, Clotilde. I want to talk to you."

She knew better than to disobey, and she stood there in bra and garter belt, dress in hand.

"It is a nice arrangement of lingerie you wear. Especially the silk stockings I gave you for our tender moments together."

He worked a cigarette into his tortoise-shell cigarette holder and lit it.

"Tell me, Clotilde. What do you think about when I am fucking you?"

Her voice was distant, exhausted.

"Today, I thought of Claire Marie Bastian. I will teach her next year. She is slow. Other children bully her. I think of Claire Marie whose mother works and who is cared for by a drunken uncle at her home across the street from the school. That is what I think of."

"You thought of nothing else? Perhaps that another man is fucking you. Did you think of another man, Clotilde?"

"I thought of a woman, a Jew."

Putnev's eyes lit up. His voice quickened.

"When you think of this woman, this Jew, what is she doing?"

"She is disappearing, dying in one of the death camps where the Germans took her this morning."

The glint in Putnev's eyes faded. He shook his head in annoyance.

"You should be screaming in ecstasy at what I do to you in that wasteland between your legs, and all you think of is a retard and a Jewess. I wonder why I bother with you."

But he knew. Obsession did that. He took a long drag on his cigarette.

"Still, I want you. I have some new ideas."

He pointed to the mirror on the armoire.

"That was one of them. I have another idea. Mrs. Borodin. She's an acquaintance of mine and is going to join us during our next interlude. She will bring a little friend."

Clotilde diverted her gaze to the floor.

"Come here, Clotilde."

She came along side of him.

"But Mrs. Borodin and her little friend won't be here until next week, and I want something more. Now. You."

With one hand, he stubbed out his cigarette in the ashtray on the night stand and with the other reached out and stroked her thighs between her legs.

"Your body, Clotilde, has three desirable openings. For eight months, we have explored two. It is time to complete the journey. Some women enjoy it. You may even beg for it."

She did not immediately understand but in a few brutal seconds, in the grasp of his hands and his twist of her body, she did.

When she regained the street 20 minutes later, she felt numb, her face so drained that a German soldier asked if she were ill. She did not answer him. She had not heard him, as she had not felt the heat of late afternoon or seen the people she had passed. All she wanted was to reach the Marais and the sanctuary of her apartment on Rue St. Claude.

But as her churning feet carried her deeper into the Marais, a hideous realization overcame her.

There was no sanctuary.

On one side, the degradation of Occupation: Paris wrapped in swastikas and awash in Wehrmacht gray. On the other, the depravity of room 8.   Its nadir - reached only a half hour earlier - would be surpassed in a week's time with the arrival of Mrs. Borodin and whatever it was she would bring with her.

Paul's final words before he set out to confront the invading Germans crashed in on her.

If there is no sanctuary, no place where hope survives, death is nobler than life.

The dark eros of self-annihilation that had driven her husband now swept over her. She had reached a crossroads. At the intersection of Rue de Turenne and Rue St. Claude, she looked down the cobblestoned roadway toward her apartment building. Two German soldiers ambled past it. Then she looked straight ahead, down Rue de Turenne. A thousand meters away flowed the Seine, where one deep inhalation of its water would confer on her the sanctuary of oblivion.

She continued toward the river but had taken only a few steps when a flutter of wings distracted her, and she watched a dove descend from the roof of St. Denys du Sacrament to the pavement below. The bird circled a cigarette butt on the pavé in front of the church then flew off.

Clotilde paused.

The front door to the church was ajar. Hardly a sign, she thought, but perhaps one last hope. She entered. At the tract table in the narthex, she searched for something, anything. Her eyes hit upon a pamphlet entitled *The Sacraments*. She picked it up. Tried to read it. But it was only words, and she dropped it to the table and walked into the airless Lady Chapel, its reredos decorated with a mural of the Virgin by Delacroix. She stood before it. Her voice thin.

"Into Thy hands, I commit my spirit."

Only silence. There was no sanctuary.

She removed from her purse what money she had and slipped it into the alms box by the statue of the Virgin.

It was time.

Making the sign of the cross, she turned to resume her journey to the river, when from behind her, out of the corner of the chapel, came a low moan. It stopped her, and in the dim light, she saw a shadowy figure raise its hand.

"Are you all right?" she managed.

A man stepped forward and swayed. She ran to his side. His body swooned. Her arm cinched around his waist.

"Danke," he muttered.

Chapter 23

The German did not resist, and Clotilde led him out of the church into the heat of the evening. A grimy tabac across rue de Turenne was still open. They entered. Behind the counter, the middle-aged proprietor looked up from his newspaper, the arch of his thick eyebrows asking what they wanted. She pointed to a table in the back and ordered tea. The young man - his thin lips and blue eyes tense - followed her to the table and sank into a wooden chair. He set his hands on the dull table top. Such delicate hands, she thought, nails manicured and polished.

"Our Lady always answers prayer," he blurted. "That is why you were there in Her chapel. I asked Her for help. Our Lady sent you."

She raised her hands to dismiss his appraisal; he waved them aside.

"Never deny Her," he said sternly. "Our Lady has sent *you* to address *my* pain."

"I was just there. Nothing more."

His voice went stubborn.

"No, it *was* more. You are Her agent. She has directed you to me. I am sure of it. I know these things."

Then he added, mingling pride with defiance, "I *will* be a priest."

Growing up, Clotilde had known boys who had professed their intention of taking holy orders. Some had been scholarly, others unsure of their masculinity, others arch with piety, but all circumscribed by the predictable biases of working-class Paris. Not one could she liken to the high-strung and pampered young man before her now, so elegantly dressed in a pin-stripe navy suit that even her father, the meticulous tailor, could not have faulted.

"But I must wait. The Reich offers no deferrals unless you are in seminary."

"Deferrals?"

"Yes, yes, deferrals," he said impatiently. "Deferrals are no longer granted in Germany. The war. Conscription. Unless you already attend seminary, they conscript you into the military."

"You're a soldier?"

His eyes rolled in sarcasm.

"What else if I am in the military?"

Clotilde leaned back, taken aback, not by his rudeness but by wonder at herself.   She should hate this soldier of the army that had killed her husband, conquered her country and filled her with despair.   But hate did not come. Only curiosity.

"What's your name?"

His shoulders squared.

"They say we shouldn't say."

"Perhaps, I can help you."

His squared shoulders sagged.

"Stull. Gerhardt Stull."

"Well, Private Stull, surely you can …"

"Lt. Stull."

"Surely, you can go to seminary later. I mean in the future."

He snorted.

"What future?   I have committed a terrible sin that clouds my future. I have not made my confession in weeks."

"Then make confession."

"You're a fool."

Stull offered no apology for the harshness of his words.

"I can't confess to a priest. Not today, not tomorrow.   A French priest would tell me to stop what I am doing. A German chaplain might report me to Commandant Schaumburg for speaking out of turn, even in the confessional. I could be court-martialed."

Her curiosity became astonishment.

"Commandant Schaumburg? The German general in charge of Paris?"

"Is there another?"

The proprietor served the tea in small white cups on cracked-glazed saucers.

"It's getting near curfew," he said.

Clotilde reached for her purse, then remembered she had no money. She looked at Stull.

"Can you pay?"

He glared at her, offended by her. She understood.

"I'm not that kind of woman. I gave all my money away in the church in the alms box."

He relented and produced a five-franc piece and threw it on the table. The proprietor picked it up and stepped away.

Stull pushed aside his cup.

"I hate tea. Why did you order this?"

"We are here," she replied, trying to suppress her amazement that she was face to face with a man who had access to the man who held Paris beneath his heel. "The owner expects ..."

Stull rolled his eyes.

"The owner expects *nothing.* He and his city have been defeated. The war is over. And that is what confounds me. The army doesn't need me. I want to be a priest, not a soldier. But they conscripted me, made me an aide to a colonel on the commandant's staff. Do you know what I do all day, every day? Railway schedules to ship Jews out of Paris."

He shook his head in disgust.

"Earlier this year, Commandant Schaumburg was called to Berlin, to a meeting in Wannsee. Deportation of Jews was the agenda. The man in charge of this deportation is named Eichmann. Last month, this Eichmann came to Paris to see the progress we were making. Commandant Schaumburg told him that before we could deport French Jews, we should first deport foreign Jews living here. What a nightmare!"

Clotilde brought a hand to her mouth.

"It is an obscenity what is happening to the Jews," she gasped.

"And to me! My colonel oversees the rail schedules for this deportation, which means that is what I do. All the time. I schedule and reschedule trains. I am nothing more than a travel agent for deported Jews. That is not what God intended for me."

He picked up his tea cup, then put it down.

"I hate tea," he repeated. "It makes me sick in my stomach, like everything in Paris. Three days ago, my colonel ordered me to deliver a confidential letter to Professor Jean LaTourette of the Curie Institute in the fifth arrondissement. I am not a mail boy, but it was a break from train schedules. That afternoon I handed the letter to Professor LaTourette. He read it and said to me, 'Tell your colonel I know no more about heavy water than he does. It is not my field of expertise.' Do you know what heavy water is? An essential element in making a bomb so powerful it could obliterate all Paris."

He pushed his cup of tea further away.

"The only good I have learned in my post is that Marshal Stalin is exploring a separate peace with us in the east. I pray God it is true. I hate the communists. I hate communists more than anything in the world, but this proposal of theirs might end the war, then I can get out of Paris and fulfill God's will for me."

Clotilde stared at him, her mind reeling. A hour ago, she had no currency to buy her way out of hell. The latest barter of her body with Putnev had driven her to despair and the Seine. But now, through this disagreeable young man, God might be providing another direction. If she were an agent of God for him, might he also be an agent of God for her?

"Lt. Stull, I can help you. I have friends who could get you away from this."

Stull's eyes squinted.

"Who are you?"

Why not be what he insisted she was?

"Perhaps, as you said, an agent of Our Lady. That is why I am here, why I was in St. Denys."

Stull closed his eyes. She had no idea if he had heard her.

"Do you know why *I* was in St. Denys?" he asked. "I'm billeted at the Hotel Meurice, and I should go to Our Lady of the Assumption. It's the closest church, but I have been seen there. Seen and reported. My colonel has asked about my interest in the church. I told him I enjoyed hearing the Latin of the mass and said nothing of my faith and vocation. I did not witness for Our Lady. So, I come here, away from prying eyes. And now I meet you."

He pushed back his chair, rose and headed toward the door. In a moment, they were on the sidewalk, he walking fast, she catching up.

"I have said too much already," he mumbled and stepped off the curb and onto the street and began to run. She started after him, but a uniformed German soldier was approaching. With a temporizing right hand, he motioned at her to slow down. In Paris, one obeyed.

Lt. Gerhardt Stull disappeared around the corner.

He did not return. But as she stood there in front of St. Denys, neither did her despair return. In the course of a half-hour -- improbably, almost impossibly -- she had come by information that might save her ... if she could use it wisely.

A slight breeze stirred the night air. She breathed in, thought of the river, thought of her flat, then stepped onto rue St. Claude and headed home.

Chapter 24

Hope worked on Clotilde that night, and she awakened in the morning with a plan. It's first step an urgent meeting with Josephine LeMans, her Christian friend of the past nine months and the same woman Putnev had ordered her to spy on.

At sunrise, Clotilde telephoned her, but Josephine had not answered, and there was no time to waste on future calls. So, Clotilde went to where she knew Josephine would be: in the Latin Quarter at the church of St. Séverin receiving holy communion.

In silence, the two women knelt at the altar, and after the celebrating priest bestowed the final blessing and retired to the sacristy, Clotilde and Josephine exited the church passing the Twisted Pillar, a corkscrew of stone rising into a swirl of shadowy vaults behind the main altar. There, in the gloom, away from prying eyes and sensitive ears, Clotilde whispered to her, "The café on the corner. Now."

In five minutes, the two women were sitting at a table beneath an umbrella, watching a street cleaner open a curbside water valve and sweep the night's detritus into the gutter. The water gurgled to a drain at the corner, then flowed into the sewer that bore it to the Seine, which hours earlier had seemed to be Clotilde's last and only sanctuary.

The two women ordered lemonades.

"I have information," Clotilde began. "Important information."

Josephine LeMans ran a sinewy hand through her short brown hair, a cut in keeping with her sharp ascetic face appropriate for a woman contemplating the convent.

"Important? You really think so?"

"But I haven't even told you what ..."

"I am being sarcastic, Clotilde. I have grown weary of *important* information. I attend what are said to be important meetings. I hear about important Resistance operations and work to advance them. I buy paper for pamphlets and ink for printing. I even have a code name, Silas, as you know. All this is said to be important. But we do nothing. The Allies do nothing, and France remains occupied. I am tired of *important.* So, when you say *you* have important information, excuse my skepticism."

They fell silent as the proprietor served their lemonades. Then, LeMans reached out and gently tapped Clotilde on the hand.

"Forgive me, Clotilde. I am just a rude Parisian. What is this information you have, this *important* information?"

In the time it took LeMans to smoke two cigarettes, one lit from the other, Clotilde had recounted her meeting and conversation with Lt. Stull, then came to the line which she had rehearsed the night before as she lie awake in her bed.

"I tell you these things, Josephine, because I believe Lt. Stull wants to defect and given his position he could provide invaluable information to our cause."

"When can you contact Lt. Stull?"

"He is billeted at the Hotel Meurice."

"Impregnable. If he doesn't come out, we can't get in."

"But he will come out because he wants out and he will return to St. Denys."

"Why St. Denys?"

"He wants to be a priest. He will come back to the church, to that church because he thinks I am answer to his prayers. And when he returns, I will be waiting. But I need a plan to present to him. He needs to hear more than my good intentions. I need to tell him 'We have contacted the Allies. They will get you out, and here is how.' That is why I am talking to you, Josephine, why I am asking you to contact London and make arrangements to get Lt. Stull to Britain."

LeMans ran her palm over the rim of her glass.

"You don't ask for much, do you?"

"I have more."

Clotilde had rehearsed this line, as well: her salvation from Putnev.

"I must go with him."

LeMans eyes went wide. She leaned forward on the edge of her wicker chair.

"Clotilde, you can't ..."

"He trusts me. He believes I am an agent of Our Lady."

"I cannot speak for Our Lady, only the Christian resistance, and the Christian Resistance will say ..."

Clotilde would not be denied.

"Never mind what the Christian Resistance says. *You* are the Christian Resistance, and I'm telling you, he won't go without me."

"Go!? He hasn't even come back to you, and if he does, we don't know if London wants him."

"That is why London must be radioed. Stull has valuable information. The deportation of Jews, Marshal Stalin, this bomb thing."

"Clotilde, you don't know if you'll see him again."

"I will. He's desperate. Desperation will work on him. Like yeast in dough. He will rise to my offer. I saw it in his eyes."

LeMans pointed a wise finger at Clotilde.

"What you saw in his eyes, Clotilde, was your own reflection."

LeMans brought her hand to her mouth with a quick "Shhhh!" as an elderly couple paused beneath the morning sun near their table, then shuffled on.

She looked to both sides of her and whispered, "Let's forget what you want and what Stull wants and concentrate instead on an important fact, or shall I call it an important limitation: Communication with London is difficult, nearly impossible. We don't have a radio. Only the communists have a radio, and they don't share it."

"But for something as big as this?"

"As big as what? A single German soldier who wants to defect?"

"A single German soldier who has access to the commandant of Paris."

LeMans opened the palms of her hands toward Clotilde.

"The best we could do is send a message via a priest with the Papal Nuncio. He travels between here and unoccupied France and Italy. He is one of us. But it will take time. Weeks."

"We don't have weeks. Lt. Stull is desperate. *We must radio.*"

"Clotilde. There is nothing *we must do* except pray that we do the will of God."

"This *is* the will of God. Stull is too important to lose."

"Clotilde, you are confusing what you want with what is best for our cause."

"I wouldn't be the first person in history to profit while serving a higher good. Not you or the Resistance or the Church can object to that."

LeMans smiled.

"Maybe *you* should be teaching theology instead of me."

"Then you'll help? You'll radio London?"

"I can't radio anyone. I have no access to a radio."

LeMans sipped her lemonade.

"However ..."

Clotilde heard the beginning of an accommodation in her friend's voice.

"... I may have a way with the communist radio operator."

LeMans' inflection of the word *way* took Clotilde aback.

"Don't look at me that way, Clotilde. I'm not a street walker."

But conceded, "I wasn't always a Christian either, least of all one preparing to take vows. I was once a communist. There wasn't much money in being a communist, so to get by, I modelled for student painters at an art school on rue du Bac."

A nostalgic smile crossed LeMans' face.

"We used to say most of the nude paintings sold to American tourists along the quais were of me."

"*We* used to say!?"

LeMans tilted her head, her lips a slight smile.

"In 1936, poverty made for strange bed fellows, and one of my bed fellows was an art student, also a communist."

"*One* of your bed fellows?"

"Don't be so judgmental, Clotilde. Through the grace of God in Christ, it's not who we were that's important, but who He allows us to become. This painting-communist also had a hobby. Shortwave radios. We would listen to Radio Moscow while he painted me. He got so good at the radio that he'd transmit messages to Moscow at the request of some Soviet agent here in Paris."

Shame tightened Clotilde's chest. The agent could only have been Putnev, whose excesses with her in room 8 made whatever happened between a painter and model in 1936 fall just short of innocence.

"For you, Clotilde, I could contact this painting radio man. He may live in the same flat in Montmartre. Perhaps, he would transmit a message to London. The message would be sent in code. A code I know, and he doesn't. Only a handful of us know the code. It was in place two years ago between the French and British armies at the time of the German invasion."

"It's perfect, Josephine."

"Perfect, unless, he resists. He won't like transmitting a message he doesn't understand. Communists are a paranoid lot; they'll assume we're hiding something. And we are. Yet, he may still have sentiment for me. But understand, Clotilde, even if I convince him to transmit, I will not ask London to reply through him. The communists would take advantage. They'd withhold London's response until we told them what was going on. Let the Allies reply through our priest from the Papal Nuncio. It's safer."

"But the radio for a first transmission?"

"If the communist radio operator agrees."

he communist radio operator agreed.

LeMans had knocked on the door of his room overlooking an airshaft on a seedy street on the Butte. He was startled but greeted her warmly and said he had often wondered what had become of her. He was not surprised she was taking vows.

Then she asked him the question that had brought her, and he said, "I don't know about that, Josephine, but while I'm considering it, you might consider enjoying yourself one last time in my bed ... before you enter the convent."

She smiled no, and he relented with a laugh.

"Well, General de Gaulle has broadcast that all factions of the French Resistance work together."

That night, the communist radioman transmitted a coded message to London, and Clotilde and LeMans made plans. LeMans would wait at St. Séverin for a response from the priest attached to the Office of the Papal Nuncio. Clotilde would wait in St. Denys du Sacrament for Lt. Stull.

Chapter 26

For six days, Clotilde did not vary her routine. She arrived for morning mass, then remained the day, leaving only to visit the tabac across the street for coffee and toilette. Twice, the priest had asked if she wished him to hear her confession. No, she lied. She just loved St. Denys and the Delacroix Madonna.

Her wait was agonizing. So many uncertainties. Not only must Stull return to St. Denys, London must also tell her what to do when he did. Time was running out. Looming the next day was her rendezvous with Putnev ... and Mrs. Borodin. And looming in its own way: the Seine. Now, in late afternoon, she sat in the back of the church watching the sacristan arrange the prayer cushions disarrayed during noon mass. He shuffled from pew to pew amid the deepening shadows, genuflecting each time he passed the altar. In 20 minutes, the church would be closed and locked. Another day gone without answers. No Stull. No word from London.

She rose and stepped into the side aisle where she genuflected before entering the Lady Chapel. She lit a candle on the iron stand in front of the mural. Then, as she made the sign of the cross, she heard the thick wooden door of the narthex creak open and watched a man enter the nave and sink into the pew she had just vacated. It was Stull.

He slid out a prayer cushion and leaned forward. She did not disturb him but waited in the chapel by the wood-paneled wall. As the sacristan approached the last pew, Stull rose and entered the chapel.

"l prayed I would find you," she whispered.

He swung around, his eyes wide with terror.

"You!"

She brought a silencing finger to her lips.

"I must talk to you. It's safe on the street. You're not in uniform. You won't be recognized."

They passed back through the door and stepped onto rue de Turenne.

Outside, the slow descent of summer night had begun, and with it a languid breeze rippled the Nazi flags draping the arms of street lamps.

In the distance, she saw two men. She slipped her arm around Stull's waist.

"Don't be alarmed. I'm not like that," she said. "But it's best if anyone seeing us believes we are a couple."

Stull did not resist, and the two men ahead of them continued on their way.

Clotilde drew a deep breath. It all came down to what she was about to say and how he would respond.

Her language needed to be precise in its duplicity: tell him London had been contacted; deprive him of the detail that London had not yet answered.

She stopped, turned him toward her.

"I have done something for you," she said. "I have taken steps to get you out of Paris and to England and seminary. We have contacted the Allies. Told them you want to defect and become a priest."

Stull brought both hands to his face.

"My God!" he muttered. "What have you done!?"

In the heat of early evening, a chill shook her. She brought her arms tight to her chest, her body trembling.

I have failed. He had never wanted to defect.

Holy Mary Mother of God pray for me now and in the hour of my death.

Stull lowered his hands from his face, clasped his hands together in front of him.

"When!?" he said, his eyes wild. "When can I get out!?"

Clotilde staggered backwards.

"Thank God," she stammered.

Her relief vanished in the moment it took Stull to shriek an answer to his own question.

"You must get me out now! Do you understand? Now!"

"Gerhardt, please. I ..."

Stull was wringing his hands, oblivious to her using his Christian name without his consent.

"Do you know why I came here, today!?"

He did not give her time to answer his question.

"To pray for strength to tell my colonel that I am sick and must be relieved of my current assignment."

Putnev's words came back to her, the words he had used when she had asked to be relieved of her assignment. *You know too much.*

"They will never let you go, Gerhardt. You're in too deep. They'll never let you walk away from the Army. They'll only recycle you within it. You'd still be a soldier, not a priest. But if you let me help you, you can get to England and to seminary. *All I need is time."*

His hands came still, his question a plea.

"How much time?"

"Soon. Be strong. We must be strong enough to live our regular lives for a few hours more."

"My regular life is not regular! It is a horror!"

So is mine, Clotilde thought. Room 8.

"Your agony will soon be over."

"How do you know!?"

She didn't, so she lied.

"London is setting up your escape. It's only a matter of hours."

"But you have nothing *now?"*

"In a day. Maybe two days."

"A moment ago, you spoke of hours, now you say days."

His shoulders slumped, and he turned away.

"You have nothing for me!"

It was her last chance.

"No, Gerhardt, it is you who have nothing. I offer you everything."

IIer voice strengthened.

"Here is what we will do. Each day at 5, return to St. Denys. I will be here. And I will have information. Trust me. Trust Our Lady. She never despised one who loved her. You *will* be delivered. We will hear quickly."

He nodded and began to

Chapter 27

The next morning, compelled by her own directive to continue their regular lives, she set out for the Hotel Splendide, trying not to think or feel or question what Putnev and Madame Borodin would do with her when she arrived. It was a matter of getting through one more day.

She had considered not showing up, but Putnev would seek her out, and that was too dangerous for Stull. Then she thought of throwing herself on Putnev's mercy amid a flood of tears. But tears would only pleasure him. She remembered a scene in de Sade's *100 Days at Sodom*. She and another girl from convent school had read the book in secret one rainy afternoon in the vertigo of puberty. The scene had detailed the anguish of a servant girl who, in the name of the Lord, begged for respite from endless debauchery, only to be beaten and raped more for having invoked the name of God.

She would submit to Putnev, one last sacrifice for the sake of her students' safety. In a week, she and Stull would be en route to England, or she to the Seine. In either case, her agony would be over.

As she turned the corner onto Place Pigalle, bracing herself for the sight of the Splendide, she stopped. Fifty feet in front of her, Putnev was talking to a woman, blonde and Slavic, who she knew must be Mrs. Borodin. Next to the woman stood a girl in a school uniform of scotch plaid skirt and white blouse. In a streetscape devoid of klaxons and rumbling engines, she heard Putnev say to her, "In a half hour. Room 8."

Then he looked up and caught Clotilde in full sight. He beckoned her with an avuncular gentility she had first seen from him before the war, when he had befriended her and her husband.

"How nice to see you, Clotilde. Come into the lobby. I have something to discuss."

Inside, Putnev motioned toward the faded red sofa. He sank into one end of it and patted the cushion next to him. She hesitated, then lowered herself down. He looked around. They were alone except for the clerk behind the front desk.

"First things first, Clotilde. We're not going upstairs today."

Hope stirred in her.

"But I do have a final assignment for you."

Two German soldiers swaggered into the foyer, each with a woman. Seeing them, Putnev barked at Clotilde, "I will pay what you want, if you do what I want. You have done such things before?"

She hesitated.

"Well!?" he yelled loud enough to make her jump. "Have you done such things!?"

The soldiers smirked when she answered, "Yes, I have done such things."

The Germans and the two women disappeared up the staircase.

"Just cover," Putnev said. "Can't be too careful. Now, about your new assignment. I want you to reinfiltrate the Christian Resistance group, those well-intentioned buffoons you spied on more than eight months ago at St. Séverin."

The hope that had stirred in her a moment earlier died. She should have known. In Paris, there was no hope, no sanctuary. If you evaded one horror, another awaited. Her world teetered between room 8 and the betrayal of friends. In the balance lie the safety of her students.

Putnev pulled himself to the edge of the sofa and looked around again. It was a gesture without artifice, a man doing his job.

"But perhaps those Christians are not buffoons. You see Clotilde, they know something. Five nights ago, a member of the Christian resistance named Silas - that's the LeMans woman you told me about months ago, the one you said was incompetent - asked my radioman if he would convey an urgent message to London. The agent said no. LeMans persisted. Finally, recklessly, the radio man agreed without consulting me. He justified his decision by citing General de Gaulle's order that all factions of the resistance work together."

A nervous little man with a wispy black moustache stepped into the foyer, consulted his pocket watch and positioned himself by the staircase. At his appearance, Putnev slipped his hand onto Clotilde's knee, saying loud enough for the man to hear, "You know what I like?"

She did not have to answer, as another man, young and muscular, strut in from the street and put his arm around the man with the wispy black moustache and led him up the stairs.

Putnev withdrew his hand.

"The message my undisciplined radio operator transmitted to London was this: *The baker and assistant want to make a home delivery of a wedding cake. But he has doubts. Can arrangements be made?"*

Clotilde squinted in confusion.

"It's code," Putnev said. "An arbitrary code. In this case, one used by the French Army at the time of the invasion. You know it, or you don't. I know it, and the message it conveys is extraordinary. *Baker* refers to someone in enemy high command. The *assistant* is an associate of the baker, maybe a wife or friend. *Home delivery* means the two want to defect. Why? That is explained by the phrase *he has doubts.* He has misgivings about what the Nazis are up to, perhaps moral or emotional or religious. What the defection will provide is exceptional information which is the significance of *wedding cake.* The *request for arrangements* is straightforward. Can the defector be gotten out?"

Putnev's tone took on an intensity Clotilde had heard from him only in bed.

"In short, the Christian resistance in Paris - as incompetent as it may be - has its hands on gold: a high-ranking Nazi who wants to defect.   Silas did not reveal the identity of this high-ranking Nazi. Probably doesn't know it. Silas told the operator the Christian resistance would not need his radio services again, which means the Christian resistance has another means of communication with London. Probably a courier. But they chose not to use their courier to make initial contact. Why? Too time consuming, indicating their situation is urgent. And if urgent for them, it is urgent for me. I cannot be kept in the dark about something this momentous.   That is where you come in, Clotilde. But let me ask you this. It may save me a lot of time and you a lot of bother. Have you heard anything about a Nazi defector?"

She hesitated, and she knew she had hesitated too long before mumbling, "No, Sergei, nothing at all."

103

Putnev pursed his lips, then relaxed them with something close to the sound of a kiss.

"In that case, you must obtain his name. That is your assignment. Contact your Christian friends. Especially Josephine LeMans at St. Séverin. She may reveal to you what I want to know. Do whatever you must, but get the name of the defector. Meet me here every day at three. I will be in the lobby. If you learn something in the middle of the night, call the telephone number you have memorized. Ask for the baron. If you succeed in obtaining the name, I promise you no more assignments for The Party. Perhaps no more trips to room 8."

Then with a smile, "But let's not be rash."

Chapter 28

As Clotilde left the hotel, Putnev stepped to the front door. He snapped his fingers, summoning Mrs. Borodin from the street.

"Tell the taxi driver parked at the corner to come here. Then go to room 8 with the girl."

She straightened her back, set her jaw.

"I charge more for two men. You will pay this?"

"Tell the driver to bring a newspaper."

Putnev returned to the lobby, picking up a copy of *Pariser Zeitung* from the front desk. He walked to the sofa, sat down and slid 5000 francs under the cushion next to him. Trafanov entered. Neither man acknowledged the other. Putnev unfolded his newspaper. Held it up, obscuring his face. Trafanov sat next to him; opened his newspaper.

"Did you do what I ordered?" Putnev asked.

"Yes, comrade."

"Any of your usual fuck-ups?"

"No, comrade."

"Then that chapter is closed. A broken neck on a dark staircase. An accident. Of course, I must find a new radioman."

Putnev turned the page of his newspaper.

"I have another job for you. Last December, you delivered a letter into the coat pocket of a teacher at the Louis Pasteur School in the Marais. A few moments ago, I asked that teacher for some information. She told me she didn't have it. She lied. She will need convincing to tell me the truth when I ask her, again. You will provide the convincing."

Putnev fell silent, not speaking until Mrs. Borodin and the girl passed through the lobby and ascended the stairs.

"Across from the Louis Pasteur School lives a child. Claire Marie Bastian. She is slow in the head and in the care of her uncle. He drinks. Find the child. Bring her to the school. It's summer; the school will be empty. There, do your business. At first, I thought to scare her, but being slow, she may not understand and treat you without concern. So, do more. Much more."

"Kill her?"

Putnev did not concur or dissent.

"Then leave the clue - the armband with the swastika - as you did in Beauvais a few months ago.   Do this today. Now. When I leave, you will find money beneath the cushion you're sitting on. The money's yours. But no fuck-ups."

Putnev rose and ascended the stairs.   Trafanov slid his hand beneath the lumpy cushion and removed the 5,000 francs, then headed for his taxi and the Marais.

Chapter 29

Striding with the gait of a woman who knew her city, Clotilde veered down rue Frochot toward Place St.-Georges, well clear of Pigalle and the ears and eyes she suspected Putnev employed in that quarter.   She reached the plaza in 15 minutes, its circular streetscape of plain trees screening three-and-four-story buildings of floor-to-ceiling windows and ironwork balconies. She crossed in front of the statue of Paul Gavarni, the artist of the Carnival of Paris. Parisians had not celebrated the pre-Lenten Carnival since the Occupation. She wondered if they ever would, again.

On the far side of the plaza, she deposited coins into a pay phone and dialed.

Josephine LeMans answered.

"Clotilde here. Don't talk. Listen. Putnev ..."

"Who?"

"A wicked man, a powerful man, crucial to the communist resistance in Paris. He has learned there is a defector. The message you transmitted got back to him. He knows the code you used. Now, he wants the defector's name."

"I warned you about this, about the communists, about using their radio."

LeMans exhaled deeply, then calmed.

"Why has this Putnev contacted you?"

"I know him."

"That's no reason."

Clotilde pressed on, not prepared to tell LeMans why it was a reason.

"Stull borders on hysteria. He wants us to move, now. Is London willing!?"

"I can't answer what I don't know, Clotilde.   But here is something I do know. You are at risk. This Putnev. Why didn't you tell me about him?"

In the tangle of betrayals Paris had become, the inference was as easy to make as it was devastating, and LeMans made it.

"Is there something between you and him, Clotilde?"

Clotilde paused.

"Is it physical, Clotilde?"

"Yes."

"Anything more?"

Clotilde paused again.

"Are you working for him, Clotilde? Is that why you sought us out last year, to spy for the communists?"

Clotilde's third pause turned LeMans' voice cold.

"What did you tell him about us, Clotilde?"

Again, silence.

"Clotilde, *what did you tell him about us?*"

The question shamed her. Also, freed her.

"That the Christian resistance was incompetent and unimportant."

"Is that what you think, Clotilde?"

"I told him *that* to shield you. So he would dismiss you."

"Did he believe you?"

"I don't know. It was months ago, and he removed me from the assignment. But now, he has learned there is a defector."

"And he wants you to spy on us, again."

"But I cannot. I will not. I no longer work for him."

"That's not what he thinks."

"Josephine, for the love of Christ, forgive me! Believe me!"

The ice in LeMans' voice had not thawed.

"Forgiveness is one thing, Clotilde. Christ commands us to forgive. But belief ... belief is another. If I believe you, am I being a fool? St. Paul says we are to be fools for Christ. Are we to be morons for Him, as well?"

"I have not worked for Putnev since December."

Clotilde pushed from her mind her weekly ordeal in room 8.

"And I brought Stull to you. Not to Putnev. *To you.* Would I have done *that* if I still worked for him?"

LeMans paused long enough for Clotilde to interrupt with a staccato, "Josephine, are you there!? Talk to me!"

"I am here, Clotilde, and I am talking to you. It is not only Stull who verges on hysteria. I hear it in your voice, as well. Hysteria is dangerous. In Paris, hysteria will betray you faster than a collaborator. Calm yourself."

"I know I don't deserve ..."

"Who am I to say what you deserve? Listen to me. Go to your apartment. Pack a small suitcase. You are in grave danger. You know too much. Communists hate people who know too much. They will not hesitate to silence you. They are as brutal as Nazis. Come to St. Séverin this evening for mass. I will give you shelter, either in the short term, as we prepare to get you and Stull out, or, if London denies our request, for longer. Be careful. Make sure no one is watching your apartment. I repeat. You are in great danger."

"Then you ..."

"Yes, Clotilde. I believe you. We will not speak of this, again."

Oblivious to the morning freshness that brightened Paris, Clotilde raced from Place St. Georges to the Marais and to rue St. Claude and her room. It occupied a corner of the second floor of a dilapidated building that had gone overlooked in Haussmann's redesign of Paris. The building housed a disparate pod of lower middle-class Parisians. Not a subversive in the group and, consequently, no reason for her to see what she now beheld. It stopped her cold. A gendarme, accompanied by her concierge, stepped through the doorway of her building and onto rue St. Claude.

From across the quiet street, Clotilde heard the woman tell the policeman, "I don't know when Mrs. deBrouillard will return."

Clotilde averted her face and retraced her steps back toward Rue de Turenne. Across the street from St. Denys du Sacrament, she took temporary sanctuary in the tabac where she had first taken Stull.

The proprietor, who recognized her from her visits of the past week, motioned her to sit where she wanted. She pulled out a chair at the back, far from the windows. He shuffled over.

"Have you heard the news?" he asked.

She shook her head no, as if spoken words might betray her.

"At the school," he said, warming to his subject and jerking a thumb over his shoulder in the direction of the Louis Pasteur School. "A little girl. They say she is very slow. Attacked. Ambulance, doctors. They dare not move her. She is unconscious. Perhaps, dead. The gendarmes have come around asking if I have seen anyone. It is terrible. What would you like?"

Chapter 30

Clotilde bolted out the tabac and rounded the corner toward the school, throwing open the front door and running past a German officer talking with the school custodian. She followed muffled words to the head mistress' office at the end of the corridor.

"Clotilde, thank God you are here!" Camille Ronsaar gasped, taking her hand. "We have been looking for you. We sent a gendarme to your apartment to fetch you. It is Claire Marie Bastian. She has been attacked. Her skull has been struck. She is unconscious, her breathing irregular."

On a cot in the corner, Claire Marie lie under a horse hair blanket, only her pale white face and cowlicked hair exposed. A doctor held salts of ammonia beneath her nose. A nurse wiped spittle from the girl's slack mouth.

"Will she live?"

"One doesn't know," Mrs. Ronsaar answered gravely. "The doctor says the longer she is unconscious the less likely she will recover."

"But when!? Why!?"

"The custodian found her in the schoolyard. Saw her body behind the trash cans. She couldn't have been there more than a few minutes. They found *that* lying next to her."

Ronsaar pointed toward the nurse's desk. On a green ink blotter lie a red armband, in its center a black swastika.

"Claire Marie may have pulled it off the arm of her assailant. But we cannot know until – unless – she comes to. We are trying to contact her uncle but have not found him."

The doctor turned from his patient toward the head mistress. He was a severe young man, with wire frame glasses and an unemotional voice.

"We dare not move her. Her condition is critical. A large edema has formed at the base of her skull. The swelling is pressing into her medulla. I will pierce the edema. It may relieve the pressure. It may not. But we run short of options."

The doctor opened his black leather bag, withdrew a stainless-steel lance, doused it with alcohol before saying to Ronsaar and Clotilde, "You may wish to turn away."

Mrs. Ronsaar did. Clotilde did not. The nurse rolled Marie Claire on her side and swabbed her neck with an alcohol-soaked sponge. The doctor inhaled deeply and pressed the lance into the gray-green edema, then handed the lance to the nurse and began to palpate the wound. Blood and lymph ran over his hands, spread into Marie Claire's matted hair and onto the cot.

The child lay motionless, then a spasm shook her, her arms flailing. Nurse and doctor holding her down.

A scream.

The closed eyes opening. A jet of vomit.

Then silence until deeper breathes and blinking eyes and a plaintive word, as if asking for an explanation.

"Mama?"

The doctor's shoulders slumped. The nurse continued to swab the back of Claire Marie's neck, then embraced Claire Marie and whispered to her, "You are alive, little one. You will live."

"She *will* live," the doctor confirmed and after toweling off his hands, drew a cigarette from his pocket and lit it.

"The crisis is over."

He exhaled a plume of smoke, then looked up, adding, "But maybe not."

Chapter 31

The blond and angular German officer Clotilde had raced past in the corridor stepped into the head mistress' office. Clotilde sighed so deeply at what she was sure would be her arrest that the German came to her side and took her arm, fearing she was about to pass out.

"Please, sit down," he said gently. "This is harrowing. No one should have to see such things. I am aghast at what has happened."

He guided her to a chair. Clotilde did not resist, her mind distracted by the Nazi officer's unexpected sympathy.

"My name is Captain Witt Halle. German State Security. The Paris police called us immediately. That is why I am here. That and the swastika there on the table."

He waggled a finger at it and cocked his head in concern.

"Perhaps, it is a ruse planted by a perverted soul to incriminate a German, or no ruse at all, and the attacker is German. In any case, the blood of this monster makes no difference to me. He is an outrage to Aryan morality. I will find him no matter where, no matter what."

He looked at Claire Marie.

"I already have a lead. The custodian encountered a man walking away from the school yard shortly before he found the child. Medium build, stocky, dark suit. Not much, but the custodian did note one striking characteristic. The man had a scar on his face beneath his right eye in the shape of a checkmark."

Clotilde gasped and spoke before she thought.

"I have seen this man!"

And in that moment, she knew she would have to lie to Captain Halle or confess to him she had been arrested by the man nine months earlier on a snowy night in George Wilson's room.

Mrs. Ronsaar came swiftly to Clotilde's side, her face angry.

"Clotilde, where? Where did you see this man? You never told me."

"Here, at the school," Clotilde lied, "before Christmas. I approached him. Asked what he wanted. He said nothing. Walked away. I didn't think ..."

"Quite correct, Clotilde, you didn't think! You know how diligent we are about strangers at the school. Especially men. You should have reported it. I am appalled you did not. Your behavior is unforgiveable. A breach of responsibility toward our children!"

Images of what she had done with Putnev in room 8 to discharge that responsibility flashed in Clotilde's mind.

"Clotilde, come to my office. This is an extremely serious matter, and I want to ..."

"Yes, extremely serious," Captain Halle interrupted, "so please, postpone your private meeting until I finish questioning this woman."

The head mistress' face registered defiance, but she did not act on her feeling, and Halle's questions began.

Had Clotilde seen this man, again? Did she know him? Could she provide a detailed description? Had the child ever spoken of a man? Had any of her children spoken of a man?

No, Clotilde said. Halle took her address and told her to be available for further questioning.

Ronsaar reasserted herself.

"And now, Clotilde, if the captain permits, come with me."

But Clotilde did not, and the last thing she heard as she walked out of the room was her head mistress suspending her and vowing she would never teach in a Paris school again.

Chapter 32

In two-step strides, Clotilde took the staircase in the Hotel Splendide, throwing open the door to room 8. Putnev stood by the bed staring at Mrs. Borodin and the girl, their nakedness barely registering with Clotilde.

"Sergei! They have attacked one of my children!"

Putnev snapped his attention back to the bed.

"Get dressed in the hall," he yelled at Borodin and the girl, and pushed them into the corridor, throwing their clothes behind them. He slammed the door and turned to Clotilde.

"She's dead!?"

"No, thank God!"

Putnev brought his hands to his face to conceal his rage. Trafanov had bungled his assignment. Again.

"It's unspeakable, Sergei! The same Gestapo agent who arrested me last November has attacked Claire Marie! I know it! Captain Halle said ..."

"Captain Halle?"

"The German policeman. He's investigating. Knows that a man with a scar was seen at the school. It's the same man who arrested me and threatened my students! Now, he's tried to kill Claire Marie! Sergei, protect my children! You promised to protect them!"

Putnev reeled. A moment earlier, he had been whiling his time in a ménage à trois awaiting the death of a child that would scare Clotilde into providing him the information he wanted: the name of a traitor to give the Gestapo in exchange for their political favor. Now, that name might be the only thing between him and a German concentration camp. Not only had Trafanov blown thc simple task of killing a seven-year old retard, he had been seen. If Halle found Trafanov, he would sweat Trafanov. And Trafanov would break; tell Halle that Putnev had ordered the attack. And Putnev would be defenseless, unless he gave Halle something greater than himself. He could wait no longer. His life was in the balance. He needed the traitor's name. His voice exploded at Clotilde.

"Who is this defector, Clotilde!? Tell me his name! Then, I will help you!"

His thunderous voice did not intimidate her. When it came to the safety of her children, nothing intimidated her.

"A barter arrangement for the safety of my students!? What kind of monster are you!?"

Her defiance stunned him. She was no longer the compliant object of his obsession. Desperation had hardened her. She couldn't be bullied, only persuaded.

What had she once told him? *I always respond to gentleness.* Gentleness was not his trait. But he had seen it in others, and he fumbled his hands around hers.

"Dear Clotilde, of course I will protect your students."

Then he resorted to a trait that was his. Dishonestly.

"Please understand why I need this man's name. I need it *to protect you.*"

Her defiant chin lowered.

"*Protect me?*"

"The Germans ordered an attack on the girl for only one reason. To force *you* to give them the name of the defector."

"For the love of God, Sergei! How do they even know there is a defector?"

"The radio transmission. They must have intercepted it. Knew the code."

"But why me!? I had nothing to do with a radio transmission."

Lies tumbled from him.

"LeMans did. They must have had St. Séverin under surveillance. Must have seen you there with her. Made the connection. And gone after you."

"But why attack a little girl!? Why didn't they come for me straightaway!? Just me!"

"A waste of time. You'd have denied any knowledge of a defector. But now, when they come, you'll give them everything they want because you know what they'll do."

Putnev let the logic of his argument penetrate before adding, "And they will come, Clotilde."

"But my children!? You must protect them!"

115

"I can only do that if I have his name."

"What does his name have to do with ..."

"Everything. If I have his name I can prepare your escape from Paris. That will save your children. They will be safe the moment you and your defector get to England."

She opened her mouth, but words did not come. Putnev didn't need to hear her words. He saw them in the wild hope in her eyes. He had reached her. Now, it was only a matter of her believing he could do what he promised.

"Clotilde, the Gestapo threatens your children *only* to get at you. If you disappear, so do Gestapo threats. And I can make you disappear, with the defector. I can get you both to England. Your Christians can't. They're incompetent. You told me so yourself. Yes, they scored a coup in learning the defector's identity, but they've botched everything since. And they'll botch getting you and him out of France. That requires skill and resources far beyond theirs: transportation, safe houses, bribery, forged documents, communications. They have none of it. If the Christians organize your escape, you won't get beyond Paris. If I organize it, you'll get to England. He'll be in the hands of the Allies. You'll be in London. And your students will be safe. But to make that happen, I need his name."

Everything she wanted was now before her. All for a name.

Could she trust him?

Nine months of room 8 told her she could not. But nine months of room 8 had spawned in her desperation enough to trust anyone who might help her, even Putnev. Yet, Josephine had promised to try to deliver that security. And she still might succeed, making any arrangement with Putnev a betrayal of Josephine, and she would not betray her friend, again. If she were to go with Putnev, she would have to tell Josephine LeMans face to face. And Josephine LeMans would have to agree.

"I'll need approval from the Christians. Without it, I cannot consider your offer."

Putnev couldn't afford to lose her. He eased back.

"Get it, Clotilde. Minutes count. For you, for him, for your little girls."

She turned to go, but he reached out again, gently grasping her right arm. He, too, stood on the brink. He needed something more, anything to give the Germans if Halle arrested Trafanov before the traitor's name was known.

"Clotilde, I must begin to make arrangements, now. But to do so I need information. Does this defector have special needs? It is essential for me to know if he's sick or incapacitated."

"No, not that ... but it might be best ..."

Her shoulders slumped. She had to give Putnev something to keep alive his offer of transport to England.

"What might be best, Clotilde? What!?""

"... if we don't emphasize The Party. The Communists. He hates them. You see ... he wants to be a priest."

Putnev nodded slowly. Keep reeling her in.

"Don't return to your flat, Clotilde. Too dangerous. Make room 8 your base of operation."

"No."

"Then, where will you go?"

"I have somewhere."

"A safe house?"

"Safe enough."

"Where?"

She didn't answer.

Don't lose her, he thought, play her on with the gravity of the situation and his readiness to help her.

"We have little time, Clotilde. Terrible clouds are gathering. I will remain here. You know the number. *Remember*. Ask for the baron."

She broke into the hallway and rushed down the stairs past Mrs. Borodin and the girl. Putnev let her go. For the moment, he had done all he could.

Or had he? Downstairs, he stopped at the front desk and pulled from his trouser pocket a 100-franc note. He threw it on the counter and grabbed the telephone receiver from the hand of the startled desk clerk. Knowing Putnev, fearing Putnev, the clerk stepped back but not before sweeping up the bill. With a quick tilt of his head, Putnev ordered the clerk to disappear. Then Putnev dialed. The call went through immediately.

"We must meet."

"Must?" the voice on the other end mused. "I'm the one who says what we must do. When?"

"Now! I have vital information."

"Tomorrow morning in my ..."

"Now!"

"*Now* will interrupt my schedule."

"It will also advance your career."

"In a half hour," the voice responded, tinged with a threat: this better be important. "At the Brest monument."

Chapter 33

Five minutes later, Putnev was sitting in the rear of Trafanov's taxi on his way to a crash meeting and wondering if he should shoot Trafanov in the back of the head before the day was over.

But retribution - or was it simply good management - would have to wait. He still needed Trafanov.

"After you drop me, contact Captain Azuir," Putnev ordered. "Get the address of a Jewess named Bloch. She was arrested in the last few days by the Paris Police at the Louis Pasteur Primary School in the Marais. Pay Azuir the usual, provided he obtains the information."

Putnev alit the taxi in front of the Madeleine and walked briskly down rue Royale. His fast step not out of place. Pedestrians, mostly German soldiers, had also picked up their pace, as dropping pressure and cool air rushing down from the upper atmosphere foretold a storm. In front of the Hotel Crillon, Putnev stepped into the Place de la Concorde. The Brest statue – a monument to one of France's great maritime cities - loomed before him, its stone base draped with a Nazi flag. He came around to the statue's far side, away from the hotel.

A skeletal man in his forties, tall and erect and dressed in a dark business suit said to him in German:

"You know, Putnev, it was right here, on January 21, 1793, that the French revolutionaries beheaded Louis XVI. Can you imagine?   Exactly where we are standing.   One young man retrieved Louis's head and shoved it in his crotch, making Louis's first act in death one of fellatio. I assume January 21 is a holy day in the Soviet Union. Death to the old regime."

Gestapo Major Manfred Keucher stood with hands on hips, his lips oddly twisted, as if what little tolerance he had for Putnev was about to vanish.

"By the way ... you're late in your payment."

"Two-thousand Reichsmarks will be deposited in your account tomorrow morning."

"The cost of keeping a cab in Paris has increased. It's now 2,500 Reichsmarks."

Keucher looked up at the threatening sky.

"Now, what's this about, Putnev? It's going to rain. If I get wet for nothing, I'll send *you* to the guillotine."

"I have urgent information."

"I'll appraise its value."

Putnev squared his shoulders.

"A German officer posted at the Hotel Meurice with access to extraordinarily sensitive material is about to defect to the Allies."

Keucher showed nothing.

"His name?"

"I don't have it. Not yet."

"What information *do you have*?"

Putnev was about to say the defector wants to be a priest but held back. Information was power and to be shared only to get something. He would keep Keucher in the dark, at least for the moment.

"That's all I know."

"That's all you know? For this, you called a crash meeting?"

"My source is excellent."

"What source?"

"The Christian Resistance in Paris."

"Which I ordered you to infiltrate."

"Yes. Very smart of you. Smarter still that you listened to me and kept those cells in place even after I had identified them for you. Had you rolled them up - as you wanted when I first informed you of them, you would have bagged only a few small fry. But having left them in place, they've become an important, if unwitting, source of information that will reward you many times over."

"Yes, yes, Putnev, all very wise, but you still don't have this traitor's name."

"I will. Within hours. Along with him and his Christian handler. No doubt, higher ups in the Resistance, as well. All I need from you is the manpower to arrest them when they show up."

"Show up where?"

"Perhaps a hotel in Pigalle or a safe house somewhere else. I'll know soon."

"It's vague. How many men will be required?"

"A dozen, so there's no chance they'll slip by."

Keucher exhaled loudly.

"But a big chance I could look ridiculous. Deploying a dozen men to surround a Pigalle whorehouse might come to the attention of my superiors in the Gestapo, especially if I don't have the name of the defector to justify the deployment."

"My information is good, as it has been in the past."

"Ah, yes, the past. You were the Soviet's premier agent here in Paris, until you saw the error of your ways and agreed to work for us on the sly ... but only after we occupied the city. You know, Putnev, I'm not quite sure about you. You'd sell out your mother. Of course, I don't care about your mother, but I care about myself. Before I do what you ask, I need better justification than your word. So, here is my offer. I will assign a dozen men once I know exactly where they are to be deployed. But to keep my generous offer open, I want the traitor's name. That way, I can justify personnel deployment to my superiors. And I want the name of the persons handling this defection for the Christians."

"Josephine LeMans and Clotilde deBrouillard."

"Where can I find them?"

"LeMans at St. Séverin in the Latin Quarter. But I wouldn't arrest her. It could send the Christians and the defector into hiding."

"I'll decide when to arrest, not you. Where's deBrouillard?"

"With the defector."

"In any case, I want the defector's name."

Putnev raised both hands in capitulation, a clap of thunder affirming his gesture. Keucher looked again at the darkening sky, then back at Putnev.

"My line will be open 24 hours. Operators will have instructions to contact me immediately. When you call, use the name *Thunder*. If you want the deployment, get me the defector's name."

Chapter 34

The first two parachute jumps exhilarated Wilson. The third had not. The first two had ended in soft landings in morning sunlight in fields on the Surrey Hills. The third was at night, and Wilson never saw the jagged fence post he crashed into until it had gashed his right shin. The wound bled heavily. A medic in attendance with Venerable did not intercede.

"Bit of good luck," Venerable observed. "Gives you a chance to practice self-administered first aid."

Wilson groaned. Venerable demurred.

"Come on, Number 765, I know it hurts, and I know you've just vomited and must be light headed, but behind enemy lines we won't be there. You'll have to tend your own wounds. You'll thank me for this later."

As Venerable and the medic stood by, Wilson tied his handkerchief to his shin, wrapping it over the wound. Only after he was up and walking did the medic turn on his flashlight and inspect the job.

"It'll do," the medic sniffed.

Back at Perran House and medicated with a large snifter of brandy pressed on him by Venerable, Wilson fell into a deep sleep interrupted eight hours later by Venerable bursting into Wilson's morning-lit room and announcing, "Big day, George. You're going to find out where we're sending you and what you'll do when you get there."

By OSS training standards, Wilson's breakfast was sumptuous. Three eggs, two sausages, toast, an orange and real coffee, not the sludge made from acorns mandated by rationing. Even the meal's setting was palatial compared to the trainees' usual mess in a converted mudroom off the kitchen. Wilson ate in the main dining hall from a polished table overseen by oil portraits of Georgian aristocrats. He was alone, peeling the orange, when Venerable entered carrying an attaché case. He set the case on the table and pulled up a chair.

"How's the leg? Sure it's fine. Not much time. Let's begin. We'll start with the big picture and detail back. We're sending you to France."

Wilson suppressed his excitement. If Venerable saw it, he'd ask about it, and what was Wilson to say, well, once I knew this girl in Paris ...

"You'll be parachuted into a field at night east of Le Havre, on the right bank of the Seine. There you'll be met by a partisan, code named Abelard. The partisan will escort you to a safe house where you will appraise your situation. Did the enemy see me drop in? Do I have access to transport? Can I begin my mission? Do you mind giving me a wedge of that orange? They're pretty rare in Britain, now days."

Wilson pried out a section from the rind and handed it to Venerable, who popped it in his mouth. He winced.

"Tastes like cardboard. Oh, well, our intentions were pure. Wanted you to have something special. Let it be a lesson to you. Appearances can be deceptive, especially in our trade, especially behind enemy lines, especially in occupied France, where who knows who's on your side. Where was I? The partisan will deliver you to one and only one contact, and you will set up a cell. In turn, that contact will deliver you to another contact with whom you will set up another cell. Let each contact know we will make arrangements in the weeks ahead to drop radios and personnel to train them and establish transmission schedules. Presently, there are few shortwave radios in France. The communists have one in Paris. There's also one in Normandy. It's the one we're using to coordinate your drop. For now, your job is to set up cells throughout Normandy, between Le Havre and Rouen, so when the time comes, they'll be ready."

"Ready for what?"

"You don't have to be Von Clausewitz to figure out the Allies are going to invade northern Europe. Stalin is in a rant about it. Wants relief from the German divisions besieging Russia. Looking at a map, that invasion must be in France. The low countries are unsuitable for an amphibious attack. The Germans can flood the lowlands in a day. We'd never get off the beaches. But France is a different kettle of fish. High ground 200 yards inland from

123

Cherbourg to Boulogne-sur-Mer. The invasion will most certainly come somewhere between the two. Precisely where, I don't know. Nor do I know when, and the cells you set up must understand that. They are sleepers and may be dormant for months. Let them know that soon we will drop radios to them, but they should not be discouraged if they hear from us infrequently, at least for now."

Venerable opened the small suitcase on the table in front of him.

"Next, you're no longer Number 765. You have a proper name. Georg Olert, or more precisely Father Georg Olert, an Alsatian priest, born a French citizen but now, thanks to the annexation of Alsace back into the Reich, a good German. And you're pleased as punch about this. This priest cover story works on several levels. First, it explains why a man your age is not in the German Army or a laborer in a munitions plant. Secondly, this identity fits perfectly with your academic work in Church history and spares us the need to bring in a real priest to show you the ropes. If some nosey Nazi asks you about a particular feast day, you can reply appropriately, even in Latin. Another benefit of you being a medievalist. We also assume you can convey a certain level of priestly piety."

"Questionable assumption."

Venerable did not smile.

"Listen closely. If a French cop stops you, and a French cop may stop you because they're in league with the Germans, show him this and answer his questions in French."

Venerable dipped his hand into the suitcase and withdrew a German passport and handed it to Wilson and continued.

"We're betting a French cop won't be able to distinguish between a German accent applied to the French language and an American accent. He'll think you're muddling through in correct but oddly pronounced French and leave you alone."

"What if I'm stopped by a German?"

Venerable smiled at his own cleverness.

"Present the same passport but speak to him in German."

"If I'm a German speaking German to a German, he's going to know I sound foreign."

"Open the passport. Look where it says Place of Birth."

"Kaiserberg."

"And where is Kaiserberg?"

"Alsace."

"When you were born there 27 years ago, Alsace was French. That means you grew up speaking French. So, of course, your German accent would be impure. Just bubble over with joy at being returned to the fatherland. Tell them you've been a German at heart all your life."

"Then why am I in France?"

"You've been assigned by the Reich to make sure the curricula of Catholic schools in Normandy reflect the German point of view. You know the diatribe. Jews are satanic. Communists are evil. The Nazis have ushered in utopia."

"I will have official documentations to that effect?"

Venerable held up an envelope.

"Signed by the Reich's Deputy Minister of Education in Berlin and countersigned by a bishop in Paris. It's a forgery but a good one."

"What if the bishop or the deputy minister is contacted?"

"If a checkpoint guard gets through to the Deputy Minister for Education in Berlin, you've had it. But we're betting ..."

"With my life."

"... that a German checkpoint guard won't even try. If he does, he'll never get to speak with the deputy minister."

"What about the bishop in Paris?"

"Not really a bishop, but he is a real priest."

"Why not get a real bishop?"

"They don't grow on trees. Besides, the Vatican is not to be trusted. The Vatican doesn't like the fascists, but prefers them to the communists and is prepared to work with brown shirts or black shirts to thwart red shirts. That appears to be Vatican policy, and its bishops are obliged to support it, so finding a bishop who is also a resister is difficult. Whereas, finding a priest who is a resister is fairly easy, such as Father Gérard, our ersatz bishop. His telephone number is on this letter. If he receives an inquiry about Father Georg Olert, he will vouch for you, provided he picks up the phone at his church. That's Ste. Hélène's in Paris."

"Are you sure he'll pick up?"

"He said he'll try."

"He'll try?"

"That's all we can expect of any one."

A shiver down Wilson's spine torqued his back.

"As to getting you home, that's the job of your contact, Abelard. When your assignment is completed, get back to him. He knows the country. We don't. He's your man. *Get back to him no matter what.* Without him, you'll never get out of France."

"What if I can't get back to Abelard?"

"Hopefully, you won't have bolloxed your operation that badly."

"Sir, with respect, *what if I can't back to Abelard?* Should I try for Switzerland? It's neutral."

Venerable exhaled wearily.

"You might get in, but we'd never get you out."

"Then south?"

"Across 500 miles of open country through Spain to Lisbon? A snowball's chance in hell."

"What about the Channel?"

"Unless you're a fish, you'd never make it. The Channel's 50 miles wide at the mouth of the Seine, but it's the heaviest fortified 50 miles on earth. The Germans would blow you out of the water in minutes. Plus, you'd never get a boat big enough. Any vessel smaller than a good fishing boat would founder in the heavy seas, and there are always heavy seas in the Channel. And don't get it into your head we'll evac you by submarine. They're for insertions not pick-ups. Too risky having an immersible sitting in German-patrolled waters waiting for a spy to float by. Just get back to Abelard. He's key. Abelard."

Venerable saw the concern in Wilson's eyes.

"Don't worry George. It won't be that bad. Besides, you'll have plenty of this."

Venerable revisited the suitcase and removed a wad of German Reichsmarks and French francs.

"Remember my lectures. Money can buy bed and breakfast from a farmer or a prostitute or anyone who might help you. Use money and hope the people who take it have scruples and help you. If not, and they turn you in, well, be creative. If there's a gun at your head, offer the gunman something better than your dead body. If you think fast enough, you may conjure an alternative to a bullet in your brain. If you can't conjure, well, there's this."

Venerable placed a capsule in front of Wilson.

"Cyanide. There's one sewn into the lining of your valise. It would be your call, but I don't recommend being taken alive."

Wilson stared at it as a gambler might eye a huge raise placed on the table by his opponent. Then, he looked at Venerable.

"Stirring pep talk."

"Now, to details of your drop. You parachute in at night. One airplane crossing the Channel generally does not disturb Jerry. A partisan with a light box will signal the landing area to your pilot. After you land, a partisan will approach you. That will be Abelard. He or she will ask you, 'Will it rain tomorrow?' You will answer, 'Who can predict the weather?' We keep the sign and countersign mundane. Should you ask the wrong person *Will it rain tomorrow?* there's no problem. It's a common question."

Venerable ordered him to repeat the sign and countersign three times. Wilson did.

"Now that you've learned it, I hope you have also figured out what to do if the person you're talking to garbles their response. Number 809 was probably right on that one. Kill him … or her. And know this Father Olert. If you don't respond correctly, he or she will kill you."

From the suitcase, Venerable removed a Latin missal, a breviary, rosary beads, a vulgate Bible and a German travel visa.

"Most of this is the normal accoutrement of a priest. The travel visa isn't. It's called an Ausweise. If the Germans stop you, and they will as part of routine checkpoint security, show the visa. It grants its bearer access to the forward area. It's a damn good copy. Our forgers are excellent. The vast majority of people can't get these visas, but you're a government agent and citizen of the Reich on a mission for the Ministry of Education. Checkpoint guards should not consider you a security threat, and after they see the Ausweise, you'll be on your way."

Venerable rose.

"Oh, by the way, George, don't wander too far. You're going out tonight."

"Tonight?"

"We don't like providing too much lead time in these matters. After dark, we'll drive you to the Woking Golf Course. A plane will be waiting on what was once the eighth fairway and is now part potato field. The weather's ideal. Thunderstorms predicted from London to the Channel to Paris. The Nazis won't be looking for an airborne insertion during an electrical storm. It's a stroke of good luck."

Wilson had once read the chances of being struck by lightning were 50 million to one. He wondered what they were for a parachutist in a thunderstorm.

"For the rest of the day concentrate on being a good Alsatian, born a Frenchman now overjoyed with the reabsorption of his homeland into the Reich."

Venerable extended his hand.

"Best of luck, George. And by the way ... that little stiffening of your back a few minutes ago? Don't do it in front of a German. It's a giveaway. Finally, use your priestly status as you deem appropriate. If you're talking to a reincarnation of Siegfried, I wouldn't press it. But if your interrogator is a good Catholic, don't be afraid to use his religion against him. Well, that's about it. If you're a praying sort, good time to give it a whirl. See you later."

Chapter 35

Late on the afternoon of the Feast of the Assumption -- as Putnev plotted with Major Keucher at the Brest Monument, and Wilson received his final orders from Venerable -- Clotilde entered St. Denys du Sacrement. She blessed herself with holy water from the stoop by the door and retired to the chapel to await Stull.

It was an agonizing wait. Impossible decisions confronted her. Should she throw in with the communists? Were they abler to get her and Stull to England? But could she trust Putnev? Eight months of enslavement and humiliation told her she couldn't. She *could* trust Josephine LeMans, but could Josephine get it right? Could she do what had to be done?

Despite her indecision – or perhaps because of it – Clotilde clung to a hope that would eliminate her having to choose, a hope that the Allies, so dazzled by a prize as tempting as Stull, would step in and take over. But even that solution posed a huge problem: managing Stull.

He had become increasingly difficult: demanding, suspicious, arrogant, fearful, all on display in his wild eyes and abrupt movement as he entered St. Denys. After reverencing the altar, he slid stiffly into her pew. He did not wait for her to speak.

"No more delays," he whispered fiercely. "We must do this thing! Now!"

"We are close, very close. Hold on a few more …"

"Are you listening? Do you hear me? You said you would help me. You are not helping me. Do you know who I am?"

"I'm asking you to hold on."

"I can't."

"You can. Return to your post in the morning."

"I can't. I left my post at noon, today. I have not returned. I will not return."

Clotilde bridled her impulse to swear at him, even curbing an incredulous *You what!?*

She breathed in deeply, trying to unknot her stomach and managed only the most obvious observation.

"They'll be looking all over Paris for you. We must hide you."

"You told me you could arrange such things."

"With enough planning and ..."

"You promised. Take me out! Now!"

"I can't take you ..."

"Now!"

His voice was rising, and she was losing him and nothing she could say would get him back, only what she did.

"I *will* find a safe place for you."

Sweet Lord, she asked in a quick, silent prayer, Putnev or LeMans? The Christians or the communists? Whom to trust?

Stull had his own idea.

"Your apartment?"

She could not tell him Putnev and LeMans had both warned her about returning there, or that a gendarme had visited her concierge earlier in the day, or that Captain Halle had taken her address. Her apartment was impossible, which left her two choices: Putnev or LeMans.

Putnev offered her everything: safety in Paris, escape from France, transit to England. LeMans only a Paris hideout. But Josephine had forgiven her betrayal. Believed in her, again. It was enough. Clotilde's conscience overwhelmed her.

"I know a Catholic, a member of the Resistance. She will help us. I will talk to her."

"*I will talk to her*. I have this right."

No point in arguing.

"Yes, yes, come with me. *You* will talk with her. You have that right."

They left St. Denys to a rumble of thunder. Clotilde opened her umbrella.

"Stay beneath this as we walk. Good cover from curious eyes."

They headed down ruede Turenne toward the river, passing door after door adorned with neatly painted yellow stars.

Clotilde spoke to reassure him.

"It's quiet in the Marais. The Jews have been taken. No need for the Nazis to come back."

Stull did not comment.

On rue des Rosiers, across from a shuttered synagogue, they stopped at a pay phone. She telephoned LeMans, would ask for a crash meeting. Tell her of Putnev's offer. Beg her advice.

She never had the chance. LeMans burst into Clotilde's salutation.

"We have heard from London! They didn't wait for a courier. This has become urgent to them. So urgent, London risked transmission through a radio in Normandy. A woman code-named Thomas has just brought their answer. London is sending someone to meet Stull. The agent will be in Paris tomorrow afternoon. For this initial meeting, London is demanding a cutout."

"Cutout?"

"An intermediary between the agent and Stull to make sure all is in order. Since you know Stull, you will be the cutout. You will rendezvous with the agent in Paris, in the church of St. Hélène's tomorrow, 3 p.m. Enter the confessional, as if you were going to make confession. The person on the other side of the grille will be the Allied agent. Tell the agent to meet Stull two hours later in the Luxembourg Gardens, by the pond. They should both carry copies of the *Pariser Zeitung.* There, Stull and the agent will employ the newspaper protocol. Say nothing more to the agent. Nothing. The sign for your meeting in Ste. Hélène's and between Stull and the agent in the Luxembourg Gardens will be, *What time is it?* The countersign, *My watch is not reliable."*

"Does London know they must get two of us out of France?"

"They were told in the initial transmission."

"If they know, then I should meet this agent, as well."

"The first meeting is Stull alone. He is the prize, Clotilde. You are extra. Once that meeting takes place, the final plan will commence. Be ready."

"Am I to go?"

LeMans' voice cut sharp.

"I don't know. I don't know if Stull is to go. That is a decision the agent will make."

"Am I to go!?"

"Don't be desperate. It's unbecoming a Christian. For now, communicate with the agent at Ste. Hélène's. You will say only what I told you. Nothing more."

131

"Is the priest at Ste. Hélène's aware of this?"

"Father Gérard knows that an Allied agent will be using the confessional protocol tomorrow at 3 p.m., and that he may have to house this agent for a night or two. This information should calm Stull. Is he better?"

Clotilde drew a deep breath.

"No," she said slowly. "He has left his post. Deserted."

"Dear God! I won't ask you how that happened. I doubt you could have prevented it. We must keep him under control for the next 20 hours. Bring him here. Now. I have made plans to shelter you. I will accommodate him, as well. Be at St. Séverin in 30 minutes."

Clotilde hung up and informed Stull of London's decision. He nodded, conveying more of it's-about-time than thank-you. They walked toward the Seine that only days before had seemed her only choice and crossed the Louis Philippe Bridge to the Ile St. Louis, then into the Latin Quarter. The flow of pedestrians along the quai enveloped them, and for a moment, Clotilde felt the comfort of urban anonymity and answered prayers. The Allies had interceded. Jumped at the chance to land Stull and saved her from choosing between communist and Christian. The Allies would get them out.

She and Stull veered off the quai and weaved through the one-lane cobblestone streets onto rue des Prêtes. There her comfort vanished. She stopped short, eyeing the scene unfolding 50 feet in front of them.

"They're arresting someone!"

Ahead of them, a black Mercedes 260D had been angle-parked to block the street, its headlamps brightening St. Séverin's soot-stained western portal. Through the doorway stepped Josephine LeMans flanked by two men in dark suits, her folded hands in front of her clutching rosary beads. The men guided her down the four stone steps beneath deeply cut Gothic arches and into the back seat of the Mercedes. The car accelerated around the corner.

Stull understood, his voice desperate.

"She was the one, wasn't she? The one who was to help me. The one with the safe house. Who will help me now!?"

Clotilde did not answer. The squeal of the Mercedes's tires filled her ears, and tears filled her eyes. Josephine LeMans was gone but Clotilde had no time to grieve and little time to devise an alternate plan to get Stull and her to England.

Now, only one plan remained.

She took Stull's hand, as if he were a child, and led him into a cafe on the corner and   sat him at a table. He hung his head in his hands. Clotilde made another telephone call.

"I must talk to the baron," she said, fighting back tears.

A minute later, Putnev took the receiver offered him by the desk clerk at the Hotel Splendide.

"Sergei," she gasped, fighting back tears, "I need a place for that someone we spoke of. For tonight. London is sending a handler for him. After tonight, the handler will take over."

Putnev brought the telephone receiver to his chest whispered to himself with something akin to conviction, "Dear God."

An Allied handler! If he could deliver Stull *and* an Allied agent, the Germans wouldn't just dismiss his attack on Claire Marie, they'd fucking reward him.

"You *know* I will help, Clotilde. I will hide them both. You, also.   But the name. I need the name of the defector."

"When can we come and where!?"

"Room 8, the Hotel Splendide in two hours, but if I am to help you and him and his handler, *I must know his name. I need to make arrangements.*"

She hesitated, praying something might intervene.   Nothing did. She had run out of time and deceptions.

"Stull," she said. "Gerhardt Stull."

"Be here in two hours, Clotilde. You won't regret this."

Chapter 36

Alerted by his adjutant that someone calling himself Thunder was on the line, Gestapo Major Manfred Keucher picked up the receiver. Putnev so excited that the rustle on the other end was all he needed to hear before blurting, "Stull. The name of your defector is Gerhardt Stull."

Keucher paused, then said indifferently, "Makes sense. He's been AWOL since midday. Tell me something I don't know."

"Stull will be here in two hours. With Clotilde."

"Where's here?"

"The Hotel Splendide in Pigalle. Rue Duperré."

"I'll make preparations."

As darkness settled on Pigalle, Putnev stood at the window of room 8 observing the narrow street below. Ignoring the impending thunderstorm, a dozen plain-clothed Gestapo agents patrolled down one side of rue Duperré and up the other, one of the men always passing in front of the hotel. A black Mercedes 260 D idled at the northwest end of the street.

Clotilde and Stull took the Metro, transferring twice before alighting at Pigalle. They turned onto rue Duperré when she saw the Mercedes fifty feet in front of them. She stopped.

"What's wrong, *now?*" Stull sulked.

"Wait for me around the corner. Give me the umbrella."

He looked at the darkening sky and reluctantly handed it to her. She opened it and held it to her shoulder and walked down the street. At the Mercedes, her pace slowed. She glanced inside. A strand of rosary beads lie on the back seat. She closed her eyes, gathered herself, crossed the street to the Hotel Splendide. Whatever else, she must warn Putnev a trap had been set. The Gestapo ready to arrest them.

As she mounted the stone stairs to the lobby, a man carrying a newspaper pushed past her. Clotilde looked up, caught glimpse of a scar beneath his right eye. She froze, watched him walk through the foyer and sit on the faded red sofa. He opened a copy of the *Pariser Zeitung.* Next to him sat Putnev, also reading a newspaper held high in front of him. Neither man acknowledged the other.

Why would Putnev and a Gestapo agent ...

From beneath the two-year nightmare of Occupied Paris, the answer broke into her consciousness: Putnev was a Nazi agent.

The revelations cascaded into place: why Putnev had insisted on knowing Stull's identity; why he was willing to shelter them; why the black Mercedes was parked at the end of the street; why Claire Marie had been attacked. Putnev knew her fears for the child would drive her to him for protection. In exchange, she would provide him the name of the defector, which he would give to his Nazi masters.

It also explained why he had known George Wilson was *a young fair-haired American student.* The Gestapo agent had told him.

She backed down the steps onto rue Duperré. In a minute, she reached Stull. He had to be told.

"It's a trap. The Gestapo. They're here."

The anger she expected from Stull did not come. Instead, he slumped against the locked door of a dressmaker's shop and brought his thin hands to his face, his voice a whimper.

"I am no better off than a Jew. Just as doomed. *Nowhere* to hide."

Her resolve flagged. He was right. They were as doomed as Ilena Bloch.

Yet, the very thought of her friend evoked in Clotilde something more than inconsolable sadness.

Hope.

"There is *somewhere,"* she said to Stull. "Come with me."

Chapter 37

Stull was beyond resisting, and she led him. They turned off rue de Turenne onto rue Anastasia, stopping in front of Ilena Bloch's apartment building. A flash of lighting illuminated a plaque by the door noting that Juliette Drouet, mistress of Victor Hugo, had once lived there. Clotilde's mind reeled. Juliette Drouet gets a plaque for sleeping with Victor Hugo; Ilena Bloch gets dragged to hell for worshiping the Lord of Hosts.

It had begun to rain. Clotilde fished two keys from her pocket and slid the larger one into the lock. The door clicked open. She and Stull stepped inside the cobblestoned foyer. To their left, a thin rectangle of light outlined the concierge's door. To their right, a narrow staircase. They made for the stairs, Stull stumbling in the dark. The door cracked open.

"Who's there?" a woman's voice asked. "Is there anyone there?"

Clotilde was about to answer, to say anything - we seek refuge from the rain; we are looking for a friend; is there an apartment for rent - when a bolt of lightning and crack of thunder shook the building, then darkened the lights in the concierge's flat. The woman cursed, stepped back into her apartment and slammed shut the door.

"Quickly," Clotilde whispered beneath another roll of thunder. "While she's searching for candles. Upstairs."

Undetected, Clotilde unlocked the apartment door. They entered. A stench of ammonia and methane wafted over them.

"Get in," she gagged. "We have no choice."

She pulled shut the door behind them, cupped both hands over her nose and mouth and stepped forward, suddenly aware that Ilena Bloch's cat, Spinoza, had not welcomed her with his customary meow and curl about her ankles. In a moment, Clotilde knew why, as her shuffling feet collided with a lump of cold fur. She bent down. Nearly vomited. In a flash of lightning, she saw Ilena's cat, its head snapped back, its jaw slack. Even the pet of a Jew had to be destroyed. Clotilde edged around it and found a dust pan in the corner by the sink. She pushed the cat's remains onto it and dumped them into the air shaft, echoing with the patter of falling rain. The stench eased.

She rejoined Stull, still standing by the door.

"You can't expect me to ..."

"I do. We stay here, tonight."

"This is no safe house. It's a holding pen. I am awaiting slaughter."

She said nothing. Their words would only attract the concierge. Besides, Stull was right.

But there was a safe house, she thought, a safer house, anyway.

In Le Havre. Ilena's uncle's flat. Ilena had said he had been arrested a few days earlier. Like the apartments of deported Jews in Paris, it would be empty. But where in Le Havre? Clotilde stepped to a small desk by the door, opened it's dropleaf front. In another flash of lightning, she eyed what she sought. A small address book. Picked it up. Found the B's. Bloch. Abraham Bloch. 1 rue Marine. Le Havre. She tore out the page. Put it in her pocket.

A safe house in Le Havre.

"Sleep Gerhardt. We are on our way."

Chapter 38

The pilot saw three short bursts of light from the dark field 4,000 feet below and gave the green light. Wilson jumped. His parachute opened flawlessly and amid the rumble of thunder and streaks of lightning, he drifted to earth. His heavy black shoes, a standard wear for Alsatian priests, sank into the loamy soil of a Norman wheat field. He was burying his parachute and jump suit beneath the rotting trunk of a fallen birch, when a man's voice asked from the dark, "Will it rain tomorrow?"

Wilson answered as Venerable had directed.

"Abelard is all you need to know about me," the man said, his face no more than a shadow in the night. "Follow me."

They trudged in silence for a half hour, never on a road or even a path, only along the edges of wheat and corn fields. Then Abelard stopped, removed a flashlight from his belt and signaled twice at the dark outline of a house 400 feet ahead. Two flashes came back. In two minutes, they were inside the house, seated in the kitchen at a gate-leg table bearing half a baguette, two glasses, a bottle of red wine and a guttering candle. Abelard pointed to the bread and poured the wine.

"You came down with no difficulty," he said, lighting a Gauloise and tossing the match into the stone hearth behind them. "Your priest outfit isn't even dirty. Good cover. Some Germans actually attend mass. Want one?"

He shook the pack of cigarettes at Wilson, who declined, wondering how a Gauloise could smell so aromatic and taste so foul. Abelard inhaled deeply, cigarette smoke catching in his black mustache.

"Your drop was coordinated with the change of guard in Le Havre. We hope the Germans were too busy doing paperwork between shifts to notice you. They're obsessed with paperwork."

Abelard poured a glass of wine. Offered it to Wilson.

"No," Wilson said, remembering St. Patrick's warning about drink.

Abelard shrugged, took a large gulp.

"You look like a priest, a German priest I mean. I met some a few years back. They were visiting the cathedral in Rouen. They don't dress like our priests. Less fancy, like you. Black suit, black bib, simple collar. No cotta and robes or whatever those things are."

Abelard finished off his wine.

"I'm going to send a quick radio transmission alerting London you arrived in one piece. They're expecting it."

"There are few radios in France."

"I've had one since the invasion. I was a radioman for the French Army. After we surrendered, I kept it. It's our only link with London, at least for now."

Abelard continued to talk as he moved the table.

"Tomorrow, you will be contacted by Pigmy. When you finish your work, Pigmy will give you the code name of another contact and where you will meet."

Abelard jettisoned his cigarette into the hearth, then sank to his knees and rolled up the worn floral rug where the table had stood. He pried back a pliant floorboard and lifted out a small black suitcase. He opened it on the table.

"Take these," he said to Wilson, handing him two wires. "String them on that ceiling rafter."

Wilson tried, but the wires fell to the floor.

"Then just hold them over your head. You'll be the antenna for this transmission, provided the battery's charged."

It was. In a moment, a high-pitched tone shot from the radio. Abelard flicked the transmission switch and said in French, "The birthday gift arrived."

He switched to receive and said to Wilson, "I don't expect anything more from them. They know it's dangerous to broadcast for long. Germans can track you down. They have trucks that triangulate your location. The shorter the transmission the better. I'll wait a few seconds more."

As he moved his right hand to turn off the radio, a crackle of static interrupted him. A woman speaking Parisian French said, "Poem needs editing. File what you have in triplicate. Publisher dispatched on same ticket."

The radio went silent.

Abelard switched it off, retrieved the wires that Wilson had held overhead and stashed the suitcase back beneath the floor boards, covering it again with the rug and table.

He lit another Gauloise and shook his head in confusion.

"London just aborted your mission. They're sending someone else. "

Wilson was too stunned to speak. Abelard continued.

"The message was in code, but that's what it meant. *Poem needs editing* means mission aborted. *File in triplicate* means do not proceed. *Publisher dispatched on same ticket* advises that someone else is coming in immediately and will be inserted the same way as you. Right now, over the Channel, there's another Halifax approaching the coast. I would expect arrival in an hour. I'll meet whoever they drop and find out what the hell's going on."

Abelard pointed to a door near the hearth.

"Get in the cellar. The person who flashed us in is upstairs. When you're below that person will come down. You don't need to know anything about that person. He or she will signal me in when I return ... hopefully with your replacement and an explanation of what the hell's going on."

With flashlight in hand, Abelard led the way down a rickety staircase. Wilson followed, descending slowly. At the bottom, Abelard shone his flashlight on a pile of burlap bags of corn seed. He slapped one with his right hand. Dust from it rose into the beam from his flashlight.

"It's the closest thing to a bed. I'll be back as soon as I can. When I return, I'll knock four times on the cellar door. If you don't hear that knock, don't open. In fact, get out. Through the cellar window, and don't look back."

"Where do I go?"

"Just run."

"Where? You're my means of exit."

Abelard rolled his eyes.

"In that case, I'll be sure to come back and knock four times."

"But if you don't come back?"

"I will."

"At least give me the name of a contact."

"Clovis."

"Where is Clovis?"

"I shouldn't have given you even that. If you have to escape head for Unoccupied France. It's not much, but it's all we have. We've never done this before."

"But ..."

"Don't worry. I'll be back."

Abelard was up the stairs and away. Wilson alone. Moonlight glinted through the dirty eyebrow window set atop the stone foundation. Wilson worked his way to the window and pushed it open.

If he had to leave quickly, his exit was ready. To where was another matter.

Chapter 39

Muffled conversation from the kitchen above stirred Wilson in the cellar below. The cellar door cracked open. In the hour he had waited, there had been no knock. Not four, not one. A beam from a flashlight swept the staircase. The door creaked shut and the muted conversation resumed. In German.

Wilson did not hesitate. He moved silently to the unlocked window, eased it open and slid through the window frame, emerging belly down onto a patch of dew-soaked sod. As he began to pull himself up, he felt a gun barrel press hard into the base of his neck, pushing his face into the wet grass. Then two clicks of a revolver being cocked. His chest tightened, his lungs refusing to exhale. Of all the memories that might have come to comfort him in his final moment – his parents, Unity, Mae, Yale, Harvard – only one came: the scent of gardenia.

"You just blew your cover," 809 said, withdrawing the pistol. "A real priest would have prayed, not cowered. Let me tell you something, Father Olert. None of us is going to live forever. To be a good agent or a good priest is a matter of not wanting to. Get up."

He did not extend his hand to Wilson but turned and marched back to the farm house. In the candlelit kitchen, he pointed sharply at Wilson's shaking hands.

"They didn't teach you that, did they? How to die. You're scared to death. Scared *of* death. OSS should only hire priests for this kind of work. Real priests, more confident of the world to come than of the world we have. Men who understand obedience. But who do they send. You, Father Olert."

"How do you know my cover name?"

"Venerable couldn't expect me to come to France and ask for Number 765."

"809 is equally ridiculous. Your name?"

"Jerome."

Jerome looked at Abelard and pointed to the door.

"Father Olert and I need to be alone."

Abelard left the kitchen, closing the door behind him.

Wilson spoke first.

"Why were you speaking German with Abelard?"

"To test you. I trust no one. Certainly not you. If you and Abelard were Nazis, and you heard me speaking German, you would have stayed in the cellar or even come upstairs, confident you were among friends. But you tried to escape. That proved you were no Nazi."

Jerome poured himself a half glass of wine and drained it in one gulp.

"Here's why they sent me. Your mission's changed. At the last minute. You had just jumped. Your old mission has been given to me. I will establish the cells you were originally sent to organize. You have a new assignment ... one that was supposed to go to me but now, in Venerable's wisdom, has gone to you."

Jerome poured himself more wine.

"I stress the extreme importance of your new assignment. It comes directly from Venerable who received it from Allied High Command in London, and it comes with a condition ... "

Jerome paused.

"... you may have to kill two people for no other reason than they won't do what you want. If you don't think you can meet that condition, I am to take your place, and you will return to the task that brought you here."

He stared at Wilson.

"I'm waiting for your answer. Do you accept the condition of this assignment?"

"I don't know what the assignment is."

"You won't until you agree to this condition."

Wilson swallowed hard, then said with more authority than he knew he had, "I will do as required."

"You will kill two people?"

"If necessary."

"A simple yes would have been more assuring."

"I don't need your approval. Give me *my* assignment. Then, shut the fuck up."

Unperturbed, Jerome sipped his wine.

"A few days ago, London received a communication from a Christian Resistance cell transmitting from Paris. The cell had managed to get access to a shortwave radio. The coded message the radio operator transmitted was this: a German officer with access to high levels of Nazi leadership in Paris wants to defect, and he is demanding that another person come with him. The message indicated he has moral doubts about his work for the Reich. We have no idea about the sex, attitude or value of the second person. But before mounting a removal operation, London must learn if this defector is legitimate. That will be your job."

Jerome's jaw clenched, then released.

"It was to have been my assignment, but Venerable thinks you're a better judge of men than I. Told me I was a butcher. For this job, he said, he needed a surgeon."

"It could be a German trap to lure an Allied spy to the bait of a potential defector."

"The London evaluators don't think so. The original radio transmission alerting London to a possible defector came from a communist radio operator code-named Marx."

"Anyone could say he was Marx. He could have been a Nazi."

Jerome ignored the interruption.

"Over the months, London radio operators have gotten to know Marx and his little ways: when he transmits and, obviously, his voice."

"Voice? What does that matter? He could have had a gun at his head."

"If he were in danger there is a signal Marx could have used in transmission. He needed only to use the French pronoun tu instead of the more formal vous. He didn't. London believes his transmission is legitimate. That's why they're ordering you to Paris. At once."

"But what if ..."

"I'm not done. When you meet this potential defector, offer him money for his efforts or women or any of the enticements our line of work provides. If he accepts, you'll know he's a fraud. Remember, he is supposed to be doing this for moral reasons, whatever they may be. Therefore, such inducements would offend him. Now, what I am about to say is critical."

Jerome stepped closer to Wilson.

"Under no circumstances are you to offer him immediate sanctuary. If he's the real item, London wants him to stay in his position and spy for us in Paris. He could be a huge asset. Stress the nobility of such action. On a regular basis, he will report to his Resistance handler and deliver information he deems appropriate for the Allied cause. He is to be a spy, not a defector. Your job is to convince him. If you can't convince him, kill him."

Wilson said nothing.

Jerome glared.

"The killing is why they should have sent me. Nonetheless, you've been chosen, so understand the rationale of why he and his companion must be liquidated if he refuses. They are already under tremendous pressure. He and/or his companion may be unhinged, and if we deny them sanctuary, they might boomerang back to the Nazis and betray their Christian handlers. That is why if he refuses to spy for us, you will kill them."

Jerome's finished his wine.

"For this assignment, your sign and countersign have changed. Your new sign is *What time is it?* The countersign is *My watch is not reliable.* Now, one last thing."

From his belt, Jerome removed a Luger.

"Despite his better judgement, Venerable wants you to have it. He reasons that if you must kill this defector, you wouldn't do it with Grandad. A pistol is so much cleaner for the weak of stomach."

He handed the weapon to Wilson, who tucked it between his belt and the small of his back. Jerome summoned Abelard from the other room.

"Not only has Father Olert's assignment changed," Jerome said to Abelard, "but yours as well. You will handle me as you had intended to handle Father Olert, but first you will deliver Father Olert to the resistance cell in Rouen. They will get him to Paris. I was told you can arrange this."

"I can try. When?"

"Now. No time to lose. Get this priest to Rouen, then come back for me. I have cells to set up between there and Le Havre."

Chapter 40

Dawn brightened the tree line along the Seine. At a weathered barn bearing a faded advertisement for Gitane cigarettes, Abelard turned off the paved motorway onto a dirt road leading down to the river. At water's edge, he stopped his car. He and Wilson got out. Abelard pointed toward the end of a wooden dock extending 15 meters into the Seine.

"That's how we're getting to Rouen."

Moored at the end of the dock, a 7-meter pilot boat with a small cabin midship bobbed in the current, the letters BRL printed in black on its bow plank.

"It's not the Normandie, but on a full tank of fuel it can go from Paris to Le Havre, almost 200 kilometers. I store the fuel in that barn we passed. The Germans actually provide me with petrol. They consider me valuable. At least what I do valuable. I'm a river pilot, and today I have a job escorting a tender from Rouen back to Le Havre. I'll ferry you upstream on route to my assignment. If we have luck, I'll connect you with someone in Rouen who'll get you to Paris. After that, I'm out of the picture. Sit in there."

He pointed to the tiny cabin, then pried back a silvery plank in the middle of the dock and removed a key tethered to an old tennis ball. He joined Wilson in the cabin and inserted the key in the ignition. The engine groaned and caught, its valves tapping in loud syncopation.

"After the war maybe I'll have the money to fix them."

Abelard eased back the throttle, and the boat pulled away from the dock and began to ply its way upstream. Fifty meters from the north bank, sight of land disappeared, lost in a heavy mist rising from the river.

"The Seine is treacherous. Silt builds up. I know where. That's why the Germans allowed me to return to my job after the invasion. They need navigators. Otherwise, I'd be slave labor in Germany."

"How long have you worked the river?"

"Long enough to know what we are doing is dangerous. I can't recall a priest hitching a ride in a pilot boat. If the Germans find us, it will be hard to explain. But this should shield us."

Abelard waved a vague hand at the mist.

"Monet painted the river fog. He never got it right. But if he painted what he saw, he'd have only a gray canvas."

Abelard pulled the wheel hard to port.

"There's a sandbar just to starboard. They're all along the river. When we reach the dock just south of Rouen, you'll get off. It's isolated. There won't be any Germans."

There weren't, when two hours later Abelard maneuvered the BRL to the end of another wooden jetty, anchored to shore by a shack.

"I'm going on to make arrangements. Wait inside the cabin for one hour. If no one comes, go on your own. Follow the dirt road up river. It comes to a paved road. Take it. It winds into Rouen. About a mile along, you'll see a timbered inn, the Auberge Jeanne d'Arc. Go inside. Do nothing to draw attention to yourself. This is enemy territory. But if all goes well, you'll be expected. Someone will approach you."

"Who? Clovis?"

"Forget Clovis."

"But ..."

"No buts, because I don't have the answers. We're making this up as we go along. Just remember. You'll be approached. I don't know by whom."

"But you're my contact to get out of France."

"Not anymore. You'll be in the hands of the Paris resistance. Talk to them. Good luck."

For a hour, Wilson waited in the shack. No one came. He set out. Thirty minutes later, he pushed open the thick door of the Auberge Jeanne d'Arc, its wooden sign swaying from two chains suspended from a yardarm above the front door. The aromas of coffee and yeasty bread filled the wood-paneled reception area just off the dining room. Three German sergeants sat at a table, eating breakfast.

Wilson made no eye contact with the soldiers and walked to the vacant front desk, a brass push bell on its counter. He did not ring it, Abelard's warning paramount. *Don't draw attention to yourself.* He would return in a half hour. He turned to leave when one of the sergeants rose from his table and approached him.

"You're a priest?" the sergeant asked in a southern German accent, wiping bread crumbs from his chin. "I don't recognize you. I know the priests attached to the cathedral, but I don't know you. Where are you from?"

Abelard had told him he would be approached; was this sergeant his contact?

"What time is it?" Wilson asked.

The sergeant looked at his wrist watch.

"9:30. Please answer my question."

Wilson had no choice.

"Alsace," Wilson responded in German, as Venerable had directed.

"Why are you in Normandy?"

"To develop curricula for diocese schools now that France is subject to the Reich."

"A strange accent, Father, but then you are Alsatian."

"It was the way the French taught German when I was a boy. They insisted on a French accent. But my family and I are happy once again to be part of the Reich. We felt as orphans after 1918. But now we're proud to be Germans. That is our blood."

Wilson handed the sergeant his travel visa. The sergeant ignored it and stole a glance over his shoulder at his colleagues, then removed an envelope from his tunic and handed it furtively to Wilson.

"Read this."

Without looking at what the sergeant had handed him, Wilson said, "I'm sure my Ausweise is in order."

"Yes, yes. Your Ausweise is not why I am talking to you. You're a German priest. That's what matters. Please, Father, read this."

Wilson unfolded the envelope and withdrew a handwritten letter.

Sergeant Koblenz,

You are defending the Fatherland, and we are proud of your service, but you should know certain facts about your wife, Frau

Koblenz, residing in Stuttgart. To be blunt, Frederich, she has been
unfaithful since your departure, not with one man but with many. It is
my duty to inform you of this so you may take appropriate action for
the sake of your own reputation and state of mind. God bless you
Frederich, in all that you do for the Reich.
  A Friend

The sergeant retrieved the note from Wilson's hands and said in a hushed voice, "I attend mass at the cathedral and am billeted here at the inn. I do not want the priests in Rouen to know what is happening. Then I saw you. I knew by your attire you were a good German priest, not French. You are an answer to my prayers. Tell me what to do, father. About my wife. I can't return to Stuttgart. I am going crazy. I can't sleep. I can't think."

"You should ignore this."

"But the letter ..."

"The letter proves nothing. Our enemies in London prey on the natural fears of good men by sending false letters of indictment, telling them their wives or sweethearts are unfaithful. You can see how powerful this weapon is. It has flattened even a man of your stature. You believe this lie, and now you are unable to perform your duty. I tell you this is a libel. Ignore it."

"How can you be sure?"

Wilson reached out and put his right hand on Sergeant Koblenz's left shoulder. It was Frederich Koblenz's first intimate physical contact with another person since leaving Stuttgart.

"The writer of this note knows your name. Frederich. And yet the writer only refers to your wife as Frau Koblenz and does not mention your address. If this letter were true, the writer would have provided her name and address to make the indictment more authentic. The writer did not mention these details because the writer does not know them. The Allies know which German divisions are here. The Resistance no doubt has supplied particular names of some soldiers. Yours included. But they have no access to the names of the wives and home addresses. Do not despair, sergeant. This letter was concocted in London, not in Stuttgart. God bless you, my son. Keep faith with your wife."

The stooped back of Sergeant Koblenz arched erect.

"You think so?"

"I am certain."

The sergeant grasped Wilson's hand with a firm single-pump handshake.

"Thank you, Father. Thank you so much."

Sergeant Koblenz returned to his table, and Wilson was making for the door when he heard from behind him a voice ask, "What time is it?"

Wilson stopped, turned slowly toward the front desk.

A brawny man in a shabby blue suit and white shirt stepped toward him. He held a plumber's wrench.

"My watch is not reliable," Wilson replied.

"I was busy," the man snapped. "Second-floor toilet problem."

Chapter 41

The innkeeper approached Wilson, his accusatory whisper betraying his nonchalant stride.

"What the hell's wrong with you!? Talking to a German. I'm risking my life to get you to Paris, and you're chatting with a German. What the hell's wrong with you!?"

The man breathed in, exhaled slowly, gathered himself.

"Go out the front door. Turn right. At a hundred meters, you'll come to a French postal truck. A yellow Renault. Its passenger door will be unlocked. Get in. Crouch down. If you're spotted in the truck, it will be hard to explain. Wait for the driver."

Wilson walked to the door and descended the three stone steps to rue Belleau. He glanced up the lane. The truck was there. He quickened his pace, then slowed as an old man with a cane shuffled toward him. The man nodded, and after he passed, Wilson opened the passenger door and slid inside, back first. He crouched to the floor of the cab bringing his knees to his chest, his arms around his legs.

He had not seen the woman seated behind the steering wheel.

"What time is it?" she asked.

"Christ!" Wilson gasped. "You scared me!"

"*Christ, you scared me?*"

Wilson took a deep breath and answered, "My watch is not reliable."

She nodded.

"Stay down until we're out of town. While you're at it, come up with some exclamation other than 'Christ you scared me!' when you're surprised. It makes you sound like the spy you are instead of the priest you're pretending to be."

The truck pulled from the curb.

"My name is Thomas. We are at great risk. Take off that God damned clerical collar."

"It's my cover."

"Not in a French mail truck. Put this on."

She wiggled out of her Postal Service jacket and handed it to him. Her short brown hair and thick features were as tough as her words.

"If we're stopped, the Germans may think you're a postal worker. But even that will be a hard sell. Technically, no one's supposed to ride with me. Nazis are very touchy about mail service. Sometimes, they even send an escort car with me to protect their precious letters. I'll tell you when you can get off the floor."

She did, a half hour later. Wilson pulled himself up and began rubbing his right leg.

"Lose circulation crammed down there?" Thomas asked.

"My leg's itchy and hot. I hurt it a couple of days ago."

"Nerves," she pronounced.

They proceeded east on an empty road, passing sun-splotched farm fields separated by low stone walls, dense copses and denser hedgerows.

"Nice country," Wilson said. "This isn't such a bad job."

"Not bad, if delivering German mail is your idea of fun."

"I meant ..."

"I know what you meant. It wasn't a bad job before the Occupation. It's still not bad ... in its way. Good cover for me as a courier between Paris and western France. It would be a shame to lose that cover if you're discovered. So, you'll masquerade as a Postal employee until we get to Paris."

"I must say," Wilson noted, "the Christian resistance is well organized."

"You call these people well organized? Well organized would not have a secret agent curled up on the floor of a mail truck."

"*These people*? You're not one of them?"

"I'm no Christian, at least not the kind you expect."

A German staff car motored toward them.

"Duck down," she ordered.

As the vehicle approached, Thomas smiled and waved at it. The driver waved back.

"I always wave to them. I want them to think I'm happy they are in my country. *They* are certainly happy to be in my country. What German soldier wouldn't want to be in France when the alternative is Russia?"

She looked in her side mirror.

"They kept driving. You can get up, now."

She adjusted herself in her seat.

"I work with the Christians because it makes it easier to curse God."

"That doesn't make a lot of ..."

"My brother was killed in June, 1940, near Étretat. The army sent him home in a box, what was left of him. We gave him a proper church send off. Prayers, hymns, a mass. It had been God's will, the priest said at the grave. After the service, I told the priest he was a fool for believing his God had anything to do with Didier's death, and if he really believed it was God's will, then he should burn down the church as an act of resistance to such a monstrous deity. The priest must have been told something like that before, because he told me he understood my anger. Three months later, the same priest came to dinner at our apartment and asked me if I were still angry with God. I laughed and said I had forgiven his God by concluding He didn't exist. The priest did not chastise me, instead asked if I'd consider working with a small band of Catholics to help subvert the German occupation. I told him the Catholics must be hard up for volunteers, if they wanted me. He said I had a special gift. I didn't compromise. To be a good resistant, he said, you can't compromise. Compromise is what the Nazis want. I was no mealy-mouth agnostic, he said. My belief was as strong as a priest's, only in the opposite direction. Anyway, I agreed to join him. He unofficially baptized me Thomas, the doubting apostle. We rendezvous in church. Only problem, we meet in Church. That's where I get my orders. That's how I found out I was to transport you to Paris."

She lifted her left hand from the steering wheel and looked at her wrist watch.

"It's eleven. I say the Our Father at eleven. Join me."

Before he could say that her reciting the Our Father made no sense, she had begun. Wilson joined in, adding the addendum he had learned at St. Mark's Methodist.

"... for Thine is the kingdom and the power and the glory and for ever and ever. Amen."

"You're Protestant."

"Of a sort. I thought you said you don't believe in God."

The truck careened through a pothole. The violence of the bump lifted Wilson from his seat.

"I should have warned you. There are lots of potholes. The Germans don't spend money to fill them. There's another one coming. Look out!"

She swerved and avoided it. The truck resumed its forward trajectory.

"I didn't believe in God. Now, I do. It's essential for my mental health. You see, my faith accommodates my hatred. If He doesn't exist, I can't hate Him, and if I can't hate Him, I'll go mad. So, to survive, I have become a Catholic. Inside Mother Church, I can rail against His treachery. Every Sunday when I consume the Host, I am not spiritually taking Him into me. I'm mangling Him, as He mangles us, as He mangled my brother. Brace yourself. Here comes another."

Thomas yanked hard on the steering wheel, but the front right wheel caught the pothole's edge, again lifting Wilson out of his seat and bouncing him toward her. His left arm flayed out. It hit hard into her right breast.

"That's another thing I like about the Church. The priest isn't after me. He has no motives in courting me other than my continual association with the Resistance and the salvation of my soul. The communion rail is where he wants me, not in his bed. It's good to have a man friend who isn't angling for sex. Not that he'd get any. I don't think he knows I'm a lesbian."

Wilson's exposure to any sexual arrangement other than the dowdy wedlock of New England and the academic celibacy of the Ivy League had been minimal. Except for two young men he had seen embracing one night on the Quai de Montebello, Wilson knew nothing about homosexuality, except that it existed in the shadows and rarely. That women might be homosexual was no more than a rumor to him.

"I shouldn't pick on my priest, just because he doesn't know I'm a lesbian. It's men in general. Germans, Nazis, communists, French, all the same when it comes to matters sexual. They assume women either don't have sex or require a man if they do. Still, I'm discreet, and being discreet, I'm good with secrets. It may be why I was asked to take you to Paris."

By early afternoon as the road swung down close to the Seine, crops and pasture began to give way to the clutter of suburban life. Thomas pointed far off to the right.

"We're coming into Paris. Way over there you can see the top of the Eiffel Tower. You get out after we pass through the checkpoint."

"Won't the Germans question me at the checkpoint?"

"If they do, we're screwed, but they're surprisingly lax around Paris. It's part of their good-manners campaign. German soldiers have behaved well. No rape. No looting. They mind their business. Hitler has demanded their good behavior. You can see it at the checkpoints. Maybe it's because I come through every day, and I know them, but they're pretty friendly. Once we're on the other side, I'll let you out by a church, Ste. Hélène's. Go inside. You'll be met by the priest, Father Gérard. He's strange. You'll see. He's the priest who buried my brother, the priest who has brought me back to the Church, so I can carry on my feud with God. Father Gérard will tell you what to do next. Your sign and countersign are the same for him as they were for me. Questions?"

"Many."

"They'll have to wait. We're coming to the checkpoint."

"Should I duck down?"

"If they see you hiding we couldn't explain it. Just smile."

Wilson smiled. Thomas smiled and told a dirty joke to the German soldier at the checkpoint. The private smiled.

The arm of the barricade lifted.

Ten minutes later, Thomas stopped the mail truck in front of Ste. Hélène's. Wilson looked up at its massive façade.

"It looks more like a bunker than a church."

"What did you expect? Chartres? It's new. Now, give me back my jacket, put on your God-damned clerical collar and get out. Good luck."

Chapter 42

Every ancient church Wilson had entered in France engaged his senses with the musty scent of incense, the flicker of candlelight and the sound of half-heard voices echoing off stone walls. But as he approached the front door of Ste. Hélène's, he doubted he'd find the same numinous atmosphere. The church's contemporary and massive façade was closer in spirit to a fortress than a temple, as out of place amid the wonders of Paris as a pyramid might be in the courtyard of the Louvre. But upon entering, Wilson's minimal expectations vanished amid a bright play of light across an airy interior of ochre stone and fruit wood.

The incongruity between the brutality of Ste. Hélène's facade and the delight of its interior diverted Wilson from the mortal pressure of his mission. But only momentarily. At the far end of the nave at the high altar, he watched a priest genuflect, then descend the three steps from the chancel and proceed toward him, his focus steadfast on Wilson. Wilson did not move, only watched the priest of wiry unkempt hair and severe demeanor come abreast of him and ask, "What time is it?"

"My watch is not reliable."

"I am Father Gérard. This is my church. You must be the one calling yourself Father Olert. I will tell you Father Olert, I do not like deception. Christ deceived no one, but here I am talking to a man who is not really a priest yet dresses as one."

"This is an extraordinary time."

"All time is extraordinary. The miracle of God's creation makes it so."

Wilson ignored the metaphysics.

"You know why I'm here?"

"This morning a communicant told me someone named Father Olert would arrive this afternoon and use the confessional protocol. It is about the confessional protocol that I want to warn you. See that?"

He pointed at the confessional next to the entrance to the chapel.

"That's holy space, the place between heaven and earth where one of the Church's sacraments is offered to Her people. Respect it."

Father Gérard walked toward the confessional. Wilson limped behind him.

"In a few minutes, you will be on the other side of the grille. Your contact, posing as a penitent, will tell you what you are to do next. What is said in that holy space will have nothing to do with our faith, only our present political distress. As a result, I will have to confess this profanation. My confessor will ask me why I allowed someone other than a priest in the confessional. If I confess the truth, I don't know what my confessor may do. If he chastises me, it will be appropriate. As a proper priest, that is all he should do. But what if he intimate with the Germans? Might he give me up? If he does, my confession will endanger the people of my cell."

"You could ignore the so-called profanation."

"That would be a sin of omission, compounding the sin I had already committed by letting you use the confessional. If I do not confess this sin, what is the point of confession? Priests do not make good resistants. We cannot serve two masters, and yet I am here, talking with you, caught between Mother Church and the demands of war. In any case, Father Olert, once you receive your instructions, leave the confessional booth immediately. It is unlikely anyone else will seek to make their confession. If they do, excuse yourself, and come to me. Under no circumstances listen to his or her sins and under no circumstance offer absolution. You're Protestant, yes?"

"I was raised a Methodist."

"I am not interested in your sect. Protestant is enough, so especially do not offer absolution. Now, get in. I don't know if we will meet again, but you will stay in the rectory tonight. It is the next building over. The door will be unlocked. Sleep on the sofa."

Father Gérard walked down the side aisle toward the high altar, then veered right toward an open door.

Wilson slipped into the fruitwood confessional and sat down. The straight wooden seat pressed the Luger that was already pressing on his conscience into his back. The air was close, and Wilson ran a finger between his neck and his clerical collar. His right leg had gone beyond the insistent itch he had felt crammed the floor of Thomas's mail truck to a throb. His throat was parched. He was about to go in search of water when he heard approaching steps and the swoosh of the confessional curtain. He slid back the wooden panel over the grille.

"Forgive me Father, for I have sinned," a woman whispered.

Wilson swallowed what little saliva he had and said, "What time is it?"

There was a pause. Seconds passed. Wilson's stomach knotted. Then, "My watch is ... not reliable."

The woman's voice lowered, but its intensity heightened.

"We must move quickly. A meeting has been arranged today, 5 p.m. in the Luxembourg Gardens by the circular pond. Take a seat on one of the metal chairs around the pond. Without drawing attention, arrange another of the chairs so it is back-to-back with yours. I will leave behind a copy of *Pariser Zeitung.* When I am gone, retrieve it and carry it with you to the Garden. After you have arranged the chairs, open it and read it. It will be a signal. The man who sits down behind you will also be carrying a copy of the *Pariser Zeitung.* You will use the words we have just used to make contact. You will not speak with him face to face. Speak loud enough into your newspaper for him to hear. He will do the same. That is all I can say."

"What does this man look like? How will he be dressed? I need more information other than he'll be carrying a newspaper. Many people carry newspapers."

Silence.

Wilson repeated his questions.

A man replied.

"Forgive me Father, for I have sinned. It has been three days since my last confession.

"What time is it?"

The man blurted, "I have betrayed a fellow worker at the library. We were lovers. She was a Jew. I told her I didn't care, then one day she said she could no longer see me, that our love making was wrong. I told her I loved her. Again, she told me it was wrong. A few weeks later, she married another man. Himself a Catholic. I was bitter. That was months ago. Yesterday, the gendarmes came to our library. They interviewed each of us. Alone.

Asked me if I knew any Jews either at work or in my neighborhood. I told them about Reni. That is the woman's name. I said that despite her Christian surname, Reni is a Jew. This morning, the gendarmes returned and took Reni away. Afterwards, one of the gendarmes thanked me for my help and gave me 1,000 francs. Oh, Father, what I did was evil, what can I ..."

"Burn the money and return tomorrow at this time for your penance. Repeat your confession again to the priest who is here. Go in peace."

"But ..."

"Go in peace."

Wilson heard receding footsteps, and he pulled back the door and walked to the other side of the confessional. Inside lie a copy of *Pariser Zeitung*. He picked it up and putting it under his arm, looked around the church. He did not see the woman or the man or Father Gérard. He was about to search for the priest to tell him about the man's confession, when something deeper than the scent of incense and waxy candles caught in his nostrils. From the newspaper rose the faint fragrance of gardenia and, for a moment the pain in Wilson's leg and the pain in his soul for the man who had betrayed his lover quieted, silenced by the ache of what might have been.

Chapter 43

Wilson hid the Luger atop the confessional. He didn't need it ... not yet. What was he to do if the defector refused to stay at his post and spy for the Allies? Shoot him in the middle of a public park in the middle of the day in the middle of Paris?

But on a deeper level, Wilson knew hiding the gun had nothing to do with secreting it away until the moment of execution and everything to do with his growing doubt that he could carry out the execution at all.

With a copy of *Pariser Zeitung* under his arm, Wilson made his way to the Luxembourg Gardens, struggling to keep his doubt at bay. Parisians helped. Passersby between Ste. Hélène's and the Porte de Clignancourt metro station in the working-class 18th nodded respectfully at him as he limped by. One thick-ankled old woman said she would pray for him, sympathizing, "Your leg must hurt terribly, father." But by the time he reached the free-thinking enclave of the Latin Quarter, polite acknowledgements had disappeared. In that quarter, he was the enemy, a medieval anachronism in an intolerant modern world. Passing through the wrought iron gates that opened to the Gardens, an austere young man carrying a copy of *On the Origin of Species* strut past Wilson and spat a wad of saliva on the earthen path in front of him. Wilson nearly welcomed the affront, a momentary diversion from the pain in his leg and the turmoil in his soul.

But by the time he reached his meeting spot at the circular pond, the call to duty had reasserted itself and with it the anguish of what that duty might entail.

Wilson stopped and scanned the landscape. In the foreground, a woman dressed in the black-and-white uniform of a governess kept watch on a small boy towing a tethered sailboat around the pond's edge. In the background, the lowering sunlight reflected across the orderly pattern of foot paths and grassy parterres around the Marie Medici Palace, now Luftwaffe headquarters in France. Ignoring the throb in his leg, he dragged a metal chair back to back with another and sat down. He opened his copy of *Pariser Zeitung,* hoping to find another diversion in the pro-German broadside. He didn't have the time.

From behind him sounded the crunch of footfalls on compressed earth, then the grate of chair legs dragged through gravel, and finally the crinkle of a newspaper being folded.

"What time is it?" Wilson asked.

"My watch is not reliable."

"Don't turn toward me. Keep the newspaper up. Who are you?"

"The one. The one who wants to be a priest. Is that why sent you, a priest, to bring me to England? I'm sure it is. It would proper for you to treat me ins this fashion. I am Stull. I want to be a priest and go to seminary in England."

Wilson reeled. The defector was said to have doubts about the Nazis, not that he wished to take holy orders.

"My vocation or yours are not relevant," Wilson said. "I am an Allied agent sent to assess your value, not to offer you asylum, at least not yet."

"Not yet!?"

"Not yet."

"Do you understand what I have said?"

There was a pause.

"I'm not to be taken out?"

"I didn't say that."

"But the woman promised!"

"Stop talking!"

"But ..."

"Shhh!"

Wilson watched the boy towing his toy sailboat around the swoop of the pond approach them. The governess hurried to the child.

"Excuse us, Father," she said, picking the boy up with one hand and retrieving his sailboat with the other. "He is only a child. I didn't mean for him to disturb you."

Wilson smiled and said, "Remember Our Lord. Suffer the little children to come unto me."

She curtsied awkwardly and headed off with the boy. Wilson waited until they were beyond earshot.

"You are of great value to us, Mr. Stull.   You are in an extraordinary position to be even more valuable. You have access to information that few people in this world have. We want you to work with us, to be part of our great common cause."

Stull's head reared back.

"I have but one cause. Our Lady."

Wilson breathed in slowly, then lied.

"Our Lady is my great cause, as well. And I know her cause and the cause we are fighting for are not opposed. If you believed the Nazi state was conducive to your religion, you wouldn't be here. That is why you must continue to work with us. You must stay in Paris and report what you learn.   When the war is over, when we win the war, we will bring you to England, but now we ask you to stay."

"No."

"I know I'm asking you to sacrifice, but sacrifice is a tenet of our faith."

"I will not stay."

"I will get you out within the year, but the condition is that you continue to work for us here in the short term to advance our great common cause."

"I do not believe in your great common cause, only in my relationship with Our Precious Lady and Her will that I become a priest."

Wilson's next sentence was a plea masquerading as a guarantee.

"I promise. We will bring you to England. We will honor that promise."

"I think you will honor nothing. You are already putting conditions on your promise."

Wilson heard the hardness in Stull's voice.

Desperately, he tacked in another direction, one he thought safer.

"And the other person. We will get the other person out, as well, just as you want."

Stull paused.

"Other person? What other person?"

"The who wants to come with you."

Stull blinked, then again, then his shoulders lumped, and his voice filled with dismissive contempt.

"You mean that woman? She said nothing about joining me. Besides, why would she wish to leave Paris? She's French. Paris is her home."

Then Stull's contempt coursed into incredulity.

"Wait a minute. Are you telling me she is why you will not take me?"

There was no safe direction with Stull. Wilson returned to his original plea.

"Work with us."

Stull's response came fast.

"No."

It was falling apart. Wilson could only play for time.

"I'll do what I can. I'll contact London. Ask if they will take you now."

It was an empty promise; Wilson had no access to a radio.

"They have to take me and take me now."

Wilson did not say what he knew was the truth. London didn't have to do anything. And if London did nothing it was up to him to act, to assassinate the man seated next to him and some unknown French woman whose only offense was her desperation to flee Nazi oppression.

"Meet me tonight," Wilson said softly, lowering his newspaper and pointing across the park, "over there at the Medici Fountain at 8:30, a half hour before curfew. It will be dark there."

Stull said nothing, folded his newspaper, rose and walked away.

Wilson pulled himself up to begin his journey back to Ste. Hélène's and the pistol he had hidden there. His mind raced, so preoccupied and horrified with the prospect of killing two innocent people that he was unaware of the increasing limp of his right leg.

Chapter 44

Wilson slumped against the white-tiled wall of the Odéon metro station.

As a taunt, Mae's words came back to him.

The big things are beyond us, Georgie. We can't control them. It's the everyday things that matter in life. That's what's real.

In Unity, Maine, she was right. There, the everyday things from doing the dishes to mowing the lawn and shoveling the snow circumscribed the passage of time. But in Occupied Paris *everyday things* had been pushed outside time, replaced by a daily and mortal struggle between the big things: mission and *morality*, betrayal and fidelity, life and death.

A train pulled in. Wilson stumbled aboard, sprawled into a wooden bench in an empty car. In a moment, the train's gentle rock and whirring tires anesthetized his mind. He did not awaken until the end of the line, where the dull lights of the Porte de Clignancourt station brought him around. He struggled from the bench and jerked open the sliding door and stepped onto the concrete platform and vomited. Perspiring and dizzy, he staggered the 400 feet to Ste. Hélène's. In the last pew in the back, he slid out a kneeling cushion and sank into it.

Once his father had confided to him, "Sometimes I pray for patients. After I have done all I can."

Having reached the point of having done all he could, Wilson began to recite the Lord's Prayer. He was unconscious before he finished it, only to awaken to shuffling feet at the far end of the nave. On the other side of the communion rail, at the high altar, Fr. Gérard genuflected, rose, opened the gilded tabernacle door, then closed it. Wilson pulled himself up and limped toward the altar. He caught the priest before he reached the sacristy.

"I didn't see you," Fr. Gérard said coldly. "Normally, I'm not here this time of day. I came to replace the reserve sacrament I took to the hospital for the sick."

"I am sick. Can you hear my confession?"

"You're not Catholic. You are not entitled to the sacrament of confession, so there is no point in learning about your sins."

164

"But ..."

"You told me you're Protestant."

"But ..."

Fr. Gérard proceeded toward the door, then stopped, turning back toward Wilson.

"All I can tell you is this: God knows you are suffering."

"That's all?"

"What else is there?"

The priest passed into the sacristy, and Wilson shuffled down the side aisle.

He reached the confessional, his breath quick and shallow. Without looking, he swept his right hand across its dusty top and found the Luger. He tucked it into his belt at the small of his back and left the church.

By the time he limped out of the Odéon station and reached once again the pond in the Luxembourg Gardens, he was spent and collapsed into the chair he had vacated three hours earlier. He bent forward and rolled up his right trouser leg. Even in the twilight, he could see scarlet lines running down to his ankle and up to his knee. A head of puss oozed from the broken wound. He dabbed it with his finger and raised the finger to his nostrils and gagged.

Wilson looked at his watch. 8:20 p.m. Ten minutes to his meeting with Stull, 300 meters away at the tree-shrouded and secluded Medici Fountain.

He would shoot there.

Wilson headed toward the fountain, one foot crunching the gravelly earth, a descant to the dragging grate of the other. He reached the base of the elevated and rectangular fountain and paused, leaving forward and vomiting. For a moment felt relief. He dropped his hand into the water and mopped his brow. To catch what still air the August night offered, he looked up. He was alone. His solitude teased him with the hope that he would remain alone, and Stull would not come. He could report to London that the contact had disappeared.

Then out of the dark ...

"What time is it?"

Wilson turned. The shadowy outline of two people stood before him. He muttered the countersign, and with one hand braced himself against the damp stones of the fountain and with the other gripped the hilt of the Luger.

"Have you reconsidered? Will you stay at your post here in Paris? My promise is good. In time, we will ..."

Then the words Wilson feared.

"I will not. I have made my decision. Here I stand. God help me. I can do no other."

A Catholic quoting Martin Luther was Wilson's last thought before the enormity of what he was about to do and the searing pain in his right leg blurred the two shapes in front of , then blended them and his consciousness into black.

 He collapsed into darkness.

Stull dropped to his knees beside him, then looked up, his eyes wild, his voice staccato.

"What do we do!? Where do we go!? We can't drag him around Paris. Why should we? He has already forsaken us. We must go! Now!"

"Go where!?" Clotilde snapped. "This man, whoever he is, is our only hope. He *alone* can get us out of hell."

"You heard him! He said he will not. He says I must stay and work for him in Paris!"

"He didn't say that, and until he comes round, we won't know what he will say. Now, do as I say. Take off your clothes, and take off his. Put on his suit and collar and dress him in your clothes. Do it!"

The severity of her tone buckled Stull's defiance. He shed his coat and fumbled off Wilson's black jacket, bib and clerical collar. Then he went silent. He had found the Luger and a wad of French francs and Reichsmarks. He held them up to her.

"This is what he's prepared to offer! A bribe or death!"

"Money and a gun. Nothing more! We've no idea what he intended to do with them."

She took them from Stull's hand and slipped them into her purse.

"Finish dressing!"

He did, and in the near dark, Clotilde could see the priest's garments were a poor fit on the diminutive Stull, swamping him with long trouser legs and shirt sleeves.   Stull's suit, now on the prostrate Wilson, was pinched and short at the wrists and ankles. Stull glared at Clotilde, as if the ill fit were proof of the idiocy of what they were doing.

"Never mind the appearance," she said. "It's night. No one will notice. As to him, it is good he appears unkempt. It is to our advantage."

"Advantage!?"

She didn't answer, only motioned to Stull to help her lift Wilson to his feet. They dragged him from the fountain toward the Garden's towering wrought-iron gate opening on rue de Médicis. The jostling restored a flicker of consciousness to Wilson. His legs began to move in a rubbery gait.

They passed through the gate to the street and the intersection with Boulevard St. Michel.

Stull shrill.

"What do I say if we're stopped?"

"If stopped, I will speak."

"What will *you* say?"

Before she could answer, a commanding voice ordered, Halt!"

They did, beneath a street lamp.

From across the roadway, a gendarme approached.

"What's this? A priest, a young woman and … and what?"

"My brother," Clotilde said, her voice cracking. "We have been looking for him for hours. Father Olert and I. My brother drinks. Too much. Too often. I must get him home to the Marais before curfew. He is a great burden to our mother. Oh, please help us!"

The policeman stepped toward Wilson and brought his hand to his face, pinching his chin then tugging down the skin beneath Wilson's left eye.

"I'll say he drinks. The man is dead drunk. Lucky we have a police van tonight. We deployed officers in this quarter earlier."

The policeman pointed to the van idling at the corner. He blew his whistle, and the van rolled to a stop in front of them.

"Take these poor people home," he ordered the driver. "They're in the Marais. Come right back."

Clotilde and Stull lugged Wilson into the back seat. The policeman poked his head inside the window and said, "God bless you father for helping this woman. Good luck, miss."

He slapped the roof of the van.

"Where to?" the driver asked, not looking from the road.

"Rue Anastasia," Clotilde directed.

The driver turned the van north and headed toward the Ile la Cite. A few streets later, the van slowed at Boulevard St. Germain. Clotilde leaned forward and, for the first time, looked closely at her comatose companion.

In the chiaroscuro of the Parisian night, she saw what she first thought was an improbable resemblance. Then she looked harder, and, in a moment, the improbable became a reality beyond all reckoning.

She lifted Wilson's hand and kissed it and kissed it again and began to cry.

Chapter 45

Stull's formative relationship with women consisted of the frequent absence of his father, the over protection of his mother and the avenging power of an elder sister who would box the ears of boys who tormented her delicate brother. If he cried, mother and sister came to his rescue. They never cried. It was not until he was 14, at his grandfather's funeral that he saw a woman weep. It was an aunt who dabbed her Bavarian eyes with a lace hankie. He couldn't comprehend why she wasn't stronger. Fifteen years later, a woman's tears still confused him.

"I don't understand," he said bitterly, his head in his hands. "This man will not help me. You should be getting rid of him, not crying for him. I don't understand."

Clotilde did not take her eyes from Wilson.

"You're right. You don't understand."

The van crossed the Pont au Change onto the deserted streets of the Marais, finally stopping at rue Anastasia.

"You're home," the driver said, then pointed to the word Juden printed in yellow paint on the door of a shuttered bakery. "Guess you got this quarter pretty much to yourself."

Clotilde and Stull hauled Wilson out of the van to the front door of number 6. The cab rolled away. She produced a small key ring and opened the thick paneled door. Inside the dark and airless cobblestone courtyard, they passed the concierge's apartment, this time without detection. Upstairs, Clotilde unlocked the door to the flat. The stench of putrefaction had eased. They lowered Wilson onto the sofa, propping his head with a throw pillow. Clotilde drew water from the tiny sink in the corner and brought a half-filled glass back to him. Wilson sipped it, most of it dribbling down his chin. His eyelids fluttered.

"You are very sick," she said softly, hoping for a recognition that did not come, "but I don't know what is wrong."

Wilson waved an exhausted hand at his right leg.

Clotilde rolled up his trouser leg to the knee. Her hand felt the pulsing heat of his calf.

"He needs a doctor," she whispered.

Stull did not whisper.

"Leave him here. Call the police! They'll find him and take him to a doctor!"

Clotilde brought a finger to her lips. It did not silence Stull. He had begun to pace on the uncarpeted floor.

"You promised me sanctuary! Last night, you told me we were on our way. Both lies. We are not on our way. We are back in this stink hole. I am in hell, and you have put me there!   I am used to women who know how to take care of things. You take care of nothing ... except him, the man who is prepared to kill me.

"You don't know he was ..."

"Why was he carrying a gun!?"

"He is a soldier in war. Why wouldn't he carry a gun?"

"To a meeting with an unarmed man? There is a name for him. Assassin!"

"Gerhardt, for God's sake, be still!"

 Stull plodded toward her in the dark, bumping into a small table by the sofa, knocking over a brass menorah. It bounced along the floor before coming to rest at Clotilde's feet.   Before she could retrieve it, she heard footsteps on the staircase. Then a hard rap on the front door.

She lowered Wilson's head to the sofa cushion and stepped to the door, cracked it open. An ample woman, salt and pepper hair pulled back tight, peered in.

"Oh," the concierge said. "It's you."

The woman craned her neck trying to see around Clotilde, then with a flash of authority in her black eyes demanded, "Why are you here?"

"I have come for the cat. Miss Bloch's cat. As you know, I took care of that cat when Miss Bloch travelled. I would like the cat now, unless you wish the cat for yourself."

"I do not wish it. Take the cat. Miss Bloch will not be returning."

"You know this for certain?"

"It is the way things are in Paris."

"I will lock up and leave the key under your mat. Good night."

Clotilde closed the door.

170

"Get him up!" she ordered Stull.   "The woman cannot be trusted. She's calling the police. We must leave."

"With him?"

"We move as three, or we do not move at all!"

"But ..."

"You have two choices, Gerhardt. Do as I say, or wait for the gendarmes."

As quietly as they had entered, they left dragging Wilson and had gotten only a hundred feet around the block before Stull stumbled, dropping Wilson's feet to the sidewalk. Clotilde pushed Stull aside and bent down.   The hard landing on the cobblestones had jogged Wilson to semi-consciousness.

"My father," he muttered, "a doctor ... knows doctor in Paris ... Jackson, Sumner ... American Hospital ... Bowdoin College."

Stull stared wildly at Clotilde.

"The American Hospital!? It's not even in Paris!   In Neuilly. On the other side of the Eiffel Tower. The curfew. We'd never get him there. Impossible!"

"Nothing is impossible. He's here, isn't he?"

"So are we, with nowhere to hide!"

Clotilde looked to heaven, then down the street. A car pulled onto rue Anastasia, headed toward them. She rose from the pavement.

"Don't!" Stull yelled. "It could be police!"

Clotilde stepped onto the roadway and strut out her right leg, her dress hiked above her knee. The car stopped abruptly. The driver rolled down the window; he wore the uniform of a Wehrmacht private. Clotilde approached him. He took her in with one long glance, conveying his hope.

"Like my car?" he asked.

Her voice was taut but under control.

"You don't see many in Paris. Yours?"

"In a way. I drive officers."

He smiled.

"And I don't have a pick-up for another hour."

She slipped her hand inside her handbag, her fingers moving between the hilt of the Luger and the roll of Reichsmarks Stull had removed from Wilson's pocket.   Either could get her the car.

The money first. She withdrew a hundred-mark note, held it in front of the driver.

"I need transport to the American Hospital in Neuilly."

She dropped the note in his lap. He picked it up, held it to the weak light from the dimmed street lamp, flexed it twice.

"There are three of us."

He waved the 100 Reichsmark note at her.

"Any more of these? It's after curfew."

She handed him another.

"My two friends are over there."

They struggled into the back seat.

In 15 minutes, the German staff car was rolling past the elegant apartment buildings along Boulevard Victor Hugo. Then the driver turned off, pulling into the hospital's emergency entrance. Stull and Clotilde hauled Wilson from the car. The automobile pulled away.   They dragged Wilson into the emergency room. Harsh light reflecting off white-tiled walls greeted them, as did a cautionary hand from an orderly. Clotilde did not wait for his question.

"Dr. Sumner. Dr. Jackson Sumner."

The orderly's face winced in confusion.

"We have no Dr. Sumner … you mean Sumner Jackson?"

"Yes, yes! Bowdoin College," she said without knowing what it meant. "Bowdoin College."

The confused orderly managed, "And you are?"

"I'm not important."

"Who are they?"

"A priest and another man. The other man is why we are here. He is dying."

Chapter 46

The operating room nurse held out the telephone receiver. "For you, Dr. Jackson."

Sumner Jackson pulled down his surgical mask and walked to the wall phone by the door of the surgery suite.

He took the receiver, listened, asked, "How do you know he is a priest? Ah, the clerical collar. And why do they want to see me? Bowdoin College?"

Dr. Jackson hung up and looked over his shoulder at the nurse untying his gown.

"The universe is an unpredictable place, sister. One minute, I am removing shrapnel from a German pilot's chest. The next called on to treat someone who knows I went to Bowdoin."

"You need rest, doctor."

"Twenty-four hours without sleep is nothing."

"It's been 36."

"Forty-eight was common when I was a resident."

"But now, you're chief surgeon."

"All the more reason to keep going."

He donned his lab coat and exited the surgery. As he pushed open the two swinging doors into the emergency room, the orderly was lifting Wilson onto a gurney.

Clotilde looked up. Looming before her a six-foot man with unrefined features that reminded her of a prize fighter, not a physician.

"I'm Sumner Jackson," he said, without taking his eyes off Wilson. "It's been a busy night. Fliers, English and German. Two suicides. Now, this."

At the sound of the doctor's bass voice, Wilson's eyes flickered. He raised his shoulders a few inches off the gurney.

"Bowdoin," Wilson muttered. "Clyde Wilson ... Mass General ... residents."

Dr. Jackson leaned over the gurney. Then the shock of recognition, the likeness of a friend's face from years ago.

"George ... George Wilson!"

Dr. Jackson turned to Clotilde and Stull, his voice incredulous.

173

"His father and I were in college together, then surgical residents at Mass General in Boston. I was with Clyde the night George was born."

"His right leg, doctor, he's ..."

Dr. Jackson returned his attention to Wilson. He rolled up the trouser leg. His diagnosis was immediate.

"I'll handle this, myself."

He ordered the attendants to transport the gurney and its patient to surgery. He walked along side of it. Before disappearing behind the swinging doors, he glanced back at the orderly.

"Take these two people to my office. I'll join them later. And Marcel, any questions from the police or our German friends refer directly to me."

The orderly beckoned Clotilde and Stull to follow him. Three corridors later, each crowded with metal-framed hospital beds bearing patients, Clotilde and Stull and Marcel ascended a shadowy staircase to another hallway, reaching a door crudely stenciled *Chief of Surgery.*

"Had been a supply room," Marcel pointing vaguely at the stark interior, "but Dr. Jackson took it for his own after he converted the chief surgeon's office to a small rehab ward. Dr. Jackson said patients needed the space more than their surgeon."

They stepped inside. A swivel chair stood behind a wooden desk covered with manila files and stacks of paper. Across from it, a metal frame chair and a Louis 16th settee. Marcel pointed to it.

"Dr. Jackson's wife is French. Insisted he have it, for elegance. Dr. Jackson will come back as soon as he can. Don't leave, and don't worry. Dr. Jackson is a brilliant surgeon. Even the Germans say so."

The orderly left, shutting the door behind him.

Clotilde sank into the swivel chair. Stull collapsed onto the settee. They did not speak.

Chapter 47

At midnight, Dr. Jackson returned. Clotilde was quick to his side.

"Will he live?"

"I lanced the site of the infection, irrigated the wound, put him on fluids, administered a strong regimen of antibiotics. He will live. We caught everything in time. He will be much improved by morning. He's asleep now. In a private room. I thought privacy best."

Dr. Jackson stepped to his desk and lowered himself into the chair Clotilde had vacated and came to the point.

"What's this all about?"

Clotilde answered. All she had left was honesty and the hope that she would use it wisely.

"I am a French national. Clotilde deBrouillard, a member of the Christian resistance. This is Lt. Gerhardt Stull. Despite appearances, he is not a priest. He is late of the Wehrmacht; he wants to defect. The Allies parachuted George Wilson into France two days ago to contact us. We were meeting with him earlier when he collapsed. We brought him here. He insisted. We had nowhere else to go. I am sorry we have involved you. But for the love of God, please help us."

Stull broke into the conversation.

"Yes, for the love of God help me, because that man and this woman cannot."

Dr. Jackson rose.

"They seem to have done a fair job so far, Lt. Stull. He's here from England, and Miss deBrouillard has protected you."

Stull scoffed.

"Only to keep me in place to spy for the Allies. I offer myself, and this is what I get. I am not on route to England but trapped here."

Dr. Jackson raised a silencing hand to Stull, then turned back to Clotilde, his look quizzical.

"Which is it?" he asked. "Is Lt. Stull to stay or to leave? If I am to help, and I am prepared to help, I must know."

"Only George Wilson knows," Clotilde replied.

"And he will keep that knowledge to himself for a few more hours. He can't be disturbed."

"We must talk with him!" Clotilde interrupted. "We're on the run. Lt. Stull has left his post. No doubt being hunted. I must talk with George Wilson."

"As I said ..." Dr. Jackson began.

Stull broke in, his voice shrill.

"She is right ... for once! I have no time! I am a fugitive. Do you know how we got here?"

It wasn't really a question. He pointed at Clotilde.

"She connived a ride from a German soldier who otherwise chauffeurs Nazi officers. He'll lead them to us ... and to you."

Dr. Jackson looked at Clotilde.

"Is this true?"

"It was that or let George Wilson die in a gutter in the Marais. I must speak to him. He alone has the information we need."

Dr. Jackson nodded slowly, his jaw set in resignation.

"The Germans *will* come here ... that is true ... but I wonder ..."

He picked up a piece of paper from his desk, examined it.

"... I wonder if when they come, we give them what they want. We give them Lt. Stull."

Chapter 48

Stull erupted to his feet. His mouth and eyes in a silent tantrum. Then an explosion of words.

"Who do you think you are!? Who do you think I am?! You can't do this! I will never! I won't ..."

Dr. Jackson's cold voice pierced Stull's hysteria.

"You will if you're dead. What's your blood type, lieutenant?"

"Do you know who I am! What I offer!? You can't ..."

Dr. Jackson repeated his request, less a question than a brutal demand for information. His words hit Stull like a punch to the chest and delivered to Dr. Jackson what he wanted.

"O positive," Stull gasped.

Dr. Jackson scanned the piece of paper in his hand.

"Good," he said, his voice modulating. "We had two suicides this evening. One was O positive. That will be you, Lt. Stull."

Stull sank back into the settee, dumfounded.

Dr. Jackson dropped the paper to his desk, looked at Stull.

"Suicide is now common in Paris. The Occupation is bad enough, but this rumor the Allies will invade North Africa has made the French nightmare worse. If the Germans must defend the southern coast, it will mean the end of Unoccupied France. The illusion of an independent Vichy France had a benefit. It provided the appearance that Hitler thought of us as near equals. If the Germans occupy all France that appearance vanishes. He will do to us what he did to Poland and Russia. France is on the brink, and our more fragile citizens are falling into the abyss. The two suicides tonight are not aberrations. One was a Jew in his late 50s. He left a note saying he saw no way out. The other man, the O positive one, is what we call in the United States, a John Doe. His identity is unknown, his body brought in by the gendarmes after he had blown his brains out. He left no note, carried no identification. His last conscious act was to put the barrel of a pistol between his eyes and squeeze the trigger. It appears he intended to fall into the Seine but didn't. He fell forward onto the Quai d'Austerlitz. He's not only your blood type, Lt. Stull, he's your size. So, we put your ID papers and a suicide note written in your hand in the breast pocket of John

Doe's suit. Then I inform the Germans what we found. The Wehrmacht will claim the body as their own. The case of would-be defector Lt. Gerhardt Stull will be closed."

Some of the bluster had left Stull's voice but not the doubt.

"But they know what I look like."

"This John Doe has no face left. It splattered all over the Quai d'Austerlitz."

Clotilde waved a problematic hand.

"Won't the Germans wonder why the hospital found Lt. Stull's ID and suicide note, and the French police did not?"

"The Germans will think it business as usual. Just another blunder by the incompetent French who overlooked his papers."

"What if the body is claimed by the deceased's family?"

"What's to claim? The Wehrmacht will have shipped the remains back to Germany."

Dr. Jackson gently clapped his hands, a quick coda to one conversation, an overture to another.

"Now that we've saved you Mr. Stull, what to do with you? And that means talking with George. He should rest. But our time grows short. We'll have to risk it. He's medicated and injured, so brining him around may be a shock. Therefore, Mrs. deBrouillard should see him first. He knows her, and, I assume, trusts her. Less disorienting for him. After he comes to, Mr. Stull and I will enter the room. Can you manage that Mrs. deBrouillard?"

Chapter 49

On a summer evening returning from a screening of *The Thin Man* at the Unity Grange Hall, George Wilson had slipped his arm around Mae Cadwallader's waist. They stopped beneath an oak tree, and he kissed her on the lips, a brief but clear assertion of his desire.

Three weeks later, on the night before they were to return to college, he to his senior year at Yale and she to her second year at Colby, he was more daring. As they sat on the glider on the porch of the parsonage serenaded by the rustle of leaves on the late summer trees, he slid his right hand along her left arm to her shoulder, then down ... before she intercepted it and rerouted it from whence it came. It was the extent of his intimacy with Mae.

So now, as a woman's hand clasped his own hand and placed it to her breast, he thought he must be dreaming.

But he wasn't dreaming, and as his mind reacquired the reality of early morning August 17, 1942 in Occupied Paris, the woman leaned across the hospital bed on which he lie and kissed him on the forehead.

He stared and stared. Then his eyes flashed wild.

"This can't be true!"

"It is the truest thing in the world," Clotilde said and kissed him on the mouth. It stiffened all of him. He raised his arms, drew her to him. The fumbling ecstasy of that snowy evening in his apartment in the Latin Quarter rushed back to him, only now the urgency of the moment was unencumbered by the need to undo snaps and buttons or discard trousers. Only a white sheet separated him from her.

"You're safe, George Wilson. Doctor Jackson brought me down. He'll be here in a second."

She was right. Hearing voices inside, Dr. Jackson pushed through the door, Stull behind him.

Wilson was too overwhelmed to speak. Clotilde was not. She took Wilson's hand in hers, looked at Dr. Jackson, then Stull.

"I must tell you something. Both of you. George Wilson and I know each other. We are friends. More than friends. I never thought I'd see him again, then last night ..."

Stull broke in.

"More than friends!? What kind of priest is he!?"

Wilson's voice returned.

"No kind. I am a lieutenant in the United States Army sent by Allied Command to appraise your situation."

"Appraise?! You've already decided! You want me to spy for the Allies, and if I refuse, you are to kill me! Isn't it so?!"

Stull stepped toward Wilson's metal frame bed.

"*Isn't it!?*"

Dr. Jackson came between them. He looked at Wilson.

"George, we have little time and much to do. If I am to help you, I must know the answer to Lt. Stull's question. What does Allied Command want you to do with Lt. Stull?"

Wilson's breaths came quickly, almost inconclusively. He was back at the Medici Fountain, its questions unanswered.

"I was sent to France to convince Lt. Stull to stay and work for us in his present position."

"And spy for the Allies?"

"And spy for the Allies."

"If he refused?" Dr. Jackson pressed.

Wilson looked at Stull, then back at Dr. Jackson.

"I was ordered ..."

His voice gave way. Dr. Jackson finished the sentence.

"... to kill him."

Stull exploded at Dr. Jackson.

"You knew! You're part of this cabal! You're in league! All of you! Assassins!"

Dr. Jackson shook his head no.

"I'm no assassin, and I didn't know. Until now. But the logic of George's order is inescapable. You have too much information, Lt. Stull. Not only about our enemy but about us. If you don't work with the Allies, you're too great a liability. You could denounce us all. In war, information is as dangerous as any weapon. If you don't use it for the Allies, you might use it against them. You have to be dealt with."

Stull stepped back toward the door and waved an encompassing hand at Clotilde and Dr. Jackson.

"What makes me so special!?   You two know as much as I! So, tell me, Lt. Wilson or Father Olert or whoever you are, if I must be dealt with because I know too much, what about them? Will you assassinate them, or will I be your only victim?"

Dr. Jackson held his ground between Wilson and Stull, and turned to Wilson, his voice the voice of a man one-upped.

"It's not only a fair question, George. It's the only question. What are you going to do?"

Wilson raised himself by his elbows and swung his legs over the side of the bed. The sheet covering him fell to the floor.   He looked at Stull, then Dr. Jackson, finally focusing on Clotilde.

"I was given another order, as well. I was ordered to kill … you."

Clotilde did not respond. Stull stone faced.

Dr. Jackson broke the silence.

"But you can't do that, can you George?"

Wilson managed two deep breaths.

"No!"

"But you'll kill me, wont' you!"

"Mr. Stull, I am taking you out of France. Alive. To England. And I'm taking Mrs. deBrouillard, as well."

Dr. Jackson bent down, retrieved the sheet, placed it in Wilson's naked lap. His voice gentle but still a warning.

"That's violating your orders, George. That's dangerous enough in peace time, but in war … you'll be executed for treason."

Wilson did not respond.

Dr. Jackson tilted his head in acquiescence.

"So be it, then. In any case, its may be academic. Your chances of getting out of France are slim.   Unless you have a reliable network of safe houses and contacts. Do you?"

"I will get him out, and Mrs. deBrouillard out."

"How?"

"Through Normandy. I have a contact there. Abelard. He will help us."

Dr. Jackson looked at his watch and said, "Right now, I must get the three of you out of *here* and report Lt. Stull's suicide.   Be ready to leave the hospital. Immediately.   I can hide you in my

181

home, 11 Avenue Foch, until tomorrow morning. It will give me time to inform the Germans about Mr. Stull and for George to recover further."

They reached 11 Avenue Foch after midnight. Masking their arrival in darkness and silence, Dr. Jackson did not turn on the lights and said little. He escorted Stull to a small room in the servants' quarters. He ensconced Wilson in the guest bedroom and assigned Clotilde to the tufted leather sofa in the salon, with the instruction, 'Get some rest. This is going to be a nightmare."

Chapter 50

Clotilde drifted off just before dawn. An hour later, she awakened to morning light streaming through floor-to-ceiling windows illuminating the accoutrement of upper-class Parisian life: walls of birch boiserie, Moroccan rugs, wall-hung tapestries, crystal chandeliers, gilt sconces, oil paintings. They enveloped her in a pre-Occupation world where she and Wilson might have ...

Dr. Jackson stepped through the paneled door of the salon. Stull slouched in behind him, stopping beneath a tapestry of hunting dogs besetting a stag.

"George is stronger," Dr. Jackson announced. "I was with him through the night. He insists on leaving, today. I agree. Your position is fragile. Informers everywhere. Fortunately, we bought some time. After we left the hospital, the Germans were informed we had Lt. Stull's body. The Gestapo arrived and tentatively confirmed the remains. They especially liked your suicide note, Mr. Stull. We have gained a few hours. Maybe more."

Stull shook his head in despair.

"A few hours, a few days, a year. What difference does it make? We can't get out of Paris. We have no visa for the train and no car."

His eyes brightened at the word car, unleashing a torrent of hope.

"But what if we took an ambulance? It could take us south into Unoccupied France. The Germans would never stop an ambulance. An ambulance could ..."

Dr. Jackson rolled his eyes.

"You're right, Mr. Stull. The Germans would never stop an ambulance. They'd escort it. They insist. They consider it a humane accompaniment, speeding medical services to those in need."

Undeterred, Stull's voice shot rapid-fire.

"Then what about your car, doctor? You're important. Why can't we have it? I'm an important man, who must be taken to England!"

The salon door swung open. George Wilson entered, his pace slow. Clotilde and Dr. Jackson were fast to his side. He motioned them away. He had heard enough to know what was being discussed.

"We will not go south. We will go west to Normandy. Le Havre."

"It's suicide!" Stull shouted. "We must go south!"

"Wherever you go," Dr. Jackson said coldly, "it will not be in my car. The Germans confiscated it two years ago."

It was Clotilde's turn.

"A car," she said, her voice a meteor amid male miasma. "Lt. Stull is correct. We need a car."

She stepped toward the wall of windows. Sunlight swept over her, penetrated her, illuminating a dark memory, an arrogant boast. Putnev's boast.

There is little in Paris I cannot arrange.

She turned back to the three arguing men, resolution in her words.

"I will return in two hours. Do nothing in that time. *Nothing.*"

Astonished questions from Dr. Jackson, Wilson and Stull collided. In the ensuing cacophony, Clotilde bolted from the salon. Twenty minutes later, she crossed the Champs-Élysées and found what she knew was there. She flung back the door of Alain Frécon Papeterie with such energy it startled the sales woman behind the counter filing her nails. Clotilde ordered a box of carbon paper and an inexpensive writing tablet.

"I'll need your pen," she demanded of the unnerved clerk.

Standing at the glass-top display counter, Clotilde removed two sheets from the tablet and inserted a piece of carbon paper between them and began to write.

Chapter 51

While Clotilde had struggled to sleep on the tufted leather sofa in the Jacksons' salon, Putnev and Keucher had waited in the lobby of the Hotel Splendide.

And waited.

At 7 a.m., a young lieutenant entered the hotel and handed Keucher a blood-stained letter. Keucher read it. Shook his head in disgust.

"We're done here," he snapped at Putnev. "We deployed a dozen men to a Pigalle whorehouse on shit information from a Russian pimp."

"What was wrong with the information?"

As if it were contaminated, Keucher held the bloody piece of paper at arm's length and read aloud:

"*The brutality of war and its destruction of hope cannot be borne. I am no longer a man. Death obsesses me, like the one note that drove Schumann to the Rhine. A bullet in my brain ends the agony.*

"The little queer killed himself. We have his body, his ID. The blood types match. The suicide note is in his own hand. It's a perfect fit to his personality."

Putnev suppressed a smile.

There might be a corpse, but it wasn't Stull's. A man who wants to be a priest does not commit suicide. Keucher had drawn the wrong conclusion because he hadn't known Stull's desire to be ordained. Putnev had withheld that information.

But Keucher was angry, and Putnev couldn't allow that. He groveled in pretended ignorance.

"Who is this Schumann the note refers to? A soldier?"

Keucher shook his head in disdain.

"Ah, yes, you're a Slav. Schumann was a great German composer. But mad, as genius can be. The musical note of A kept sounding in his mind day after day. It drove him insane. In desperation, he threw himself into the Rhine. But someone fished him out. No such luck for Stull. And no luck for you."

Putnev heard the threat. It was time to defend himself. He had the information to do it.

"But good luck for you. I have a plan."

"Your last plan was shit. Russian shit."

"Stull may be dead, but his handler isn't. He's still here."

"You mean that pissant Christian at St. Séverin? I've already arrested LeMans. As to the deBrouillard woman, we'll find her. You've got nothing for me, Putnev."

"But I do."

"What?"

"Another handler, an Allied handler sent from London to get Stull out. We almost got him, tonight, and I can still get him. When I do, he's yours. He and his information. Names, places, connections. A gold mine of information. I can deliver him."

In the barely visible tightening of his eyes, Keucher told Putnev he wanted to know more.

"I can deliver him … if I have real freedom to get the job done."

Keucher rolled his eyes.

"On your whim, I called out the German security apparatus in Paris. If that's not freedom to get the job done, what is?"

"A travel visa."

Keucher scoffed.

"To where?"

"Normandy. This handler had to be inserted quickly. That means he came into France cross Channel by boat or air and landed on the Norman coast. There, he needed local assistance, and it's there he will return to get out. If you give me freedom of operation, I can bag him for you. That would be quite a catch."

Keucher feigned disinterest.

"Even if you're right about this handler, he'd never run west into Normandy. He'd go south through Unoccupied France."

"Who does he know in the south? He entered through Normandy. It's where he'll go to get out. He will return to the resistance cells who helped him when he arrived. That's where I come in. Last year, when you ordered me to infiltrate the Christian

Resistance in Paris I learned of their contacts in Normandy. I know them. I can contact them. They'll confide in me."

"They'll confide in me, too … after a few hours in a Gestapo detention center."

"Perhaps. But Christians are a sticky lot. They believe in something greater than themselves. That makes for martyrs. Your torture chamber might not break them. At least not fast enough, and time is running short."

"You can do better?"

"I told you. They trust me. Trust has loosened more tongues than all the branding irons in history. But I have to make contact with them."

Keucher did not interrupt. Putnev continued.

"You were wise to leave those cells in place, even after I identified them for you. Had you rolled them up, you would have netted only a few French partisans. But by leaving them in place, you've given them a false sense of security and positioned them to play a bigger role. Just the way you left the Paris Christian cells in place, and you see what that's gotten us: invaluable information about Lt. Stull."

Keucher arched an eyebrow at Putnev.

"Why should I trust you after this evening's fiasco?"

"You have nothing to lose. Everything to gain. If I fail, it costs you nothing more than a travel visa. If I succeed, you get an Allied agent. That would turn heads in Berlin."

"Travel visas are rare. Only issued for state business."

"This *is* state business."

Keucher's eyes tightened again, and he walked across the lobby to the lieutenant who had handed him Stull's suicide note. They conferred. Keucher returned to Putnev, his voice hard.

"I expect results. You have five days. My lieutenant is preparing a visa for you. My line will be open around the clock. And Putnev, this time don't fuck up."

Chapter 52

An hour later, Putnev had a five-day travel visa for Occupied France.

Now, it was a matter of finding Stull. He thought he knew where to look. Clotilde had said she had a safe house or at least a house that was safe enough. It could be Ilena Bloch's.

He climbed into the back seat of Trafanov's cab parked in front of the Splendide. His rage at Trafanov had not diminished, only been subordinated to the more compelling need of locating Stull.

"Did Captain Azuir give you Ilena Bloch's address?"

"Number six rue Anastasia in the Marais, but she's not there. She's being held with a thousand other Jews in the Velodome d'Hiver on the Boulevard Grenelle. Maybe dead. Last month, the Germans didn't supply food or water. It's the same, now."

"Rue Anastasia, then."

Trafanov waited in his cab at the corner. Putnev knocked on the door of number six. It opened, framing the concierge.

"Miss Bloch. Is she in?"

"Who wants to know?"

It was a challenge, not a question.

Putnev withdrew his Ausweise from the breast pocket of his suit and held it up to her eyes.

"Know what this is?"

She examined it, nodded that she did.

"Then you know they are impossible to obtain unless one is working with the Germans. I am part of German state security in Paris."

Her look was skeptical. She knew about forged documents, had one herself for food coupons.

"Putnev is a Russian name, not German," she countered.

"Names are deceptive. There are as many Schmidts and Bachs and Brauns in Paris as there are in Berlin, and they are French. Miss Bloch. Is she in?"

"I haven't seen her."

"Has anyone called for her in the past day?"

The concierge's hesitation told him the answer was yes.

"Who?"

"A friend, a woman."

"Young and pretty?"

"I guess. It was dark."

"Why didn't you inform the gendarmes? You must have known Bloch was a Jew, an enemy of the state."

The concierge's chin was rising, her back stiffening.

"How do you think the gendarmes learned Bloch was a Jew in the first place? Besides, I called the gendarmerie. By the time the police arrived, they were gone."

"They?"

"The woman was with a man. A little man. She told me they came to get Miss Bloch's cat. That was last night. They left in a matter of minutes."

Clotilde had been there and gone, had used the apartment as a safe house. He was too late.

Or was he?

There might be another safe house. Clotilde had told him about Bloch caring for a relative. He looked back at the concierge.

"Miss Bloch had an uncle she visited. Outside Paris. Where?"

"Le Havre. But he's gone, arrested."

"What was his address in Le Havre?"

"I don't know."

Putnev removed 500 francs from his pocket. Handed them to the concierge.

"You have a key to Bloch's apartment?"

The concierge plucked the money from his hand and stepped back into her flat, removing a key from a peg board next to her door. She handed it to Putnev.

Within five minutes, he had found what he sought. From a draw in small table by the sofa, he withdrew a black leather-bound address book. He opened it to the Bs.   The page had been torn out. Now, he knew the uncle's name was Bloch. That was the good news but he still didn't have the address, the address of a house that Clotilde would most certainly use as a safe house or her flight through Normandy to England.

189

Putnev moved to the door, urgency in his steps, then stopped. Someone was coming up the stairs.

The apartment door swung open.

"The concierge told me a man was here," Wehrmacht Captain Witt Halle said, stepping into the flat. "German State Security, she said. I know most agents of German State Security in Paris, but I don't know you. Who are you? Why are you here?"

Putnev countered with bravado.

"I don't recognize you."

"Halle. I'm investigating the brutal attack on a little girl. This is the apartment of her teacher. I ask you again. Who are you? Why are you here?"

"I am a Russian émigré, ostensibly working with the Resistance but in fact a German agent. I report to Major Keucher."

"Your name?"

"Sergei Putnev."

Putnev handed Halle his Ausweise, who held it up toward the ceiling light and said, "This means nothing to me, Putnev. Paris is awash in forged documents, from ration coupons to travel visas. Although, this one is rather good."

He handed it back to Putnev and continued.

"A few days before the attack on the child, French police arrested the child's teacher, Ilena Bloch. This teacher wore the yellow star of David. It occurred to me, her arrest and the attack on the child could be related. Perhaps a Jew, or Jew sympathizer, in support of Miss Bloch wanted to wreak vengeance upon us and chose a little girl as his target. An attack on a little girl is hard to ignore."

"Attacking a French girl makes no sense"

"It does when you consider an armband with a swastika was found at the scene of the attack. It may have been planted deliberately to throw suspicion on a German. It is the kind of slur on German morality that a Jew or a Frenchman or even a Russian might find satisfying."

Putnev nodded.

"Russians are no better than anyone else. Still, the assailant could be anyone. Even German."

Halle did not respond. Putnev pressed.

"Any description of the attacker?"

Halle brought the tip of his index finger of his right hand to his cheek beneath his right eye.

"He has a scar here, and I see you have no such scar. But you may be a colleague of the man with the scar, come to remove evidence connecting him to the Bloch woman or the little girl."

Putnev's rage with Trafanov returned. He fought to control it.

"I assure you Captain Halle. I would never ..."

Putnev did not complete the thought, another thought coming to him.

An amazing, life-saving thought.

In an instant, his anger with Trafanov vanished, replaced by a perverse appreciation for what his incompetent assistant had given him: a way out of Halle's investigation and a way forward in pursuit of Stull.

Simple, elegant.

He would identify Trafanov as the attacker of Claire Marie and the rapist of the 12-year-old at the Hotel Etoile, and he would tell Halle where to find Trafanov. But when Halle got there, Trafanov would be dead. That would close both cases: the attack on Claire Marie and the rape of a 12-year-old. Maxim Trafanov, condemned by the scar beneath his right eye, would take the fall for both crimes, unable in death to deny his guilt or incriminate Putnev.

Putnev lowered his voice to a conspiratorial hush.

"I know of such a man. I have seen him in a café in Pigalle."

Halle's eyes widened.

"You know his name?"

"No."

"You frequent the cafes of Pigalle, and you don't know his name?"

"I saw him only once."

"Only once, yet you remember him?"

"The scar was striking. If to me, then to others. Someone must know his name."

"Obviously."

"I can ask."

"So can I."

191

"Better if I ask. A Russian asking for the name of another Russian is no serious matter."

Halle allowed himself a brief and uncomedic smile.

"Unless one is asking in Moscow."

"Yes, yes, quite right, unless one is asking in Moscow. But in Paris, a Russian asking after a Russian means nothing. But a German asking … it will sound an alarm, and this monster will go to ground. If he drops out of sight, he will be free to recruit other young girls."

"Recruit?"

"I'm sure he intended to recruit the little girl you speak of for prostitution, but she resisted, and he tried to silence her."

"You know this?"

"Only conjecture, but it fits the facts."

"What facts?"

"The man with the scar … he is said to traffic in young girls."

Halle stroked his chin.

"You say you're a German agent?"

"Ask Major Keucher."

"I'm asking you, and you still haven't answered my second question. Why are you here?"

Putnev lowered his voice still further.

"I'm sure you know a German officer in Paris has deserted his post, deserted with intention of defecting to the Allies."

Halle showed nothing.

"I learned of this defector through my contacts and reported it to Major Keucher. The major informs me this individual has killed himself."

"His name?"

"Lt. Gerhardt Stull. His body and suicide note have been found. But there is still the matter of the Allied agent who was sent from London to get him out. He is still certainly in France. This agent may be abetted by a woman who was a friend of the Jewess Bloch. I came here to see if the agent and woman had used this flat as a safe house."

"How do you know them?"

"It is my business to know such people. That is why Major Keucher values my work."

"Had they used this flat as a safe house?"

192

"The concierge says yes. They were here last night."

Halle tilted his head, almost in agreement.

"Well, that is between you and Major Keucher. As to what is between you and me … make immediate inquiries about this man with the scar. I will bring him to justice. We Germans must set an example of moral strength … unlike the French who turn a blind eye on such filth. It is urgent."

Halle handed Putnev a card with a telephone number printed on it. Putnev accepted it with a solemn nod.

"I will be back to you with more information, perhaps within hours. If you need me, Major Keucher knows where I can be found. As you said, it is urgent."

Just how urgent, only Putnev knew. He must kill Trafanov before Halle found him, then convince Halle it had been Trafanov who assaulted the two little girls. It was a fool proof plan, a plan that now only awaited execution. Literal execution. Trafanov would have to be killed. But by whom? Putnev knew he was not the one to do the killing. Since The Great War, he had not lifted a hand against anyone except to slap a woman or girl in his bed. In matters of violence, he only chose the victims, then ordered Trafanov to carry out the sentence. Trafanov, the brutal Ukrainian had murdered 24 Russian emigres in France, alone, three dozen more counter-revolutionaries in Russia.

But Trafanov's very skill at murder made him wise in its ways and always on guard. Putnev hurried along rue de Turenne, where finding Trafanov waiting his taxi, and climbed into the back seat.

"Take me back to the Splendide," he ordered, "and cancel any plans you have for the rest of the day. Wait for me in the cab on the street. I will have something for you later."

Chapter 53

Forty minutes after Putnev left rue Anastasia, Clotilde stormed into the lobby of the Hotel Splendide. Putnev did not immediately see her, his intense conversation with the clerk at the front desk commanding his full attention.

"If the Borodin woman asks for me," he lectured the desk clerk, "tell her I have gone. For good!"

"The Borodin is the one with the young girls?" the clerk asked indifferently.

Putnev exploded.

"Never say such a thing! Never!"

The clerk squinted in confusion.

"But you said you liked ..."

"Never! Never!"

Putnev stepped back, reordered himself with a curt tug at his lapels.

"Do as I have ordered," Putnev said, then turned toward the door. The sight of Clotilde routed his momentary restoration of calm.

"Where the hell have you been!?" he yelled.

She did not answer but ascended the staircase to room 8, opened the door. Putnev barged in behind her, about to yell *Where the hell is Stull?* when she preempted him.

"I need something," she said coldly.

"You need something! Do you know what I ..."

He caught himself. Her need might give him advantage.

"I need a car, and you can get one, Sergei. You told me once, there is little in Paris you cannot arrange."

"Where's Stull?"

"Stull's not coming."

"I risked my life to provide you with a safe house, Clotilde. Now, you say Stull's not coming!"

"That's not all I say. You set a trap for us! With the Gestapo!"

Putnev blinked hard. How did she know? His tone turned earnest.

"I would never betray you, Clotilde!"

Her words came fast enough to silence the doubt he had planted.

"You can't deny you met with a Gestapo agent yesterday in the lobby! I saw you! The same man who arrested me in November and who attacked Claire Marie! The man with the scar!"

Putnev understood. She had seen him with Trafanov and concluded his collusion with the Gestapo.

"You *did* see me talking to a Gestapo agent. I'll explain that in a moment, but answer me this, Clotilde. Just to set your paranoia in perspective. If I'm working for the Germans, why have you come back? You'd be committing suicide."

"Not when Captain Halle is involved. He's different. He doesn't want me. He wants Claire Marie's assailant."

"What's that to do with me?"

Clotilde withdrew from her pocket a folded carbon copy of the letter she had written in the stationery shop. She read it aloud.

"Captain Halle,
One of the men you seek in the attack on Claire Marie Bastian is Sergei Putnev, a Soviet agent and habitué of the Hotel Splendide in Pigalle. He arranged the attempted murder of Claire Marie, in collaboration with a Gestapo agent – the man with the scar. Putnev is as responsible for that abomination as the man who attacked Claire Marie.
Clotilde deBrouillard
Teacher at the Louis Pasteur School"

She returned the letter to her pocket.

"Get me a car, Sergei, and this letter won't be delivered to Captain Halle.

Putnev shrugged.

"Send it. Every day in Paris hundreds of Parisians denounce their neighbors to the Germans. Why do you think it's so easy to round up Jews? Captain Halle will know this. He might question me, but he'll learn nothing."

She had anticipated his indifference.

195

"I have another letter, Sergei. It will take longer to deliver, but eventually it will get to Moscow, apprising your superiors you're collaborating with the Nazis. Moscow will deal with you, even if the Germans don't."

Putnev affected an unconcerned smile, then his eyes tightened.

"I'm a spy, not an agricultural advisor. I do what I must to advance The Revolution. For Christ's sake, Stalin collaborated with the Nazis for two years. Remember the Non-Aggression Pact? I'm just working with the Germans on a smaller scale."

She brought her hand to her throat. Putnev saw her doubt. Now, he had to make that doubt overwhelm her.

Or did he?

With the force of revelation, it came to him.

Let her think she *had* cornered him. It would give him what he needed. A means of killing Trafanov.

Putnev's voice verged on accommodation.

"Nonetheless, Clotilde, I'd prefer these letters remain unsent. For that to happen, I have to supply you a car. All well and good, but if I get you a car, what guarantee do I have you won't send those letters, anyway? I don't think I can trust you. I need something more from you."

She stepped toward him, arching her back a little, her breasts rising. She had resigned herself to giving him sex, if it were the price he demanded.

He looked at her, wanted her, his old obsession with her nearly overcoming him, but she wasn't begging him, as he had once insisted. Now, she was defiant, strong. Her strength weakened his desire.

"You think I am only interested in your ... still, Clotilde, we might do business. I don't want your letters sent, lies though they be. But I need a guarantee you won't turn me in, despite my good deed. That guarantee can only be that *I* have something *you* don't want the world to know."

She managed a cynical laugh.

"You mean, what we did in this room? It was foul and humiliating, but I'm not afraid to admit it. You have nothing to use against me."

Putnev rolled his neck, and she saw a satisfaction in his eyes she had seen only in bed.

"I do have something ... provided you kill Maxim Trafanov."

Stunned silence. Then, Putnev repeated what he had just said, and Clotilde brought both hands to her chest.

"What!? Who!?"

"It's perfect, Clotilde," Putnev said, his tone airy, as if they agreed to split the bill at lunch. "You get what you want. A car. I get what I want. The assurance you won't send those letters."

His audacity reduced her to a blither of moral platitudes.

"I will not kill! I cannot murder! I cannot ..."

"Don't be so squeamish, Clotilde. You eat meat, but you don't chop off the heads of cows. You leave that to someone else, yet you're as complicit in their slaughter as the butcher. I'm just reversing the order of things. Now, you get to wield the cleaver."

"It's murder! Maxim whoever-he-is is a man, a ..."

"Do you know who this Maxim is?"

Putnev didn't give her time to answer.

"The man who beat Claire Marie and arrested you last December and held you for 24 hours in that room by the St. Martin Canal."

"*That*'s Trafanov!?"

She lowered her hands from her chest, her voice cold.

"Then why were you talking to him yesterday in the lobby!?"

"I told you I would explain. Trafanov is Russian, now working for the Germans here in Paris. Years ago, he did some work for me, spying on Russian emigres plotting to restore the Romanoffs. He's muscle for hire. Yesterday, the Gestapo sent him around to troll the emigre quarters to see if Stull had put in with the Russian expatriates. That's when you saw me talking with him. They thought if I knew the name, I would tell Trafanov. Of course, I said nothing. You concluded I was collaborating. In fact, I was being interrogated."

Clotilde's shoulders slumped. Her plan was disintegrating, it's basic assumption wrong. Putnev was no Nazi.

A grim realization came to her, her voice beaten and weary.

"That's how you knew the man I met last November at the Grand Palais was American and young and fair-haired?"

"That's how I knew, Clotilde. Sometimes, I give Trafanov information. Sometimes, he gives me information. It's not collaboration. It's real politic."

She was down to her last argument.

"But he tried to kill Claire Marie!"

"He did. One of my agents heard him joking about it in a café in Pigalle only this afternoon. I didn't know until moments ago. You see, Clotilde, Trafanov likes little girls. It wasn't merely that he was scaring you into a confession, although that was the principal reason for the attack. Trafanov thought he'd have a little fun before he beat her. So, he tried to undress her in the school yard. He touched her. She resisted. For that sin, he hit her. Not just once as the Germans had instructed repeatedly. To teach her a lesson."

Putnev brought a comforting hand to Clotilde's shoulder.

"I was aghast, Clotilde. I want him dead as much as you. Killing a monster like Trafanov should appeal to your sense of justice."

"Dear God! Turn him over to Captain Halle!"

"If I turn him over to Halle, we're back where we began. You holding all the cards, Clotilde. But if you kill Trafanov, I get my guarantee you won't send those letters, because I'd have something I could use against you. We'd have reach parity. Our fear of mutual destruction would keep us both honest."

She shook her head no.

"I can't kill."

"You can, and I'll tell you why. *Maxim Trafanov has a car.* That car can be yours. All it takes is one bullet in his chest. That bullet serves justice and gets you what you want."

"I have never done such a thing," she stammered. "I don't know how."

Putnev heard the resignation in her voice. It was no longer the immorality of the thing but her ignorance of how to do it.

"It's just a matter of pulling the trigger. Only you must not shoot this monster in the face. Under no circumstances in the face. Halle must see the scar on Trafanov's cheek. That way Halle will know the man responsible for attacking Claire Marie has been brought to justice."

"I could never get away with it. He's a brute. He would never let down his guard."

It was the very problem that had perplexed Putnev; Trafanov was never defenseless. Except when he was …

"He would let down his defenses for you, Clotilde. If you offered him something he could not resist. Something that would distract him."

Putnev took her hands gently into his.

"I'll arrange for him and his taxi to be out front at 8 tonight. Engage his services. Tell him you don't have enough money to pay full fare to Montmartre, but you're sure an accommodation can be reached. He will understand. Tell him you wish to be taken to rue Hermel. It's a sleepy little street. Once you reach your destination, hand him half the fare and invite him into the back seat for full payment. When he climbs in, shoot him in the chest. Remember. The chest. He'll fall back, out of the cab, and you'll slip behind the wheel and drive away. News of his death will reach Captain Halle within hours. I'll see to it. Halle will reason his way to the appropriate conclusion: the monster who attacked Claire Marie Bastian has been executed, and his investigation will be closed. I will be spared having to answer your letter of lies, and you'll have a car."

"I have no gun," she said weakly.

Putnev opened the armoire and from beneath a crumpled towel removed an automatic Mauser and silencer. He screwed the silencer onto the barrel and handed it to her.

"Now, you do. It's no louder than the pop of a champagne cork. Meet me here tonight. An hour before curfew. By 8:30, you'll have your car, and justice will have been done. A good night's work, Clotilde. Of course, you may keep the car as long as you need it, but I recommend you abandon it within a day. It will take the French and Germans that long to identify Trafanov, but when they do, they'll put out an alert for his car – less to find the murderer than to retrieve the vehicle. It wouldn't do for you to be caught in it."

One last detail, Putnev thought but an essential detail.

"Tell me, Clotilde, where will you leave the car?"

Amid the emotional storm swirling within her, Putnev's question confused her with its banality. Putnev saw her confusion. Addressed it.

"Think of it as a present for me. It will impress the Gestapo that I knew where to look for the car."

Choice. She had no choice.

"Rue Marine, number one, Le Havre."

Putnev nodded.

"That is satisfactory. The car is yours. But how will you leave Paris? Have you a visa?"

She didn't answer but back-stepped out of room 8. Putnev did not stop her. Don't interrupt her, he thought. She was on her way. So was he. As the door clicked shut, he clapped his hands, his excitement spinning him around in a circle. It had all come together. In a matter of hours, Trafanov would be dead along with Halle's investigation into the near murder of one little girl and the rape of another. The monster responsible for both killed by an unknown but heaven-sent assassin. And by end of day, Clotilde and Stull and their Allied handler would stumble into an apartment at 1 rue Marine in Le Havre.

It was only a matter of Putnev being there when they did and handing them to the Nazis and claiming his reward.

Chapter 54

Clotilde returned to the Jackson apartment with the same determination she had left it but as a very different person and in no mood for explanations or compromise. In the course of a morning, the war had made her someone she no longer recognized but was bound to obey. This new woman had renounced the morality that had guided the former. She had consented to murder and, on her trip back to Avenue Foch, had devised a plan to get away with it.

The door to the Jacksons' salon had not closed behind her before she said, "We leave tonight. I at 7:00, you at 7:30. Meet me an hour later on rue Hermel, in Montmartre. I will have a car. Lt. Stull and I will drive west out of Paris. To Saint-Germaine-en-Laye. You, George Wilson, will join us at first light. Take a train from Paris to St. Germain. Then, with luck, to Le Havre."

Stull bolted from the settee, his arms outstretched in a bloodless crucifixion.

"Luck! You disappear for two hours, race back and tell us we need luck! I don't know who is worse, you, who count on chance to deliver us, or he who counts me insignificant enough to kill!"

Wilson was quick to her side.

"Clotilde, what in God's name is going on?"

"I have secured a car. You don't need to know more."

Stull moved hard toward her.

"I need to know! It's my life!"

"Just do as I say."

"I have done as you say, and see what has become of me!"

"I see we are about to get out of Paris."

"Out of Paris!?" How!?"

Wilson came between them.

"Your choices are few, Mr. Stull. You have burned your bridges. Mrs. deBrouillard is your only hope."

"I have only one hope," Stull said stubbornly. "That Our Lady will deliver me."

"In that case, Clotilde will be Her agent."

"Blasphemy!"

"Not if it works."

"If what works? There is no plan except luck."

"Luck by another word is Providence."

Clotilde interrupted the theology with a voice hard and decisive.

"This is what we do. George Wilson will continue to masquerade as a priest.   He has an Ausweise. If he is stopped, he has authorization from the Germans to be in the forward area."

"But what of us?" Stull shouted. "We have no travel documents."

"You, lieutenant, will need a uniform and a new ID. Dr. Jackson can obtain those. His hospital is full of dead Germans. You are best a Wehrmacht private. Fewer questions if we are stopped. You will be our driver, assigned to Father Olert."

"A driver!   A private! I am a lieutenant. My family is ..."

He cut himself short.

"As for me," Clotilde continued, "I have my identification card as a teacher in the Paris school system. That is part of the plan ... the original cover story. Father Olert is an Alsatian priest in the employ of the Reich, sent to Normandy to reorganize curricula for Catholic schools. That is how he has come to have an Ausweise.   We are part of his entourage. You the driver. I, an administrator, assigned to assist Father Olert in this service to the fatherland."

Stull shook his head furiously.

"One travel pass for three people will never work!"

"That is why George Wilson will not go with us tonight. Only you and I will leave Paris, tonight."

"And how do we get out of Paris!? We have no Ausweise!"

Stull was wringing his hands.

She stepped around Wilson, confronting Stull.

"I will do whatever is required to get us out. *Whatever!*"

The force of her words silenced him. They had a deeper impact on Wilson.

She was no longer the woman he had known that night months ago in the Latin Quarter, if he had even known her then. And he was not the same man who had proposed to her on that night, not even the same man who had parachuted into France just two days ago. He had forsaken his mission for love and, looking at her, he knew she had forsaken something, as well.

Stull's voice returned.

"Even if you manage it. Even if we get out of Paris. What then? *What then?*"

Clotilde was fast to respond.

"I have a safe house in Normandy."

"What do we do in this safe house?"

"Wait."

"For what?"

She looked at Wilson. Wilson understood.

"My contact in La Havre. Abelard. He will get us out."

Stull turned away and began to weep.

An hour later, Wilson sat across from Sumner Jackson in the salon of 11 Avenue Foch. They were alone. Silent Clotilde and sullen Stull drank coffee in the dining room. Poised uneasily on the edge of a Louis XVI bergere, Wilson examined the military identification card of a dead German solider: Private Rudi Koegl, assigned to light duty in Paris due to severe asthma.

"Mrs. deBrouillard wanted an ID card for a German soldier," Dr. Jackson said, seated on the tufted leather sofa next to Wilson. "Now, she's got one, thanks to Private Koegl's death last night from congested lungs. You'll have his uniform shortly. An orderly is bringing it from the hospital. It will fit Stull."

"Then we have done all we can."

Dr. Jackson offered a half smile.

"Except come up with a better plan. I have grave doubts about this, George. Not only the plan but about Stull himself. Is he worth it?"

"No."

"Then why risk your life and hers to get him out?"

"Because I'm not prepared to kill him."

"Walk away."

"That's the same as killing him. He's a deserter. Nowhere to hide. I alone might save him."

"Perhaps ... but ..."

Dr. Jackson dug into his suit jacket pocket and withdrew a brown apothecary's bottle containing capsules. He looked at the bottle, then at Wilson.

"I'm sure you know about these. Give one to her, one to Stull. The Germans will be brutal if they arrest you."

Dr. Jackson glanced again at the bottle.

"They work fast. The pain is brief, much briefer than what the Germans will inflict. It's the best I can do."

"I'll offer it to Clotilde and Stull."

"Not yourself?"

Wilson was silent.

"You haven't reached that point, have you George? The point of lethal desperation.   You're still hoping the universe is charitable, that God or fate or chance will spare you. Clotilde has no such hope. I heard it in her voice this morning. Saw it in her eyes. I've seen it in others. In some pilots brought to the hospital for emergency surgery. They're decent boys. Even the Germans. They sign up to fly. Great romance. High drama. Then in one unthinkable moment in the sky over France, they find themselves in an impossible situation, driven by something beyond them … a code or instinct or desperation.   Language, reason, sentiment can't reach them. They're beyond all things human. They kill without thinking, sacrifice without thinking. A perfect soldier's state of mind. The point of lethal desperation. Clotilde deBrouillard has reached that point."

Dr. Jackson looked at his wrist watch.

"I must go. Surgery, rounds, more surgery."

"You saved my life, Dr. Jackson."

"I hope for a long time. In any case, you'll need luck, and I wish you all the luck in the world."

The two men rose and shook hands.

"You're in an extremely volatile situation, George. Stull teeters on hysteria. Be firm with him. He responds to strength. Clotilde has silenced him just by the force of her tone. As to her, firmness will not work. With Clotilde you can only be the small voice of conscience. That voice may rein her in. It may not, and you may have to do more."

"I understand."

"Do you?"

Dr. Jackson released Wilson's hand.

"When you took this assignment, you were prepared to kill both Stull and his companion if necessary. Are you still prepared to do that?"

A knock on the door. Dr. Jackson opened it. An orderly arrived with Private Koegl's uniform, packaged in brown paper. Dr. Jackson accepted it and turned back to Wilson. His question unanswerable, until future events forced a decision.

"Tell your father I hope to see him after the war. Perhaps at a Bowdoin reunion. You know, he was always a better student than I. Smarter. I hope the apple hasn't fallen too far from the tree."

Chapter 55

Clotilde met Putnev in room 8. He stood by the window overlooking rue Duperré and pointed down to the street.

"Trafanov is there. In his car. He expects to drive me to the Latin Quarter. I'll tell him my plans have changed, and I no longer need him. After I speak to him, approach him. It's dark enough. He won't recognize you.   You have the pistol?"

She nodded.

"Let me see."

She removed the Mauser from her purse and handed it to him. Putnev shook his head in annoyance.

"The safety's on."

He held the pistol to the light, clicked the release.

"Now, it's ready to fire. But no more mistakes, and remember, not in the face.   Shoot him in the chest. *In the chest.* He needs to be identified. The scar on his face will do that, but only if it's visible."

She returned the pistol to her handbag. In a moment, she was crossing the lobby, her mind uncluttered except for her resolve to finish what she had started. Putnev walked to the cab. He tapped on its front passenger window and spoke. As he turned away, Clotilde stepped forward and said to Trafanov, "I want to go to Montmartre, rue Hermel. I can pay for most of the fare, but we can reach an agreement for the rest. Yes?"

"Yes."

Trafanov started the engine. She opened the back door and slid onto the gray felt seat and shut the door behind her. The cab pulled onto the roadway then turned right, passing the Montmartre Cemetery and headed toward the Butte. Moments later, it stopped halfway down rue Hermel, the only light on the street a faint luminescence falling from a dozen mullioned windows suffused through a canopy of plain trees. He turned off the engine, climbed out and swung open the rear passenger door.

"The fare is 100 francs."

She handed him 50. He pocketed the money and said, "Move over," and pushed into the back seat, wrapping his left arm around her head.

Clotilde pulled back. Trafanov unrelenting.

"You want a slap in the face or something?"

And he grabbed her right hand. His free hand fumbled with the buttons on his trousers. In a burst of profanity, he told her what to do.

He wrenched her hand backwards and jerked it to his lap and groaned and never saw her reach into her bag with her free hand and withdraw the pistol. She squeezed its trigger. The flash from its muzzle illumined Trafanov's face, his eyes still intent on the pleasure in his groin. The discharge from the pistol drove him back through the open passenger door, his arms splayed out. His head hit hard on the cobblestone pavement.

"What was that!?" a terrified Stull asked. "It sounded like a champagne cork."

From under the dark limbs of a plain tree, Wilson took a tentative step in the direction of the sound. A moment later, he and Stull stood next to the car, staring at a bleeding corpse on the roadway.

"My God!" Stull gasped.

Clotilde came around from the side of the car, "You, Stull, drive! Now!"

Wilson opened the back door. Tried to enter. She pushed him away.

"No, not you George Wilson! Stay in Paris, tonight. At first light, take a train to St. Germain en Laye. You have a visa. We will be there in the lot by the platform."

Wilson wild-eyed.

"How will *you* get through the checkpoint!?"

"Go! Until morning."

She slipped into the back seat. Slammed shut the door. Told Stull where to drive.

The car rolled away. Wilson scanned rue Hermel. No pedestrians. Not even a nosy neighbor at a window. He dragged Trafanov to the base of a plain tree. Propped him up. The corpse might be ignored until morning. Just a drunk sleeping it off.   Wilson walked away. His pace even, his soul churning.

Amid the terror – within and without – he headed to Ste. Hélène's to arrange final details for what he now felt certain had become a doomed journey.

Chapter 56

The taxi passed Sacré-Coeur, ghostly in the summer night. Stull spoke first.

"That man back there. Did you ..."

"Yes," Clotilde said flatly.

"But the shooting of a man ..."

"We needed his car. Now, we have his car, and we are going to keep his car."

"The St. Ouen checkpoint," Stull warned, his voice trembling. "It's coming. In a kilometer. We'll never get through. We have no visa to leave Paris!"

Her voice a cold, commanding force.

"I will get us through. *Just do as I say!*"

"Do what!?"

"At the St. Ouen checkpoint, they'll ask you for papers. Show them. You are Private Rudi Koegl, light duty due to asthma, assigned to Paris as a driver for a German general in Normandy!"

"What German general!?"

"You're the German officer! What's the name of a German general in Normandy!"

"Blechmann. August Blechmann."

"You are General Blechmann's driver. He has ordered you to bring me, a prostitute from Pigalle, to his billet in St. Germain-en-Laye. When you say this to the soldier who will examine your identity papers at the checkpoint, add that General Blechmann has paid a lot of money for me. Then nod your head. Tell the guard any man would pay a lot of money for me. Tell him this with a filthy smile on your face, as if women are good for only one thing."

"But the car! It's a Paris taxi!"

"Requisitioned by the Germans. It's what you've been given to drive. Then tell the guard General Blechmann would not want his staff car seen in Pigalle. Slow down. We're almost there."

At the approaching headlights of the taxi, a private – thin and pimply – shuffled out from behind a wall of sandbags. Stull stopped the car in front of the black-and-white striped barricade arm and presented his ID. The private examined it in the beam of his flashlight.

"The car. This cab. It's not a staff car."

Stull tilted his head toward the backseat with a look of she-can-explain-everything. The private shone his flashlight in the back of the cab.

"General Blechmann," Clotilde said warmly, as if the name could open all doors. "I am his guest. Private Koegl is his driver. He is taking me to General Blechmann's billet in St. Germane en Laye. For the night."

The private looked at Stull. Stull looked straight ahead but whispered, "General Blechmann has paid a lot of money for this one."

"The cab is not a staff car," the private repeated.

Stull's voice deepened.

"It's what I've been given at General Blechmann's command. The general would not want his staff car seen in Pigalle."

The sentry hesitated.

Clotilde's eyes scanned the checkpoint. No one else was visible, and she said, "I want to talk to you, private. Are you alone?"

"My sergeant is … over there. He's using the …"

He pointed to a small café across the street.

She opened the back door, slid out of the cab, the hem of her dress high on her thighs, the ribbons of her garter belt reflecting in the dim light. Her fingers tightened around the hilt of the Mauser in her handbag.

"General Blechmann will be disappointed – angry – if I do not come."

"You need an Ausweise to leave Paris," the guard repeated.

Clotilde smiled.

"Do you really believe General Blechmann would offer a Paris whore an Ausweise? What's your name?"

The guard tried to look away but couldn't.

"Krauss. Johann Krauss."

She beckoned him toward her. The private stepped from the driver's window toward the rear of the cab. Stull looked straight ahead.

"I will be coming back tomorrow, Johann," she promised, and she reached out her hand to his belt buckle, then lowered her hand, pressing it into him, her fingers squeezing.

"It won't do to keep the General waiting ... but tomorrow, Johann ... what time are you off duty? I am tired of old men. I like men my own age. Do you know what else I like?"

She answered her own question.

"Whatever you like, Johann. Whisper in my ear what you like, Johann."

His chest tightened, and he bent forward and whispered to her what he had never said to a woman. She smiled.

"I like that, too. I could do that to you now, behind the sandbags."

Three minutes later, she was back in the car. The private stepped to the barricade, pushed down the cement counterweight. The cab passed through.

A half hour later, the taxi crunched to a stop in the gravel lot by the railroad station in St. Germain en Laye. She told Stull to park the car and to stay in the front seat. She stayed in the back. Shut her eyes. Tried to sleep. But what she had done in the past hour, would not let her rest.

Chapter 57

As Clotilde had predicted, Wilson's travel visa and clerical collar smoothed his train trip out of Paris the next morning to the extent a German lieutenant, seeing a limping priest, offered Wilson a hand and helped him onto the train.

Wilson disembarked at St. Germain en Laye and stepped down the four concrete steps from platform to lot. One-hundred meters away, the taxi sat in the morning sun, its rear passenger door ajar. Reaching the cab, he nodded to Stull before sliding onto the backseat next to Clotilde. He took her hand. She pulled it away.

"Clotilde, I ... "

She shook her head no.

"But ..."

"Go," she ordered Stull

"Not yet," Wilson said. "We're waiting for ..."

Clotilde turned toward him, her voice clipped.

"For what? Waiting for what?"

Any words from her were a relief to him.

"At Ste. Hélène's, I asked the priest to contact a woman, Thomas. She drives the mail truck between Paris and Rouen. Sometimes the mail truck is accompanied. We can follow as an escort. It will be our cover."

Wilson saw the calculation in Clotilde's face.

"When will Thomas arrive?"

At the far end of the lot, the mail truck came to a stop. Wilson emerged from the taxi but didn't look in the direction of the van. The headlights on the postal truck flashed once.

"She's seen us," he said, climbing back into the taxi and telling Stull, "Follow it. As close as you can."

"I don't see how following ..."

Dr. Jackson's admonition came back to Wilson. Show strength.

"You're right. You don't see. Just do it."

Stull's shoulders slumped in sulky compliance.

The two-vehicle caravan rolled out of the lot and past the St. Germain-en-Laye chateau, now a museum. Wilson had visited the museum a year earlier to view the Venus of Willendorf, a limestone bust of a woman no larger than a chess piece carved 20,000 years earlier, her sculpted hair parted as neatly as the garden parterres surrounding the palace. The Venus had disturbed him. He, the historian and interpreter of the past, unable to grasp its meaning.

He turned to Clotilde. Needed to talk to her, but words eluded him. The right words, anyway.

"Stay below the window line," was all he managed.

She slouched down and shut her eyes.

Chapter 58

The cab reached open country in minutes, travelling so close to the mail truck it was impossible to see oncoming traffic until the approaching vehicle had passed.

"Keep this distance," he ordered Stull. "If you stay close enough, a passing German car will think we're an escort and ignore us."

The Germans did. Three times Nazi staff cars sped by, drivers and passengers not even glancing at the taxi in the wake of the van.

At the whitewashed milestone reading eight kilometers to Rouen, Wilson broke the silence enshrouding them since St. Germain.

"Rouen is the first test. We're coming to the checkpoint."

The car slowed to a crawl.

"Thomas will vouch for us, but if the guard stops us, I'll talk."

"What can you possibly say?" Stull whimpered. "One Ausweise … three people … I mean …"

The van stopped. Wilson peaked ahead. The guard approached the van, and Wilson watched Thomas's left hand gesticulate up and down, then point casually back toward the taxi. Then her hand eased into a friendly wave to the guard who nodded and waved the van through. The mail truck pulled ahead, and the guard turned away.

For the next few miles, the two vehicles followed Gothic-printed detour signs into Rouen. Wilson pulled himself from the floor and looked through the passenger window. The three towers of the Rouen cathedral loomed above the city's roof line.

"Drive another hundred meters and park," Wilson ordered.

Stull eased the cab to the curb in front of a timber and white-plaster house set in an irregular square of timber and white-plaster houses where, 510 years earlier, Jeanne d'Arc had burned at the stake.

He took in the streetscape and said in a trembling voice, "There are soldiers everywhere."

"You'll fit in," Wilson snapped. "Get out. Buy us some bread and milk."

He handed Stull 200 francs.

"What if I'm stopped?"

"You'll know how to behave. You were a German soldier, and you're dressed like a German soldier. Get to it."

Stull climbed from the taxi and made his way down the lane.

Wilson turned again to Clotilde.

"Clotilde, I ..."

"What next?"

"Clotilde, I have to ..."

"What next?"

He relented.

"Auberge Jeanne d'Arc, across the street. At the inn is a man who can contact Abelard. I must see this man and find Abelard. Abelard will get us out. Clotilde, I ..."

An insistent rap on the trunk interrupted him. Wilson rolled down the window. A German private wearing a military police armband bent forward.

"This taxi has a Paris license plate. What is a Paris cab doing in Rouen?"

Wilson did not answer and handed the soldier his papers, including the Ausweise. The private examined them but did not return them.

"Now, hers," he demanded.

Clotilde presented her identity card from the Paris school system.

"Any other papers?" the soldier asked.

She looked confused.

"Should there be?"

The soldier ignored Clotilde's question.

"Where is the driver of this cab?" he asked Wilson.

"I drove myself."

"Then why are you in the backseat?"

"We needed to confer."

The soldier showed nothing.

"Come with me," he ordered. "Over there."

He pointed across the plaza toward a building of faded Second Empire grandeur: heavy gables, cupolas and arched windows. Printed in black letters on the semi-circular glass transom was the word *Kommandozentrale.*

They entered, stepping into the once grand lobby, now a maze of filing cabinets, stacked boxes and a dozen desks manned by German soldiers. A second-story gallery overlooked their activity.

The private directed them to a desk in the rear. A corporal with matted black hair looked up, annoyed. The look did not dissuade the private from his duty.

"Corporal, I observed Father Olert and Mrs. deBrouillard in the backseat of a Paris taxi parked off the square."

The corporal ran his right hand through his hair.

"You seem to find new lawbreakers every day, Private Gauditz. But I remind you. There is no law against a priest and a woman sitting in a taxi."

"It is a Paris taxi. A Paris taxi here in Rouen. Although the priest's papers are in order, her papers are not. She has no Ausweise allowing her to leave Paris."

The private handed the corporal both sets of papers. Wilson saw the resignation on the corporal's face. Private Gauditz had a point.

The corporal looked at Wilson.

"Can you explain?"

Wilson did. The school story. He was setting up curricula for Catholic schools in Le Havre. Mrs. deBrouillard was assisting him. She was a teacher. Wilson made no mention of Stull.

"A good explanation," the corporal said, "as far as it goes, which isn't very far. It doesn't explain why Mrs. deBrouillard has no visa, or what you're doing in a Paris taxi."

Wilson shrugged.

"The taxi was requisitioned by the German army in Paris. They could not give me a German staff car. Gave me the taxi instead. I must visit many schools in upper and lower Normandy. A car is necessary."

The corporal nodded reluctantly.

"I'm aware of such requisitions. What about Mrs. deBrouillard? She has no Ausweise."

"I am a priest," Wilson said, his voice tinged with naïveté, "and unaccustomed to this new way. In the past, such things were not required."

"You are French, then?"

"German. I was French, but with the liberation of Alsace, I am proud to be German, once again. It is a reunification my family has prayed for since 1918. God bless the fatherland."

The corporal tilted his head in appreciation.

"I wish all Alsatians felt as you. If only we can remove that French accent from your German."

Wilson forced a grin, but the corporal's good humor faded. He held up the Reich's Education Ministry authorization for curriculum reorganization.

"I've never seen one of these," he said.

"I'm sure the Ministry in Berlin can verify that I ..."

The corporal cut Wilson short.

"You think the Minister of Education will take my call? Berlin has more rigamarole than the army. If I called, I'd wind up waiting weeks for some clerk to get back to me. Anyway, it's not you that concerns me. It's her."

He looked at Clotilde.

"You're an instructor at the Louis Pasteur School. That is a secular school. Why are you with a priest? Why is he not attended by a nun?"

"The Reich asked me to assist. Curriculum development is my specialty. The Reich wishes all schools, lay and religious, to speak with one voice."

"What will that one voice say, Mrs. deBrouillard?"

"It will say the Reich is the sole arbiter in matters of civil conduct. When it comes to moral vision, the German state must be preeminent."

"Well said. Which makes what I am about to say difficult. I must detain you. The absence of a travel visa is a matter for my superiors."

Clotilde broke in.

"In that case, I will return to Paris and sort things out there, while Father Olert goes about his work in Le Havre. After all, his documents are in order."

"No, no," Wilson interrupted.

The corporal quieted him.

"Be patient."

He looked at Private Gauditz.

"Escort these two people to the sergeant. I'll call and brief him."

Clotilde and Wilson followed Private Gauditz up the staircase and along the gallery to the front of the building and into a small office, its window overlooking the square.

The private withdrew and shut the door behind him. Clotilde and Wilson were alone. He reached out for her, but the pad of feet along the gallery checked his advance. The door opened. A rotund sergeant, his neck bulging at the collar of his tunic, stood in the doorway, a look of recognition on his face.

"Father Olert! Sergeant Frederich Bregenz. We met the other day. So nice to see you."

"Of course, my son, I remember."

"I called home, to my wife, as you suggested. All is well. All is well. Thank you, again."

With a wave of his right hand, Sgt. Bregenz motioned at two chairs semi-circled in front of his desk. Clotilde and Wilson sat in them. Sergeant Bregenz seated himself on the side of the desk.

"Now ... what's this all about?"

Wilson repeated his cover story. As he concluded, he watched Sgt. Bregenz's hopeful countenance veer toward skepticism.

The story wasn't going to be enough.

Wilson took his chance.

"Sergeant Bregenz, may I suggest you call my superior, Bishop Gérard at Ste. Hélène's in Paris. He is crucial in assisting the Reich in curriculum development in Catholic schools. He will vouch for me. I have his telephone number here."

The sergeant nodded thankfully.

"Excellent suggestion."

"The number is ..."

"No, no, father, I'll call Ste. Hélène's myself. It's not that I distrust you. How could I after our first meeting? But my lieutenant will ask how I obtained the number to verify what you say. It is essential I obtain it from what he would consider a reliable source."

He rose from the desk and fished out a Paris telephone directory from the bookcase by the open window.

"And this is a reliable source. Let's see. Ste. Hélène's …"

A few flipped pages later, he said "Ah," and placed a call. Wilson was frantically conjuring an explanation if Father Gérard did not answer.

"Good morning," Sergeant Bregenz said. "I'd like to speak with Bishop Gérard. My name is Sergeant Bregenz attached to Military Security in Rouen."

He paused.

"Ah, I do have the pleasure of talking to the bishop. How nice."

For the next minute, Sergeant Bregenz asked what he wanted to learn. Only the barely audible croak of a voice on the other end of the line signified the priest portraying a bishop was responding. And responding.

Sergeant Bregenz held the receiver away from his ear, shook his head back and forth and smiled at Wilson. The sergeant finally asked, "Tell me Bishop, what about Mrs. deBrouillard's travel visa?"

Another minute of explanation from Father Gérard. This time, however, Sergeant Bregenz did not mock the priest's excess.

"Thank you very much, Bishop Gérard. You have been most helpful."

He returned the receiver to the cradle and opened his hands toward Wilson.

"Bishop Gérard vouches for you."

The tension across Wilson's back released, only to return as Sergeant Bregenz added, "But only you. As to Mrs. deBrouillard he knew she was assisting you but didn't know she needed a visa. He believed she could travel on your visa."

The sergeant pulled at his left ear lobe.

"Hard to believe a bishop wouldn't know what is a fact of daily life in Occupied France."

"Sometimes bishops are unmindful of daily life."

The sergeant looked at Clotilde.

"I need someone to vouch for you, madame. The bishop could only tell me what you have told me. That is not enough. If I am later asked by my lieutenant why I released you, he'll want to know what informed my decision. Perhaps your school head master could help? He would do nicely."

"*She* is on summer holiday. I don't think you'd be able to ..."

Sergeant Bregenz's voice hardened.

"Nonetheless, her name and the name of your school."

Like every situation Clotilde had found herself in during the past weeks, she had no choice.

"The Louis Pasteur Primary School. In the fourth arrondissement. Mrs. Ronsaar is head mistress."

She did not offer the number; Sergeant Bregenz did not expect it and consulted the Paris directory, again. He placed the call.

"I'd like to speak with Mrs. Ronsaar ... I see ... and when will she return ... the hospital ... I am sorry ... it is a tragedy when a child is attacked ... perhaps you can help me ... I need to verify that Mrs. Clotilde deBrouillard teaches at your school ... oh, she no longer works at your school ... dismissed two days ago ... thank you very much ... I hope the child recovers."

As Sergeant Bregenz hung up, Clotilde blurted, "I can explain."

The sergeant raised a non-threatening hand toward her.

"No need. I understand. Of course you no longer work there. If you did, how could you assist Father Olert with his duties here in Normandy? The secretary demonstrated a German accuracy I do not associate with the French. A precise woman. I like precision. Precision eliminates so many problems. Yes, you worked at the school for the past two years, but that relationship terminated 48 hours ago. Just as it had to terminate. Otherwise, how could you carry out your present assignment?"

The sergeant smiled in satisfaction.

"I have only one more question my lieutenant will want answered. Where will you stay in Le Havre? The corporal said you will be housed there. We need to keep tabs on such things."

Wilson had not anticipated the question and struck the pose of a man who knew the answer but couldn't quite remember it. He waggled his fingers in the air, as if they might pluck the address out of the ether.

"Rue Marine," Clotilde interjected. "1 rue Marine."

"Whose apartment is that, Mrs. deBrouillard?"

"I don't recall. It was assigned from the Paris School System and given to them by the German Army in Le Havre."

The sergeant shrugged.

"The address should be easy to verify. I will call back your school. Someone there may know."

Clotilde could not allow that. Another call was too dangerous. So was revealing the name of Abraham Bloch. Staying with a Jew was treason.

"I think the name was Blonde. Something like that."

Sergeant Bregenz pursed his lips and shook his head no.

"I need to be precise."

He returned to the bookcase and pulled out another telephone book.

"Reverse directory," he said blithely. "Wonderful resource for my kind of work. You look up an address, and it tells you who lives there. Let's see who's billeted at 1 rue Marine."

His right index finger descended a column of fine print.

"1 rue Marine," he said wistfully.

"Oh, I see … not Blonde at all. Bloch."

His eyes squinted, then relaxed.

"I see why they gave you this apartment. You'll have the place to yourself. With a name like Bloch, he was certainly rounded up in the most recent sweep. I think this matter is closed. As to the absence of an Ausweise, my office will issue one. The Wehrmacht is always prepared to help the Reich's Ministry of Education."

He buzzed in the corporal, then neatly printed on Wehrmacht stationery a request for an Ausweise. He looked up at Wilson.

"Rue Marine is on the river. Not quite in Le Havre. On the north bank. As you approach from the east, along the river, you'll see an old barn with a cigarette advertisement painted on it. It's about two kilometers after that. I was posted in Le Havre for over a year. It should be cool there in the August heat."

The corporal entered.

"Corporal, show these good people to the travel section and present this."

The sergeant handed the corporal the sheet of official stationery.

"It is a request for an Ausweise. They are a priest and teacher. It is understandable why they were not familiar with the process. And corporal, rein in Private Gauditz. Occupation is hard enough without his kind of enthusiasm. It only encourages the locals to resent us."

He turned to Wilson and Clotilde.

"You should be on your way in fifteen minutes. I apologize for the delay. In fact, I'll make it up to you. I'll call Le Havre and alert security you're coming through in a couple of hours. It may expedite your journey."

"Not necessary, sergeant, I assure you ..."

"Of course not necessary, but I'd like to be of service, as you were of service to me."

Wilson offered a weak smiled. Their address in Normandy was now known, not only to Sergeant Bregenz but to security in Le Havre.

1 Rue Marine - their safe house – was safe no longer.

Chapter 59

Stull was already behind the wheel of the cab when Wilson and Clotilde climbed in the back. He pointed at a loaf of bread and bottle of white wine on the passenger seat.

"They didn't have milk. Where have you been?"

"Explaining."

"Then explain to me. I could be caught. I could be ..."

Wilson's voice turned severe.

"Drive around the corner. Stop at the Auberge Jeanne d'Arc. Just do it."

Stull did, but in his aggravated slap of the steering wheel, Wilson saw he was reaching his limit.

So was Wilson. Thanks to the amiable Sergeant Bregenz, the Germans now knew where they were going. The safe house at 1 rue Marine was no longer safe. He had to find Abelard. Abelard would arrange their escape.

Stull parked across the street from the Jeanne d'Arc. Seeing a German sergeant enter the hotel, Wilson averted his eyes and went around to the rear of the building. The hotel manager was coming out the back door, his left hand lugging a cracked toilet, the other hand holding a plumber's wrench.

"Thank God," Wilson gasped and ran up to him.

He wasted no time on preliminaries.

"Tell Abelard I must see him! As soon as possible in Le Havre!"

The innkeeper reared back, glared at Wilson

"Abelard was arrested yesterday. Dragged from his house by the Gestapo."

"Good God," Wilson muttered. "Abelard was our only contact to get us out of France. What about his radio!?"

"Radio!? Did you hear me!? Abelard's arrested. And you ask only about his radio!?"

He dropped the toilet bowl to the ground.

"Who the hell are you!?"

A desperate man, Wilson thought.

"I'm transporting two people out of France. You must understand. *Abelard was my only contact* to organize our escape. *My only contact!*"

Wilson's stress of the word *only* did not move the hotel manager, but it did penetrate Wilson's desperation.

Abelard *wasn't* his only contact. There was another. Abelard had named him. The name came back to Wilson.

"Can you get me to Clovis!?"

The hotel manager's eyes widened in understanding.

"You want me to take *you* to Clovis!? Now, I understand!"

"Understand what!?"

"Jerome was right about you! Saw right through you."

"Jerome? Right about what!?"

"I should have seen it, too. From the moment you walked in here. When you were in the dining room with the German soldiers. You were making contact, weren't you? Contact with your Nazi handlers. It makes sense. Forty-eight hours after you show up, Abelard is taken. You're one of them."

There was no finessing an answer. Only denial.

"I'm no collaborator! I'm an Allied agent! And I must find Clovis, or we're dead, I and the people I'm taking out of France!"

The man took another step toward Wilson, sprayed Wilson's face with his words.

"*I am Clovis*! And you *are* dead!"

He raised the wrench. Swung it. Wilson ducked and replied with a rapid fist to the man's groin. The man crumpled. The wrench dropped.

Wilson fled, Venerable's words in his head, *Without Abelard you'll never get out of France.*

Wilson staggered to the car, dove into the back seat and ordered Stull to drive on.

Stull did nothing. Looked ahead, his voice without hope.

"Abelard wasn't there, was he? That was our last chance. It's over."

All Wilson had left was lies.

"Not over. We must go to Le Havre. Abelard is in Le Havre. We must get to Le Havre."

224

Chapter 60

For luncheon at L'Auberge Jeanne d'Arc, Sergeant Frederich Bregenz abjured the regular mess and ordered his favorite: bacon larded boiled cabbage and knackwurst, an indulgence he normally reserved for Sunday dinner. But this day, his self-discipline had softened. He had been able to do a good turn for a good man who had done a good turn for him. All accomplished without compromising military discipline or intelligence.

"Helmut," he said to his fellow sergeant as the platter of kraut and sausage arrived at their table. "If ever I had doubts about our absorption of Alsace, they were calmed by this priest I met. He was a Frenchman but is now proud to be part of the Reich. I wish others felt the same as Father Olert."

The name caught the ear of the hobbling hotel manager, who was bringing a crockpot of mustard to Sergeant Bregenz's table. After setting it in front of the sergeant, he lingered within earshot, still coping with the pain in his groin and seething at his betrayal.

"But Frederich, how does this priest feel about the Jewish thing," Helmut asked. "Priests can be difficult about that."

"Not Father Olert. Where he is staying in Le Havre, 1 Rue Marine, was formerly occupied by one Abraham Bloch. Was there ever such a Jewish name? I think Father Olert understands that Europe will benefit from our work to resolve the Jewish problem. It benefits not only France and Germany but also The Church. Jews have been no friends of Catholics and more than friends to the Bolsheviks. I hope Bloch left his apartment clean."

Sergeant Bregenz impaled the sausage on his fork and sliced it with his knife. As he ate, the hotel manager discretely tore a piece of paper from his order pad and scrawled on it:

Jerome,
The address you want is in Le Havre. 1 rue Marine. You were right about Father Olert. A collaborator.

Chapter 61

They drove west from Rouen, Ausweises speeding their passage through German checkpoints. Stull silent, sullen. Clotilde withdrawn. Wilson increasingly distraught; they were reaching the critical moment, but without a means to get through it.

At the five-kilometer milestone to Le Havre, Wilson told Stull to pull over. The car decelerated onto the chalky shoulder, kicking up a cloud of dust. Wilson could now only temporize, try to buy a few more hours. He pointed toward a barn with a faded ad for Gitanes painted on its side. It stood above a corn field sloping down to the north bank of the Seine. The river sparkled in the late afternoon sunlight, and Wilson said to Stull: "Walk through that field to the river and follow it west west toward Le Havre. In 20 minutes, you'll come to a roadway. That's rue Marine. We'll meet you there. Number one on the right."

Stull shook his head in disgust.

"Why must I walk? You're riding. Why can't I ride?"

"The guards will want an explanation why you don't have a visa. We can't risk it."

"We risked it at the checkpoint getting out of Rouen. Why not here?"

Wilson spoke before he thought.

"The Gestapo called ahead from Rouen. Told them two of us were coming, not three."

The moment he said the word Gestapo, Wilson knew he had blundered. The word hit Stull hard, releasing all his fear.

"Gestapo?! The Gestapo knows?! We are doomed. We were doomed from the start. There is no Abelard, is there. First, you said Rouen. But he wasn't there. Then you said Le Havre. And we are in le Habre and Abelard is not. He's not anywhere, is he!? He was never here! You lied!"

Wilson looked toward the river, as if waiting for some miraculous answer to rise from its depths and calm Stull. But nothing came except the terrible truth: he had lied to Stull, and it was a lie no longer sustainable. Abelard was gone. The safe house at 1 rue Marine compromised. They might be able to hide there an hour, maybe two, but the Gestapo would come looking. And soon. It was over.

He turned to Stull. For Wilson the faux priest, it was time for confession. He looked one last time across the corn field toward the river. If only they might sail away on that river as he had sailed months ago from Lisbon to New York, or even two days ago from Le Havre to Rouen.

"Lt. Stull," Wilson began, "Abelard is not here. And we will not find him. He is gone."

Stull's hands dropped from the steering wheel to his lap. Clotilde leaned forward, pressed her hands into Stull's shoulders, a gesture without impact on the German. She spoke to Wilson.

"It's all lost, isn't it?"

"Without Abelard, it's all ..."

Or was it?

Hope – desperate, far flung, unexpected – seized Wilson and energized his next words to Stull.

"Abelard's not here, *but his boat is*. The boat's marked BRL. You'll see it as you walk to the house. That boat is our ark. It will carry us through the flood. It will take us down the Seine and across the Channel. It's out way out. First, we go to 1 rue Marine. Wait until nightfall. Then go to the boat under cover of darkness."

Stull shook his head.

"Day or night! What difference does it make!? The banks of the Seine are crawling with soldiers. Gunboats. A Luftwaffe airfield at Octeville. We'll never get out."

"*We will get out.* Just as we got out of the Marais, out of hospital, out of Paris, out of St. Germain-en-Laye, out of Rouen. We will get to the Channel and cross to England. Simple."

"Simple!?"

"Simple! Yes! Because we have no other choices. This or nothing. We begin now. You to rue Marine, we to follow. We can be in England in 12 hours. We have a boat!"

Wilson's wild tone had resonated with the last shred of hope in Gerhart Stull. He pushed open the driver's door and crossed the road before disappearing through the field of corn.

Wilson climbed into the driver's seat and accelerated the car onto the roadway. Five minutes later, a gothic-lettered detour sign announced a checkpoint. Five-hundred meters ahead, a black-and-white striped barricade arm blocked the road. Wilson stopped the car and rolled down the window. The private attending the checkpoint shook his left hand impatiently. Wilson handed him their travel visas.

"May we proceed, my son?"

"I am not your son," the guard snapped. "Park by the guard house, and give me the car key."

Wilson did. As they sat in the car by the guard house, he said, "Clotilde, speak to me. We must ..."

"Shhh," was all she said.

The next half hour passed in silence. The private returned. He walked around the car and opened the trunk, examined it, then slammed it shut and returned the key to Wilson.

"Go on," he said sharply.

Chapter 62

Putnev walked the four kilometers from the Le Havre railway station to 1 rue Marine, stopping first at a tabac 300 meters up the lane from Abraham Bloch's room to make arrangement with the proprietor for a telephone call later in the evening to Major Keucher in Paris. By the time Putnev reached the Bloch apartment, the sun had set, but, in its afterglow, he could see the word JUDEN printed across the top panel of the door, its sloppy letters and dribbles of dried paint confirming a violent and sudden application. So sloppy, Putnev thought. But what could one expect? This was the provinces, not Paris, where neatly stenciled stars of David identified the doorways of Jewish homes.

Putnev scanned the street for pedestrians and seeing none, worked a skeleton key into the dull lock. The door opened. He stepped inside and pulled the frayed cord to the overhead fixture. Light from a bare bulb revealed two chairs flanking a battered card table bearing a hard crust of bread and cup of moldering coffee. Both testaments to a textbook Nazi raid: an early morning knock on the door, a man blindsided as he ate breakfast. Behind the table, a book case. Putnev scanned it for pornography. He might get lucky, he thought, and find something to amuse himself while he waited. When it came to sex, Jews were no holier than anyone else, and, if you believed the Nazis, far worse. He found only a worn copy of the *Torah,* a seed catalog and flashlight. He pocketed the flashlight and stepped to the brass-frame twin bed on the other side of the room. He pressed his fingers into its sagging mattress, then lowered himself onto it. A moment of rest, even indulgence, as awaited his quarry and anticipated how Keucher might reward him for his work. His imagination accelerated past mere Gestapo appreciation of his efforts to a German offer of administering a conquered Soviet city, Minsk or Kiev or Lvov. But as his fantasies grew, so did a disquiet within him. Something was missing: Clotilde, and he thought of her standing before him in room 8 in garters and hose, and he wanted her and he ...

The front door creaked open, a man in the uniform of a German private stepped inside. Evening light seeped around him,

nd in the murk, Putnev saw the man's sleeve insignia denoting
ervice in the German military force occupying Paris. This was no
Wehrmacht soldier manning the Atlantic Wall. It could only be Stull,
he means of Putnev's fantasies becoming reality.

A sincere smile filled Putnev's face.

"Come in my friend," he said, cordially.

Stull startled back. Putnev's voice oozed reassurance.

"Don't be afraid. I'm here to help you."

Stull clasped his arms across his chest trying to control his
apid breathing. Putnev crossed the room to the corner sink. He
rew water into a glass and handed it to Stull.

"Drink, my friend. You're safe. I'll see to it."

Stull grasped the glass with both hands and drained it. His
reathing modulated.

"Who are you?"

"Resistance. That's all you need to know. You are very, very
mportant to us. I am here to help you. Where are the others?"

Stull's eyes flashed anger.

"They left me on the road. They have visas. They didn't get
ne for me. I came ahead on foot, through a field and along the river
ank. They drove."

"I'm sure they're excellent handlers."

"They are not!"

"You've gotten this far, haven't you?"

"I'll never get further. Do you know what they plan to do?"

This was easier than Putnev had imagined.

"Well, naturally ... get you to England."

"But do you know *how?!* By boat. Down the Seine to the
hannel and across."

Putnev shook his head, his mouth open, his eyes dubious, all
istrionics to show his agreement with Stull.

"Boat across the Channel? Madness."

Stull stepped toward him, his arms open.

"That is what I say! Madness! We have no chance. Even if
ve make it past Le Havre and the airfield at Octeville, we'd be
ntercepted in the Channel by German gunboats!"

Stull began to sob. Putnev pointed to the two chairs by the
able.

"Sit down, my friend. I can offer you a better way. Not across the Channel but through unoccupied France, into Spain and on to Portugal. I have safe houses. A network. Colleagues. Resources. If you listen to me, next week this time, you'll be in England. Tell me about this boat. Where is it?"

"There's a barn. About a mile up river. It's weathered with a cigarette advertisement painted on its side. In front of it, a dirt road leading down to the river and a dock. The boat's there. It's marked BRL. But no matter. It will never make it across the Channel. It's no more than a row boat."

Putnev shook his head in grave agreement.

"You are right to have doubts. I will talk to your handlers. Trust me, my friend."

Stull's stiffened back relaxed. He didn't have to say what Putnev saw. Stull *did* trust him. Putnev struck a casual tone.

"When were you to leave?"

"Tonight. In the dark. From the dock. They said darkness will protect us."

Putnev laughed sadly.

"The darkness will protect nothing. The Luftwaffe and Wehrmacht are everywhere in Normandy, especially along the river. You said so yourself. And you needn't have worried about the seaworthiness of your boat. They'd pick you up or sink you, before you reached the Channel. Here, let me get you more water."

Gently, Putnev took the glass from Stull's hand, and for the first time in a week, the knot in Stull's stomach loosened.

His relief was short lived. The door to 1 rue Marine slowly creaked open. Clotilde entered first, Wilson close behind. Her eyes flashed from Stull to Putnev.

"You!"

Putnev raised a quieting hand. Wilson's right hand went into his trouser pocket, his fingers curling around the Grandad.

"Clotilde," Putnev said warmly, "why such surprise? I told you I'd be picking up Mr. Trafanov's car. That's all I want. Well, it was all I wanted until a few minutes ago, until I had a chat with Mr. Stull. Now, I want something else. I want to save your lives."

Putnev pointed to Wilson but looked at Clotilde

"He's the handler sent from England?"

"Father Olert," Clotilde answered.

"Father?" Putnev sniffed. "That's providential. With the escape plan he's cooked up, you'll need divine help. Mr. Stull explained it to me. He's dead worried and should be. Father Olert's plan won't work."

He turned to Wilson.

"What on earth made you opt for a suicidal boat ride down the Seine and across the Channel?"

Wilson leaned against the door, the throb in his leg returning.

"Any less suicidal than the alternative; three people walking through France to Portugal? We'd be caught in hours and the Christian network rolled up. Torture would make that inevitable."

Putnev smirked

"Surely, you weren't recruited because the Allies thought you'd succumb to torture."

Wilson ignored the taunt.

"The Channel is our only chance."

"Then be happy I'm here. I'm giving you another chance. In a matter of hours, I can arrange secure passage for the three of you out of Occupied France via a soft route to England. You won't be stopped. Torture will not be an issue, and you won't have to worry about betraying the Christian network. It will be *my* network that's engaged, my network that can get the job done. It's just a matter of *allowing me* the privilege of doing it."

Stull stepped defiantly toward Wilson.

"It's not a matter of *them* allowing anything," Stull cried. "It is I who will allow it. They have nothing to say in this matter. You have the means and the skill."

Clotilde saw the glimmer of triumph in Putnev's eyes. He had won.

Or had he? She had one last play because she knew he had one last vulnerability.

"Sergei's right," she said and stepped toward him, her hands open, her eyes setting on his and offering submission to his will.

"Sergei. *I beg you.* Help us. How much time do you need?"

Putnev's self-control waivered, his desire for her charging. And she saw it.

"How much time, Sergei? How much time do you need?!"

His fists clenched.

"One hour. I need only one hour. I'll make arrangements, now."

"How?"

"A telephone in the cafe up the street. Then southeast into unoccupied France. You have the car. I have a visa. We'll be in Spain in three days."

"No," Wilson exploded. "We have no time. Stull is fragile. He'll break. Our only hope is to get him out *now*."

Putnev scoffed.

"Mr. Stull will not break. A precise exit plan and a night's sleep in a true safe house will restore him."

Clotilde looked at Wilson. Her voice, denied to him for hours now definitive.

"Sergei's right. His soft route through Unoccupied France. Our only chance. Go, Sergei! Now! Make arrangements! I beg you! You're our only hope!"

Stull's hands fluttered in front of him.

"Yes, yes, go! Now!"

Putnev was out the door. It slammed hard behind him. Clotilde fast to the window. Wilson tried to speak, but she repulsed him with a quick wave of her right hand. She scanned rue Marine.

"He's gone," she said. "So are we! Now! To the boat!"

Stull erupted.

"But the man has a plan for me!"

"Yes, a plan to deliver you to the Germans. He's arranging it this moment!"

"No!" Stull bellowed. "If he wanted to betray us he would have had soldiers here with him."

"He couldn't risk it. If we didn't show, he'd look like a fool, as he did the other night at the Hotel Splendide. No, he had to be sure we were here, and he has. And now, he brings on the hounds. We have no more time! George Wilson take us to this boat!"

Wilson nodded a quick assent, then raised an open palm in momentary restraint. He dug into his pants pocket, withdrawing two capsules from the apothecary bottle Dr. Jackson had given him.

"We *are* going to make it," he said decisively. "But ..."

He handed one each to Stull and Clotilde.

"Your choice, of course. But at least you'll have a choice."
They stepped into the twilight and headed up river.

Chapter 63

As Clotilde delivered her instructions to Wilson and Stull, Putnev hid across the road, screened by a wispy hedgerow. He would give them five minutes. No matter their course – cautious waiting or rapid flight -- he was ready. He had arranged for an open telephone line in the tabac up the lane. Once he knew what they would do, he knew what he would do: call Keucher, tell Keucher the Allied handler and his resistance contact were on their way to a dock on the Seine or hiding in an apartment at 1 rue Marine.

In either case, he would collect his reward.

Yet, now on the verge of getting everything he wanted – Gestapo esteem and Gestapo favor – disquiet overcame him, the fear he might not get what he wanted most. Clotilde.

Her words – *I beg you, Sergei! I beg you!* – had inflamed him and ignited in him what was most important to him: owning her.

As he crouched behind the hedge, straining to see through the gathering darkness, he knew his obsession with Clotilde was no longer a sexual compulsion such as he had felt decades earlier with the peasant girl his father had procured for him behind a piggery on an estate in East Russia. It was deeper, darker, nearly overwhelming him with scarlet images of what he wanted to do to her and with what she had already done to him. Consumed him.

Whatever the Nazis might give him, it wouldn't be enough if it excluded Clotilde.

He tried to calm himself. Surely, the Germans would not deny her to him. What was she to the Nazis in light of all he had delivered to them? All he needed was to demand her, and they would hand her over.

Then his reverie snapped, broken by three dark shapes bursting from the door of Abraham Bloch's apartment. Clotilde was first out, Stull next, then Wilson, all running toward the end of the road to the path that led to the barn and the dock and the boat. Very well, then. They would make it difficult, but he would have her in the end. As they raced toward the river, Putnev ran up the lane to the tabac. Gasping for breath, he staggered through its open front door.

"I need to make a call," he sputtered.

From behind the wooden counter, a dyspeptic woman arched her eyebrows.

"What do you expect me to do?"

"The owner promised," Putnev coughed.

"That would be my husband. He's not here. If he promised you could use the telephone after dark, he's a fool. You know the rules of Occupation. No calls from public telephones after dark."

She pointed a gnarly finger in the direction of the oaken box phone on the wall.

"And that's a public telephone."

Putnev pulled a fist full of francs from his pocket and tossed them on the counter.

She eyed the money.

"I could get in trouble. The Germans made it clear. No calls from public telephones after dark."

"This call *is to the Germans*! You'll be rewarded!"

She paused. Putnev fumbled forth his Ausweise.

"Know what this is? Impossible to obtain unless ..."

She knew how the sentence would end and swept the money from the counter top and nodded toward the wall telephone.

"Make it quick."

Putnev did.

"This is Thunder."

The soldier answering the telephone at the Hotel Meurice in Paris immediately passed the call to Major Keucher.

"Tell me what I want to hear, Putnev."

"I know where they are," he coughed.

"That's what you said last night."

"Tonight is different! I've just come from them!"

"Where do I dispatch men from the Le Havre garrison?"

"A dock on the north bank of the Seine, three kilometers east of Le Havre. Follow the river road toward a weathered barn at the edge of a cornfield. On the side of the barn is a faded advertisement for cigarettes. From the barn, a dirt path leads down to the dock. There's a boat. Marked BRL. Stull's Allied handlers will be there."

He did not mention that Stull would also be there. The pleasure of that revelation would come later. That Stull would prove Keucher wrong and make would is demand for Clotilde easier to meet. Give me her, Putnev would say, and I will lie for you and vouch for your belief that Stull was not dead but still at large, and you were in pursuit of him.

"When will they reach the boat?"

"Send your men now!"

Keucher hung up, and Putnev stood a moment longer, struggling to regain his breath, his mind returning again on Clotilde.

The woman behind the counter interrupted his reverie.

"The Germans will reward me? You said they would reward me."

But Putnev ignored her and bolted from the shop, his obsession churning his legs and blinding him to the disturbing fact that as he lumbered past 1 rue Marine on his charge to a dock on the Seine, someone had just turned off the ceiling light in Abraham Bloch's apartment.

Chapter 64

In the moonless night, starlight alone etched the outline of the barn against the dark sky. Wilson approached it. The faded painting of a ten-foot packet of Gitanes confirmed their destination. Stull struggled along behind him, prodded on by Clotilde.

"It's just ahead. You can make it. Keep moving."

Wilson came around to the barn's double doors. Swung them open, remembering Abelard's information about the stash of fuel.

"Gas is inside," he said. "We carry as much as we can to the boat and get out of here."

"Carry?" Stull sputtered and sagged into the open barn door. I ... I can't."

"I can," Wilson said and limped into the barn. Just inside the doors he found two ten-gallon cans of fuel.

"I've got them," he yelled to Clotilde. "Take Stull. Don't let him rest until he's on board. If he stops again, he'll never get up."

It was too late. Stull's legs buckled, and he sank to the white-chalk earth. Clotilde dropped to a knee and leaned over him, sliding both hands under his arms.

"The boat's only a few more steps from here," she cajoled. "We'll be safe there."

He lifted his head, shut his eyes, his voice barely audible.

"Not safe. That man ... the man who called me his friend ... he knows we have a boat ... knows where it is."

"Impossible!"

But she knew it wasn't impossible. Stull had told him.

And now Stull had given up.

From the same dark corner of her soul where anger and hate and fear had pulled the trigger that fired the gun that blew open Maxim Trafanov's chest, she withdrew her hand from Stull's side and slapped it hard across his mouth. It snapped back his head, less remonstrance than a jolt of energy. When Clotilde again thrust her hands under his arms and pushed upward, Stull wobbled to his feet. She threw her arm around his waist. They stumbled on behind Wilson toward the river.

A dense mist rolling in off the Channel had begun to coat the landscape in condensation.   Twice, Wilson's fingers lost their grip on the fuel cans. Twice they fell to the wet earth, each time battering his injured right leg. Every 50 meters, he had to stop, dry his hands on his black clerical bib and regrasp the gas canisters.

Finally, the Seine.

"Up there ... a few hundred meters ... the boat ... go on!"

Clotilde hauled Stull past him. When they reached the dock, she did not wait for Wilson and pulled the German toward the pilot boat tethered at the end of the wharf. She spanned her feet between the steady pier and the vessel, its lines drawn taut by the river's current and guided him aboard. He sank to his knees, curling like a fetus on the floor of the midship cabin.

Wilson reached the wharf and stepped onto it, but his right foot slipped on the wet planking, and he fell hard onto the dock, the fuel canister in his right hand gouging his right leg, opening the sutures. Blood pulsed out, leaving a red streak as he crawled toward the boat before stopping and prying back a slick plank and fishing out the ignition key to the BRL, tied to a tennis ball.

Clotilde ran back to Wilson. He waved an exhausted hand at the fuel canisters.

"Get the cans aboard ... we're out of here ... now!"

She dragged them along the dew-slick dock. At the boat, she again angled her feet between wharf and deck.

"Start fueling," Wilson sputtered.

Behind the cabin, she unscrewed the cap on the fuel tank. Gasoline slopped onto the deck.

"It's full!" she yelled. "The fuel tank's full!"

Abelard's words returned to Wilson.

"On a full take it can cover 200 kilometers."

"Throw the goddam things into the river! If the tank's full, we don't need them. We can make it. They're just extra weight!"

"And tell the Germans we were here!?"

Wilson looked at her in astonishment.

"The Germans!? They don't know about the boat or the dock or ..."

"Stull told Putnev. By now Putnev has told the Germans. If they see the cans, they'll know we were here. If they see nothing, they might think there was no boat at all and look for us on land."

It flashed across Wilson's exhausted mind that if they got to England it would be only because of her. Clotilde was hauling the cans into the cabin when a beam of light from the river bank caught her face. She looked up.

"Brava, Clotilde," a gasping voice sounded from the embankment. "You are a smart one. That I could never deny."

Clotilde jerked her head toward shore. Her ears had already told her what her eyes now confirmed: Sergei Putnev. He brandished a Luger in one hand and Abraham Bloch's flashlight in the other. He set the lit flashlight on the edge of the dock, its ghostly beam illuminating the pilot boat. He waved the pistol at Wilson.

"Stay where you are!" he said, still gasping. "Where's Stull?"

Putnev did not wait for an answer. In the flashlight's beam, he saw Stull coiled on the floor of the cabin.

"Get him out."

"Let him rest," Wilson pleaded.

Putnev braced himself on a piling at the shore line.

"Germans are on their way, Clotilde. Be here any moment. I'd like to deliver the three of you ... alive and talking, but if I have to, I'll shoot. To kill. Get Stull off the boat."

Clotilde did. Stull crawled onto the dock, looked up at Putnev.

"You said you were my friend."

Putnev offered a weak smile, his chest heaving.

"I am. I told you the truth about your colleagues. I said they'd never get you out of France, and I was right. And now, I've just got you off a doomed boat, a boat that if it sails down the Seine will be blown out of the water by the Luftwaffe or sink under the waves of the Channel. So, you see, I have saved your life ... at least for a few more days. After that, who knows? Maybe you can talk your way out of this. I've given you a fair chance, which is more than these two have."

Putnev saw Clotilde slip a hand into her skirt pocket.

"Easy, Clotilde! Don't do anything stupid."

Slowly, she removed the letter she had written in the stationery store in Paris and held it out.

Putnev recognized it.

"Oh, that. Give it to Captain Halle. It's harmless enough. It might point a finger at me, but with Trafanov dead you're the only one who can speak against me. It's your work against mine. And you have no credibility. Look at the people you're consorting with: a defector and an Allied spy. Do you really think German State Security will take you seriously, especially after I give them the real Gerhardt Stull and his Allied handler? The Germans won't question me. They'll pin a medal on my chest."

His omission crashed in on her. He had not included her name among his deliverables to the Germans. He had the pistol, and she knew she might have to submit, but she also knew in that moment that he was hers.

She stepped toward him, and in the light from his flashlight saw in his eyes his desire for her, a desire deeper than flesh. They stared at each other, Putnev at her eyes and her mouth, feeling again the power of his obsession. She at him, ready to play the accommodation he had taught her in Room 8.

Wilson pulled himself to his feet, limped down the wharf behind her, reached her, swung her around. He knew.

"No, Clotilde! Don't! I can still get us out! You, me, Stull to England! For the love of God, let me try!"

His words brought Putnev back to where he was and what he needed to complete his triumph: reinforcements, and he summoned them, aiming his pistol over Clotilde's head and squeezing the trigger. She stood unmoved. Wilson coiled and cringed, hearing the bullet cut through the river air a foot above their heads.

Then from the embankment another sound. A pistol being cocked.

Putnev also heard it.

"I told you the Germans would be here," he said, satisfaction tinging his voice. "Now, I suggest we all ..."

Out of a rustle of underbrush, a figure stepped onto the dock, backlit by the beam from Putnev's flashlight.

"Jerome!" Wilson yelled. "Thank God!"

Jerome stepped cautiously behind Putnev and jammed his pistol into the small of Putnev's back.

"Drop your weapon."

Putnev did. Wilson stepped forward to retrieve it.

"Hold your ground!" Jerome yelled.

"It's me, Father Olert. How did you find us!?"

"The innkeeper at the Auberge Jeanne d'Arc. I went there first, then followed this gentleman here from 1 rue Marine."

He pressed the barrel of his pistol deeper into Putnev's back. The Russian stiffened.

"And exactly who are you?" Jerome asked.

Wilson answered for him.

"A Nazi agent."

"Maybe," Jerome answered, "but he could also be OSS on the verge of carrying out the sentence of execution you can't. I'll sort that out later. As to her, she's clearly with you, Father Olert. Therefore, equally unable to follow orders, orders which were easy to understand. You either persuaded the target to remain and spy, or you killed him. But what did I learn just now, listening there on the riverbank as you spoke with her? You and she plan to bring the defector to England."

Jerome shook his head in disdain.

"I knew you were not reliable. I saw it in your face three nights ago in the farm house. I should have dealt with you then."

He beckoned Clotilde toward him and stepped out from behind Putnev. Wilson knew what was coming because he knew Jerome would not hesitate. Wilson slipped his right hand into his coat pocket, his fingers curling around the small wooden hilt of the grandad.

"What's your name?" Jerome demanded of Clotilde.

"Clotilde deBrouillard, a French citizen and member of the Christian Resistance. We're getting Lt. Stull out of France."

"In that case, I have a question for you, Miss Clotilde. What time is it?"

She hesitated, her mind racing, then said, "My watch is unreliable."

"Your watch is *not reliable,* Mademoiselle deBrouillard. Like you."

Jerome took aim.

Chapter 65

Wilson drove off his left foot, his right fist tight around the knife. The blade slashed down and across Jerome's carotid artery, blood gushing from his neck, Jerome collapsing unconscious to the dock, his pistol dropping to his feet.

Putnev was first to the weapon, scooped it off the deck, held it overhead. Pulled the trigger. The blast echoed down the river. Another summons to Keucher's men. As if in response, a siren wailed upland from the direction of the barn.

Jerome's body lie sprawled across the slippery planks. Wilson gaped at it, horrified by what he had done, more horrified by how easy it had been to do. He had reached Dr. Jackson's point of lethal desperation.

"You killed him, you son of a bitch!" Putnev yelled above the encroaching siren. "The information he had – cells, safe houses, contacts – my prize lost!"

Putnev raised the pistol, again. Aimed it at Wilson's head.

Venerable's admonition screamed in Wilson's mind.

If a gun's at your head, offer the gunman something better than your dead body.

Wilson had no time to think, only speak.

"I'm no value to you dead," he said.

Putnev's tautened body eased, as if the logic of Wilson's assertion was incontrovertible. Wilson kept talking.

"The Gestapo will give you nothing. You're Russian. An Untermensch, sub-human."

Putnev's chin was rising.

"They'll think different after I give them you… along with Stull."

Wilson snorted.

"Stull!? Are you mad!? A Slavic stooge humiliating the Gestapo by giving them a man they had pronounced dead!?"

Wilson jerked a finger at the wretched Stull lying on the dock by the boat, knees bent, arms around his legs.

"The Gestapo officer you're working with has, no doubt, informed Berlin that Gerhardt Stull is dead. Make a fool of that officer by proving otherwise, and you won't get out of Normandy alive. You won't get off this dock alive. But if the Germans continue to believe Stull is dead, you've got a chance."

"Yes, I *do* have a chance. You. They'll reward me for you."

"Reward? You'll be lucky if they give you the taxi we came in. This isn't a game of penalties and reward. This is war, and Germany's losing. It's in a fight for its life, and it won't take time to pat you on the head and throw you a bone."

Putnev did no respond. Wilson now a river of words.

"Know why I was assigned to France? To organize resistance cells for the invasion of Western Europe. It's coming! The invasion of North Africa is coming. Your Russian winter is coming. And America has just begun to fight. The Reich will be overwhelmed. Then where will you be? Back in Moscow? No chance! Some Nazi on the run will sell you out to the Russians to save himself, tell anyone who'll listen you were a German agent working against Mother Russia. Don't you see, Putnev? You're in no-mans land. All the ground cut out from under you. A traitor to Moscow, an Untermensch to Berlin. But if you see things my way .. if you let us get on that boat, you would be an agent for Britain and the U.S. At the end of the war, on the winning side."

"A pipe dream. How do I survive tonight, without you and Stull to offer the Gestapo?"

Wilson pointed to Jerome's body.

"By offering the Gestapo him. You deliver Stull's handler, an Ally spy. Dead but undeniably killed by you. The Germans might not reward you, after all you were doing your duty as a Nazi agent, but they won't shoot you for killing an enemy of the Reich."

"How would the Gestapo know he's Stull's handler? That corpse could be an innocent Frenchmen I killed to give credence to this story you're concocting."

Wilson pointed to the Grandad lying at his feet, the weapon he had killed with.

"Show that to the Nazis. They've never seen anything like it. Made in England, especially for Allied spies. And show them this."

245

Slowly, Wilson knelt beside Jerome's body and slipped his hand into the breast pocket of Jerome's blood-soaked jacket and removed a wallet. Wilson opened it, took out what he knew was there.

"An Ausweise," he said. "It's a forgery, a good forgery, but it won't take German intelligence long to declare it a forgery. The weapon and the fake visa will convince the Gestapo he was an Allied agent, and who could it be but Stull's handler."

Putnev waved an unconvinced hand.

"And for that, I just let you float away?"

"No, for much more. By letting us go, you will have demonstrated your commitment to the Allies. And I can promise you our commitment to you. You become a double agent for us, in Paris. You provide us information. In exchange, we grant you safe harbor after the war."

"And if the Nazis win?"

"Don't talk nonsense."

"And if the Nazis win?"

"If you're a good spy, they'll never know you worked for us."

"How do I know you'd keep your word and tell London what I've done?"

"Self-interest. In London, I get a medal for recruiting you."

"What do I get?"

"To live. Not in a concentration camp or a gulag, but in Paris or London after the war."

"It's fantasy."

"It's fantasy to believe the Gestapo will give you anything worth having. I'm offering you a future, all for letting the three of us get on that boat and push off for the Channel. You have Stull's handler. And the Germans think Stull is dead."

"You'll never make it past Le Havre."

"We shouldn't have made it out of Paris. But we did. This is life and death. I offer you a chance to survive the war. I want a chance to survive tonight."

Putnev looked back over his shoulder. Bursts of light from automobile head lamps strobed through the trees.

"Almost convincing, Father Olert. But no deal. My reinforcements arrive. A bird in the hand, not two in the bush. I'll take my chances with the Gestapo and give them you and Stull."

Again, he had not said Clotilde, and again Clotilde had heard his omission – he did not say he would turn her over to the Germans -- and in that omission she knew she still had power over him, power to convince him in a way Wilson's argument had not.

She stepped between Wilson and Putnev. Stared at Putnev.

"Sergei, I beg you! Let them go. What he said is true. The Allies will take care of you."

She came close to him, her arms spread open. Everything spread open.

"I beg you!"

Putnev's chest tightened. He lowered the pistol, and Clotilde brought her hand to his waist. She did not look at Wilson but said, "Go, George Wilson! I am giving you this gift."

She took Putnev's free hand to her breast.

"Go, George Wilson! Go!"

Putnev picked up the flashlight from the dock and shone it on Jerome's body, then toward the embankment at the approaching German soldiers, cursing as they slid in the dark along the muddy path to the river.

At the sound of his native language, Stull lifted his head toward Wilson.

"My God, we must go!"

Wilson stared at Clotilde. But she did not look back, having turned with Putnev toward the embankment.

Wilson pulled Stull into the boat. Untied the taut mooring rope at the end of the dock and dropped it into the water. The outbound current caught the BRL, carrying it downstream and into the mists of the Seine and toward the Channel.

Chapter 66

Hidden in the mist, the BRL drifted silently down river provoking no sign from the embankments that the Germans knew what they were missing. After three hours, Stull stirred from the door of the cabin, his voice a plea, a few decibels higher than the woosh of the current carrying the boat toward the Channel.

"Why don't you start the engine! We must make speed before daylight!"

Wilson only stared into the fog, tortured by the awful knowledge that Clotilde had exchanged her life for his, and he had been powerless to stop her.

Stull, again.

"Why don't you start the engine! The sun's coming up. The mist will burn off. We must get to the Channel before daylight! Why don't you start the engine! We must …"

The rest of Stull's words fell inaudible beneath the rasp of sand grating against the boat's hull. The stern swung hard to starboard tossing Wilson to the floor of the cabin next to Stull.

"A sandbar! Get up!"

Wilson slid open the cabin door. Mingled with the whoosh of water around the hull, German voices wondered about the sound that had just come off the river.

"Oh, dear God," Stull whispered. "They hear us!"

And hearing them, Wilson knew the boat was only a few meters from shore.

"Get in the water," he whispered, "and push off! It's our only …"

Wilson felt the deck shift, again.   The current was driving the bow deeper into the sand. He had no choice. His hand groped through the dark along the console until it found the ignition and inserted the key. He pulled out the choke. The engine groaned, caught. The piercing tap of unadjusted valves that Abelard was to fix when the war was over, pulsed across the river.

"What's that!?" a German voice shouted. "On the river! In front of us! Shine the spot!"

Someone did, but the beam did not penetrate the mist only suffused it in silvery light.

Wilson shifted the engine into reverse.

The engine struggled, but the sandbar held fast.

"Get to the stern!" he ordered Stull. "Too much weight at midships!"

Stull crawled toward the rear of the boat. Again, Wilson threw the engine full ahead, then into reverse. Then twice more. The boat began to rock. The fourth time a billow of water and silt churned to the river's surface as suction between sandbar and hull gave way. The boat backed off, and Wilson eased the engine into forward. He turned the wheel hard to port, making for the middle of the river.

"Are we safe!?" Stull gasped.

Wilson didn't have to answer.

The fog was lifting, and a beam of light from the opposite bank, drawn by the insistent tap of the engine, swept toward them. Wilson could do nothing but watch as the shaft of light from the north bank approached.

And then went black, but the darkness could not mask what they heard: the drone of airplane engines.

"They're going to strafe us!" Stull screamed. "Planes! They have planes!"

The first Messerschmitt was over them. Then another and another, twenty-eight planes in all, at one-minute intervals, soaring a hundred meters overhead and rising. Wilson understood. The soldiers on the north bank had killed the spotlight to prevent it from blinding the Luftwaffe pilots taking off from the south bank. Wilson did not hesitate and threw open the throttle. The last plane gained altitude well to their stern. Wilson turned, watching it bear north soaring above the massed trees on the embankment, that in a moment gave way to the low barren rise of the river's flood plain. They had reached the mouth of the Channel. As first light broke across the boat's deck, a heavy chop broke over its bow.

Six hours, Wilson thought. If our luck holds, we can be in England in six hours.

They had gone no more than a kilometer into the Channel, when Wilson knew their luck had not held.

249

A gunboat was gaining on them, spray rising from the bounce of its hull through the gray waves. Even amid the rising wind and rolling sea, he could hear through the crackle of the gunboat's bullhorn an uncompromising German accent.

"Heave to! Prepare to be boarded!"

Wilson hesitated, not from defiance but from despair; they had come so far only to fail. Clotilde's sacrifice had been for nothing.

"It's over," he called to Stull, still on the floor of the cabin. "Come out. Put your hands over your head."

A hundred meters away, the gun boat was closing on them. Three German sailors manned its deck. One sailor held a length of heavy rope, the other men machines guns trained on the BRL.

The gunboat came alongside, its deck crew stutter-stepping to compensate for the pitch of the vessel in the Channel waves.

"We will throw you a line," yelled the sailor with the rope. "Secure it to your bow. We're towing you in."

The sailor raised the rope.

Then dropped it.

From inside the cabin the pilot was waving his hand, yelling to the three sailors on deck to get below. The gunboat's engine revved, and the vessel accelerated past the BRL and up Channel.

Wilson did not understand. Nor did he hesitate. He restarted his engine, threw open the throttle.

"We'll never make it," Stull sobbed. "I told you! I told you!"

Five hours later, three nautical miles southeast of Ventnor on the Isle of Wight, a Royal Navy Shore patrol Mayburn intercepted pilot boat BRL and, throwing it a line, towed it into port.

As Wilson set foot on the stone bulkhead, he didn't allow himself the satisfaction of an improbable salvation. He glanced at Stull, the man he was supposed to convince to stay in Paris to spy for the Allies or shoot if he refused. He had failed to carry out the first order and had ignored the second.

Dr. Jackson's warning came back to him: *Ignoring orders in peace time is dangerous. But in time of war ... you'll be executed for treason.*

Chapter 67

The debriefing in the Royal Navy barracks at Ventnor had been cursory. Who, what, when, where, why tossed out to Stull and Wilson, both exhausted, dehydrated and famished. Ten minutes into their interview, Stull demanded time to sleep and to thank the Blessed Lady for his deliverance. Wilson demanded nothing. It wasn't necessary. Blood dripping from his blood-soaked right sock was enough for his interlocutors to suspend questioning and send him to surgery. The next morning Wilson came out of his dreamless sleep, not as he had two days earlier in the American Hospital, nursed to consciousness by the miracle of Clotilde deBrouillard, but by a Royal Navy lieutenant who said to him, "They want you at Perran House this afternoon. We're transporting you within the hour."

He did not wish Wilson a good day.

Why should he, Wilson thought. Nothing good about it. The day held only infamy for him. He had blown his mission; Stull was not in Paris spying for the Allies but alive in England. Jerome was dead, his throat slashed by Wilson's own hand as Jerome was about to carry out the order Wilson could not. And then there was Clotilde. Sacrificed for nothing.

Court martial and execution awaited him. Both deserved.

He could, of course, lie. Tell his OSS evaluators the Germans had killed Jerome. Seen it with his own eyes, had witnessed the brave Jerome endure torture only to be shot in the back of the head when the Nazis found him unbreakable.

The story was fool proof, except for Stull who witnessed the entire debacle. But it was more than Stull's that would keep Wilson from lying. It was his own sense of shame. He didn't deserve reprieve. He deserved punishment. He had failed. Most painfully, he had failed Clotilde.

His death would be some recompense.

It would, he knew, shatter his parents. Still, an arrangement might be reached. In exchange for his full confession, St. Patrick or Venerable could grant the humane favor of keeping the shame of his treason from them. His parents could find comfort in the story that

251

heir boy had been killed in the line of duty while on special
ssignment in Europe.

A taciturn British Army sergeant escorted Wilson to the
entnor air strip where a two-seat RAF DH Mosquito idled.   Wilson
oarded. In 15 minutes, he was 4,000 feet above the Soylent,
earing northeast on route to his reckoning.

Chapter 68

An hour later, carrying only a wooden cane, Wilson hobbled from the plane onto the sun-splotched earthen runway that had once been the eighth fairway of Woking Golf Course.

A military Jeep and its driver, the same sullen corporal who had supplied Wilson with a bicycle for his excursion into Woking a few weeks earlier, transported Wilson to Perran House. As the car pulled into the gravel driveway, the corporal said, "You know your way from here."

Wilson limped inside, heading for the wing chair in the corner of the reception hall, when the door from the library opened. Venerable emerged.

"Come in, Father Olert. We have things to talk over."

Wilson leaned heavily on his cane. No matter the remonstrance and verdict, he had made his decision. The truth would prevail.

Venerable pointed to the empty chair in front of his desk. Wilson lowered himself into it, and then, to his surprise, Venerable handed him a Waterford tumbler, a third filled with whisky. And to Wilson's even greater surprise, he was smiling.

"Congratulations, George. One in a million. Never seen such a string of good luck, good judgment and good outcomes."

Wilson downed the whisky with one swallow.

"First of all," Venerable said. "Your timing was impeccable. Know what happened yesterday?"

Wilson was too stunned to answer.

"Of course not. How could you? Top secret. Operation Jubilee. A surprise Allied raid at Dieppe, across the Channel. Mostly Canadian lads."

Venerable looked wistfully toward the French doors opening onto the garden, radiant in mid-summer bloom.

"And mostly dead. Their objective was to seize the German fortification at Dieppe. Hold it for 24 hours, inflict as much damage as possible and pick up some intelligence. The invasion was a shambles. 6,000 Allied soldiers crossing the Channel ran into a German convoy that alerted the defenders what was coming. The

Canucks landed at dawn. Light was up. Germans prepared. The only good thing: the invasion coincided with your trip down the Seine and into the Channel. The Nazis dispatched all their planes from Octeville air station and all their shoreline gunboats to meet the invaders to the north. That's why they let you go. Needed elsewhere. Timing was as immaculate as your ingenuity. Stull told us about it. A master stroke to substitute a dead Parisian for Stull. Then getting out of Paris, through Rouen, down the river, across the Channel. Exceptional initiative. Of course, you had luck. But you positioned yourself to let luck work its charms. Brilliant."

"You don't know what really happened. An extraordinary man named Sumner Jackson ..."

Venerable took Wilson's glass, carried it to the sideboard behind his desk and poured another whisky and talked over Wilson's objection.

"As you know, we wanted Lt. Stull kept in Paris. We thought him ideally situated to help us. You decided differently. As it turns out, our evaluators endorse your decision. It is obvious to them that Stull could never have endured the pressure of being a double agent. Would have cracked and taken God knows how many of the Resistance with him. But that's not why we're pleased you brought him over. I think you know why."

Wilson drained his second drink. He didn't know why, and hoped, as the last drop of whisky burned the back of his throat, Venerable would tell him. Venerable did.

"There's a reason little Gerhardt got a plush assignment in Paris at the Hotel Meurice. He's the son of Konrad Stull, the Reich's Deputy Ambassador in Tokyo. We'll wait a few days before back-channeling information to Deputy Ambassador Stull that his little bundle of joy is alive."

Suddenly it made sense to Wilson: Stull's veiled references to his family, his personal elegance and epic egotism had been borne of a life of ease and privilege.

"Won't Ambassador Stull run to the Nazis with that information?"

"We think not. And I'm sure it's just as you assumed. Deputy Ambassador Konrad Stull is old line German Catholic, one of those who thought they could control Hitler, who in turn, would provide a

254

bulwark against Bolshevism. Ambassador Stull is not really a Nazi, not like Goebbels or Himmler. They're gutter. Stull's not. Degree from Marburg University. Took a first in philosophy. Then entered the German foreign service. Quickly came to the attention of the Weimar Republic. Stull's career advanced. Postings in Washington and London. When the Nazis came to power in '33, they were eager to present the face of German competence to the world. They kept Konrad. He was never awarded ambassadorial rank – the Nazis reserve that for party loyalists -- but he played well on the international circuit. We're hoping, as I'm sure you had hoped, Konrad Stull values his baby boy a lot more than he values his Nazi bosses, and consequently, will work with us. Excellent call, George, excellent."

Wilson felt none of Venerable's pleasure. There was Jerome and, overwhelmingly, Clotilde.

"The other agent you sent in," Wilson began, "Jerome …"

"I know," Venerable interrupted. "He didn't make it. You said that at your initial debriefing down in Ventnor. Stull spoke about that, too. Said you killed him."

Finally, Wilson thought, the truth. A cathartic slump of his shoulders.

"I *did* kill him."

Venerable shrugged pensively.

"We'll tell his mother her son died in action. Which is true. We'll throw in that he died a hero. It's not accurate, but it will spare the woman some pain."

"But *I killed him*, not the Germans."

"Stull told us Jerome was about to shoot you and him. That got Stull's attention. I think I'll join you."

Venerable stepped to the sideboard and poured himself a whisky. Sipped it, winced at the pleasure of it.

"Difficult breed, spies. We're never sure if we've gotten dross, as we did with Jerome, or gold, as we did with you. Two OSS evaluators wondered about him from the start, and my friend, St. Patrick, thought him a bad fit."

Venerable sipped his whisky.

"George … I earn my bread and serve my king by following orders and, when necessary, by making brutal decisions. I don't pologize for any of it, but I think you're entitled to more than a flip wave of my hand as to what happened to you over the last few days. No doubt, you're wondering why, at the last minute, I switched assignments. You to appraise Stull, and Jerome to set up the cells that originally had been your mission."

"Jerome told me something about him being a butcher and me a surgeon."

"Some truth in that. But you deserve all the truth. When I initially gave Jerome his assignment and told him what he was to do with Stull if Stull did not cooperate, Jerome said, 'I will.'"

Wilson's guilt boiled up. He had done the same.

"So did I. Jerome told me what he – and you – expected of me. I said I would meet that expectation and, if necessary, execute Stull."

The flip hand Venerable had said he wouldn't employ now waved at Wilson.

"I'm sure you did. And if that had been all Jerome had done – simply told me he'd follow orders – I would not have switched assignments. But that *wasn't all he did.*"

Venerable picked up the decanter and poured himself two more fingers of scotch.

"You see, George, after I gave Jerome that order, Jerome smiled. *Smiled.*"

Now, Wilson flourished a flip hand, his tone aggressive.

"You once told me you appreciated that kind of obedience, the kind that followed orders, *no matter what.*"

"Yes, I said that. Our service requires men and women to do unspeakable things without balking. But Jerome's smile told me he'd not only carry out the order, he'd enjoy carrying it out. That gave me pause. If he enjoyed it, he might not think twice about it. But you *would* think twice about it, and in our line of work, George, you need to think twice about everything. You need to be agile, reevaluating every situation at every moment. In the OSS, reevaluation is not an end-of-the-day exercise as you make plans for the next morning. It's a minute-by-minute requirement."

Venerable brought his glass of whisky to his lips, then lowered it.

"Of course, Jerome objected to the switch. Said you didn't have the stomach to do what he was prepared to do. Said you'd hesitate and that would give Stull a chance to escape, or you'd flat out disobey the order to kill Stull and jeopardize everything. He might have been right, but as I explained, every situation is a freak of nature, requiring an agile response. Jerome didn't have that agility. You do."

Venerable's did nothing to ease the ache in Wilson's soul, nothing to stop him from saying, "There was also a woman."

"We know. Stull told us. Clotilde deBrouillard. Christian Resistance."

"I am here because of her. Stull is here because of her."

Venerable sipped his drink, needed it for what he was about to say.

"Not according to Stull. She was, in his word, 'impure.' He told us about how she got him out of Paris. I'm sure you know."

"She killed a man."

"And prostituted herself with another. Stull thought the whole thing immoral or disgusting, depending on which of her actions he was discussing. Says the only reason he got out was through the intercession of the Blessed Virgin, not the genius of Clotilde deBrouillard and George Wilson."

Wilson could no longer contain it. He had to know.

"Is she alive?"

Venerable gathered himself.

"The Germans would never have allowed her to walk away. They would have arrested her and that Russian, Putnev. I know you said he agreed to spy for us, but we doubt he'll have the chance. In any case, we haven't heard a word from him. We're sure he's dead."

Venerable cleared his throat, continued.

"And I'm afraid, so is Clotilde deBrouillard. It's the uniform consensus of our intelligence wing that the Germans captured her and executed her. Probably after they ..."

Wilson brought his hands to his face.

"I'm sorry George. Stull told us you gave her a poison capsule. I hope she had time to use it."

Venerable's voice turned matter of fact.

"The doctors in Ventnor say you have serious muscle and tendon damage in your right leg. We're sending you to our rehab center in Tunbridge-Wells, down in Sussex for a few months. After what you've been through, it will be boring, but boring might be good."

Wilson did not answer, nor did he lower his hands from his face.

Chapter 69

Nine weeks after arriving at hospital in Tunbridge-Wells, Wilson received a note from Venerable.

Doctors say you are healing well and ready for reassignment. Report to Perran House in two days, noon.

Healing well was inaccurate. While his right leg was much improved, his soul still roiled in torment. Not an hour passed, when he did not see Clotilde, hear Clotilde say to him, "Go, George Wilson. I am giving you this gift. Go."

During his convalescence, he knew he would go. He would go to Venerable and say, *I'm returning to the regular Army. The Aleutians, North Africa, the Pacific. I don't care where. But no more OSS. No more hideous choices with hideous outcomes. No more lethal desperation.*

A Medical Corps staff car transported Wilson from Sussex to Surrey. He arrived at Perran House on a bright October morning. The same lugubrious corporal who had directed him to his bicycle for his "final exam" two weeks ago, now showed him to Venerable's office. Venerable had just finished his morning lecture to the latest class of OSS recruits. He welcomed Wilson warmly. Invited him into his office and came to the point.

"We have a new assignment for you, George."

"Sir, I'm requesting, I'm demanding ..."

"Oh, by the way, George, this came down an hour ago from our people in London."

Venerable held up an envelope.

"They got it from our embassy in Lisbon, which in turn got it from a priest in the French Papal Nuncio's office. It's a miracle of mail delivery. The address on the envelope reads *George Wilson, OSS, London.* Fortunately, our embassy person in Lisbon knew about OSS and passed it along to Allied Intelligence Command, which sent it down here this morning."

He handed the envelope to Wilson. Wilson withdrew a sheet of paper and read:

George Wilson,

The last time we met, many things happened. So many, it is improbable either one of us is alive. But I am alive, and perhaps the same Power that preserved me has saved you.   I pray so, because I think of you often, not of our last moments but of our first moments on that snowy night an eternity ago in the Latin Quarter. I hope someday we meet again. Until that day, should it come, I send you my love.

Clotilde

PS – I did not use the pill you gave me. After all, it was only the second-best thing you gave me. As it turned out, your best gift was all I needed. What you first gave me. Your love.

Wilson folded the paper and slipped it into his pants pocket. Venerable did not ask for it back.

"The doctors say you're ready for reassignment," Venerable said. "We have something in mind. You know the lay of the land in Paris. And by a freak of luck, even have friends. We'd like you to go back."

Second Lieutenant Galahad George Wilson squeezed the letter in his pocket and, for the first time in ten weeks, smiled.

"Yes," he said. "Paris. Yes."

The End

Made in the USA
Monee, IL
18 May 2023

34015168R00152